MURDER ON ST. MARK'S PLACE
Nominated for the Edgar® Award

"Lovers of history, mystery, and romance won't be disappointed. Exciting . . . Will hold the reader in thrall."
—*Romantic Times*

MURDER ON GRAMERCY PARK

"The inclusions of [historical] facts make this novel . . . superior to most of those found in the subgenre . . . The lead protagonists are a winning combination."
—*BookBrowser*

MURDER ON WASHINGTON SQUARE

"Victoria Thompson's Gaslight Mysteries are always . . . exciting treats to read."
—*BookBrowser*

MURDER ON ASTOR PLACE
*Nominated for the Best First Mystery Award
by* Romantic Times *magazine*

"Victoria Thompson is off to a blazing start with Sarah Brandt and Frank Malloy in *Murder on Astor Place*. I do hope she's starting at the beginning of the alphabet. Don't miss her first tantalizing mystery."
—Catherine Coulter, *New York Times* bestselling author

"A marvelous debut mystery with compelling characters, a fascinating setting, and a stunning resolution. It's the best mystery I've read in ages."
—Jill Churchill, author of *The Merchant of Menace*

Berkley Prime Crime titles by Victoria Thompson

MURDER ON ASTOR PLACE
MURDER ON ST. MARK'S PLACE
MURDER ON GRAMERCY PARK
MURDER ON WASHINGTON SQUARE
MURDER ON MULBERRY BEND
MURDER ON MARBLE ROW
MURDER ON LENOX HILL
MURDER IN LITTLE ITALY
MURDER IN CHINATOWN
MURDER ON BANK STREET

continued . . .

MURDER ON MARBLE ROW

"Victoria Thompson has crafted another Victorian page-turner." —Robin Paige, author of *Death on the Lizard*

"Cleverly plotted . . . Provides abundant fair play and plenty of convincing period detail. This light, quick read engages the readers' emotions." —*Publishers Weekly*

"Engaging characters . . . An enjoyable read." —Margaret Frazer, author of *The Hunter's Tale*

"Victoria Thompson has a knack for putting the reader inside her characters' heads, and her detailed descriptions of New York at the turn of the century bring the setting vividly to life." —Kate Kingsbury, author of *Slay Bells*

"Each novel in the Gaslight Mystery series just keeps getting better . . . [*Murder on Marble Row*] is well-executed and the ending will come as a complete surprise." —*Midwest Book Review*

MURDER ON MULBERRY BEND

"An exciting intrigue of murder, deception, and bigotry. *Gangs of New York* eat your heart out—this book is the real thing." —*Mystery Scene*

"A thrilling, informative, challenging mystery." —*The Drood Review of Mystery*

"There are few mysteries set back in history that I enjoy reading. This mystery series is one of those. The characters and settings are so real . . . I highly recommend this book and series." —*The Best Reviews*

MURDER ON
LENOX HILL

A Gaslight Mystery

Victoria Thompson

BERKLEY PRIME CRIME, NEW YORK

THE BERKLEY PUBLISHING GROUP
Published by the Penguin Group
Penguin Group (USA) Inc.
375 Hudson Street, New York, New York 10014, USA
Penguin Group (Canada), 90 Eglinton Avenue East, Suite 700, Toronto, Ontario M4P 2Y3, Canada
(a division of Pearson Penguin Canada Inc.)
Penguin Books Ltd., 80 Strand, London WC2R 0RL, England
Penguin Group Ireland, 25 St. Stephen's Green, Dublin 2, Ireland (a division of Penguin Books Ltd.)
Penguin Group (Australia), 250 Camberwell Road, Camberwell, Victoria 3124, Australia
(a division of Pearson Australia Group Pty. Ltd.)
Penguin Books India Pvt. Ltd., 11 Community Centre, Panchsheel Park, New Delhi—110 017, India
Penguin Group (NZ), Cnr. Airborne and Rosedale Roads, Albany, Auckland 1310, New Zealand
(a division of Pearson New Zealand Ltd.)
Penguin Books (South Africa) (Pty.) Ltd., 24 Sturdee Avenue, Rosebank, Johannesburg 2196,
South Africa

Penguin Books Ltd., Registered Offices: 80 Strand, London WC2R 0RL, England

This is a work of fiction. Names, characters, places, and incidents either are the product of the author's imagination or are used fictitiously, and any resemblance to actual persons, living or dead, business establishments, events, or locales is entirely coincidental. The publisher does not have any control over and does not assume any responsibility for author or third-party websites or their content.

The Edgar® name is a registered service mark of the Mystery Writers of America, Inc.

MURDER ON LENOX HILL

A Berkley Prime Crime Book / published by arrangement with the author

PRINTING HISTORY
Berkley Prime Crime hardcover edition / June 2005
Berkley Prime Crime mass-market edition / June 2006

Copyright © 2006 by Victoria Thompson.
Cover art by Karen Chandler.
Cover design by Rita Frangie.

ISBN: 978-0-425-20610-2

BERKLEY ® PRIME CRIME
Berkley Prime Crime Books are published by The Berkley Publishing Group,
a division of Penguin Group (USA) Inc.,
375 Hudson Street, New York, New York 10014.
The name BERKLEY PRIME CRIME and the BERKLEY PRIME CRIME design
are trademarks belonging to Penguin Group (USA) Inc.

PRINTED IN THE UNITED STATES OF AMERICA

10 9 8 7 6 5 4

To Liam, my favorite little boy, and his mommy Lisa who gave me the solution to this one!

I

THE WEATHER WAS SO MISERABLE, EVEN MRS. ELLSWORTH was indoors, Sarah Brandt noted as she hurried down the windy street to her house. Her next-door neighbor could nearly always be found sweeping her front stoop in order to keep track of the comings and goings of the other residents of Bank Street. Today Sarah passed unnoticed, hurrying up her front steps and fumbling with her key before finally finding refuge inside.

Slamming the front door against the cold, Sarah immediately dropped her medical bag, the one that still bore the brass plate with the inscription "Dr. Thomas Brandt." Her husband had been dead nearly four years, but she still used his bag. It was the one tangible reminder she had left of him.

She stood still for a moment, chafing the feeling back into her gloved hands before removing her cape. Then, just as she had expected, she heard the clatter of running feet across the floor above and down the uncarpeted steps into the foyer where she waited. Her heart lifted with joy at the sound.

"Be careful!" she cried instinctively, half-expecting to hear a small body start to tumble down the stairs.

But the footsteps were as sure as they were swift, and in another instant, that small body emerged from the stairwell and launched itself at Sarah, wrapping surprisingly strong arms around her knees through the thickness of her skirts.

"Don't knock her over, Aggie!" a warning voice called from the stairway, and then Maeve appeared, moving more sedately but equally happy to see Sarah, if her smile was any indication.

Sarah reached down and pulled Aggie up into her arms. "How's my girl today?" she asked, knowing she wouldn't receive a reply. Although Sarah estimated that Aggie had to be at least four years old, she hadn't uttered a word since the day she'd been found sleeping on the doorstep of the Prodigal Son Mission last spring. No one knew where she'd come from or even what her real name was.

"She's been good," Maeve reported. "Ate two pieces of butter bread for breakfast, and let me braid her hair, she did." Maeve was another refugee from the mission, a girl whose family had turned her out to fend for herself in the streets because they could no longer afford to feed her. She was proving to be a very satisfactory nanny for Aggie.

"That explains why she's getting so heavy," Sarah said, playfully bouncing the child in her arms. "Do you like your braids?"

Aggie grinned and shook her head vigorously, making the neat, brown braids whip around the sides of her head and forcing Sarah to draw her own head back to keep from getting slapped, too.

"I think she means yes," Maeve said, unable to conceal her pride. "She's been doing that all morning. Come along now, Aggie, and let Mrs. Brandt get her coat off."

Aggie let Maeve take her from Sarah's arms and set her on the floor, but her shining brown eyes never left Sarah's face as she removed her cloak and hat and hung them on the rack by the door. Sarah reached for her medical bag, but Aggie beat her to it. Using both hands and a great deal of effort, she half-carried, half-dragged the heavy bag into the adjoining room, which served as Sarah's office, and set it beside her desk.

"Is . . . was everything all right?" Maeve asked hesitantly as she and Sarah followed Aggie into the room.

"Oh, yes," Sarah said. "A healthy baby boy, and the mother is doing fine."

In the weeks that Maeve and Aggie had been living with Sarah, Maeve had learned that Sarah's job as a midwife didn't always result in healthy mothers and babies.

Aggie looked up curiously at the mention of a baby. "That's right, Aggie," Sarah explained. "I helped a lady with her new baby today. It was a little boy, and they named him Jacob."

Aggie smiled with pleasure.

"You must be so tired, Mrs. Brandt," Maeve said. Sarah had been summoned to the delivery just after supper last night, and it had been a very long night. "Are you hungry? I can make you some eggs or something before you go to sleep."

Sarah was perfectly capable of making her own eggs, but she said, "That would be wonderful. I'm starving." She knew how eager Maeve was to demonstrate her new cooking skills. "Did the mail come?" she added.

"Not yet, but I almost forgot, a man left a note for you. It's there on the desk."

"A man?" Sarah asked, picking up the envelope. The paper was good quality, and the handwriting a woman's.

"Nice-looking gent, for all he was kind of old. Clean and polite, and not in a hurry either," she reported as she headed for the kitchen. "I told him you was out, in case it was a baby being born, but he said it wasn't no emergency," she added over her shoulder.

Ordinarily, Sarah would have corrected her grammar, but she was too interested in opening the note. Inside was a request for her to call at the home of Mr. and Mrs. Wilfred Linton at her earliest convenience for a consultation. The address was on the Upper East Side in the Lenox Hill neighborhood. That told her the Lintons were comfortably middle class. They could most likely afford a doctor to attend Mrs. Linton's pregnancy, but perhaps they preferred a midwife because of Mrs. Linton's delicate sensibilities. Whatever the case, Sarah could at least expect to collect her full fee from this family. That didn't always happen when she delivered a baby on the *Lower* East Side of the city.

Sarah was pleased that someone as respectable as the Lintons had sought her out, because they must have been referred by one of her other patients. "Isn't that nice?" she asked Aggie, not expecting a reply. "Why don't you show me what you've been doing this morning while Maeve cooks my breakfast?"

The small girl grinned hugely, grabbed Sarah's hand, and began dragging her back toward the stairs to the floor above. Those upstairs rooms had been originally intended for the children Sarah had never been able to bear Tom. Long empty, now they finally held the family Sarah had longed for.

AFTER A NICE, LONG NAP, SARAH FELT RECOVERED enough to call on the Lintons late that afternoon, when she expected Mrs. Linton would be "at home" for visitors. She walked up to Fourteenth Street and took the Ninth Avenue elevated train to Fifty-ninth Street and then took a streetcar across town to the Lenox Hill area. The afternoon sun had warmed the winter chill somewhat, but Sarah was still glad to be admitted to the comfortable warmth of the Linton home.

A young Irish girl took her wrap and showed her into the fashionably furnished parlor where Mrs. Linton had just put aside some needlework and her husband laid down a book. They both rose somewhat anxiously when Sarah was announced, and she was a little surprised to see how old they were, at least in their fifties. If Mrs. Linton were indeed pregnant, it would be somewhat of a miracle and certainly a cause for concern.

"Mrs. Brandt, how good of you to come so quickly," Mrs. Linton said after she'd introduced herself and her husband. "Please sit down. Kathleen, would you bring Mrs. Brandt some fresh tea?"

While they waited for the maid to return with Sarah's tea, the two women engaged in polite small talk while Mr. Linton sat in strained silence, as if too shy to participate but too polite to walk out. Mrs. Linton was small with fine features and neat, ash-brown hair that was nearly half-gray. She'd been a pretty girl who had matured into a handsome woman. Mr. Linton was balding and his waist had thickened with age, but he carried himself with an air of confidence that told even a casual observer that he considered himself a successful man and was proud of his accomplishments.

Sarah and Mrs. Linton complained about the weather and hoped spring would be early this year. Mrs. Linton told Sarah the name of the lady who had referred her to Sarah and reported that she and her child were still doing nicely. No one wanted to discuss delicate matters until they could be sure the serving girl would not accidentally overhear.

Finally, Kathleen delivered the tea things, and Mrs. Linton informed her they were not to be disturbed again. Mrs. Linton waited until the doors had closed behind her, and then another few moments, to be sure she was well away.

"I'm sure you must be wondering why we needed to see you, Mrs. Brandt," Mrs. Linton began, folding her hands tightly in her lap, as if to steady herself.

Sarah tried a reassuring smile. "I assumed that you needed my professional services."

To Sarah's surprise, Mrs. Linton's eyes filled with tears. "Yes, we . . ." Her voice broke, and she looked at her husband helplessly.

"Now, Mother," he said more kindly than Sarah could have imagined. "We must be brave." But Sarah saw his eyes were moist, too.

"Yes, dear, of course," Mrs. Linton said, dabbing at her eyes with a lacy handkerchief and stiffening her back purposefully. "I'm sorry, but when you know, you'll understand. You see, it's our daughter . . ."

"Grace," Mr. Linton supplied when his wife nearly lost her composure again. "Our little Gracie," he said more softly and with a tenderness that touched Sarah's heart. "She's seventeen."

"She's our only child," Mrs. Linton quickly explained. "We'd given up all hope of ever having a family. I was one week shy of turning forty when she was born. We were so happy . . ."

Sarah could see something had marred that happiness, and she could guess what. "Was something wrong?"

"We never guessed, not at first," Mrs. Linton assured her anxiously.

"She's a beautiful girl," Mr. Linton said with a combination of sadness and pride. "Perfect in every way."

"Except . . ." Mrs. Linton dropped her gaze to the handkerchief she clutched in her lap.

Sarah waited, giving them time to tell her in their own way what she already knew.

"She was the sweetest child," Mrs. Linton said so softly that Sarah could hardly hear her. "But slow. Slower than most to do everything—walking and talking. She was almost three before she said more than a few words."

"We thought it was our fault," her husband explained. "We thought we must have spoiled her or made things too easy."

"But after a while we had to accept the truth," Mrs. Linton said, absently dabbing at a tear that had escaped to run down her cheek. "She never really learned to read properly, and sums are beyond her."

"She sews beautifully," Mr. Linton added defensively, as if to say she wasn't completely worthless.

"Oh, yes, she's good with her hands. She can draw, too. But we had to take her out of school very early. Since then, she's led a very sheltered life."

"We aren't ashamed of her," Mr. Linton hastened to explain. "But people can be cruel. We never wanted her to be unhappy, you see, so we kept her at home."

Sarah knew only too well how people would have shunned a girl who was judged simpleminded or "touched in the head." She thought of Brian Malloy, the son of her friend Detective Sergeant Frank Malloy. He had been judged simpleminded, too, and kept secreted away so no one could make fun of him. "I'm sure you did the best you could to protect her," she said.

"Yes, we did," Mrs. Linton said, pleased that Sarah had understood so easily. "Which is why this is so difficult . . ." Once again she looked down and twisted the handkerchief until Sarah thought it would tear.

"You believe your daughter is with child?" Sarah guessed, trying to help them by saying what they could not bring themselves to admit.

"We aren't sure," Mrs. Linton said at the same instant Mr. Linton said, "It's impossible!"

They exchanged a glance, and Mr. Linton silently agreed to allow his wife to explain.

"As my husband said, it's impossible, and yet . . . Well, our maid, Barbara, came to me a few days ago to tell me that Grace hasn't had her . . ." She glanced at her husband apologetically, "her monthly flux in several months. At least four, she thought."

"That isn't unusual for young girls," Sarah said, thinking she could probably put their minds at ease if this was their only cause for concern.

"I knew it," Mr. Linton said almost hopefully.

"There's more," Mrs. Linton said, ignoring him. "Barbara wasn't concerned at first, either, but then she noticed that Grace is . . . is plumper. Not that she's getting fat, precisely, but that her stomach is noticeably larger. And so is her . . . her bosom. Grace's clothes no longer fit her properly."

"She's probably still growing," Mr. Linton insisted, but Sarah could hear the thin thread of fear beneath the words.

"She isn't growing anywhere else," Mrs. Linton said, holding her composure with difficulty.

Sarah's mind was spinning, trying to think of a logical explanation that would reassure these people. "You said you've kept her at home," she tried. A pregnancy would require a male contribution. Where could that have come from?

"Not literally," Mrs. Linton said. "She goes to church, and I take her visiting with me to close friends who . . . who know her and are kind."

"But she's never alone when she's away from the house," Mr. Linton insisted. "How could this have happened? As I keep saying, it's impossible!"

Sarah had to agree, it seemed so. "Perhaps there's another explanation for Grace's symptoms," Sarah said, although the other explanations weren't likely to be simple or even necessarily good. Ailments that simulated pregnancy were often fatal, even to young girls like Grace. "Have you taken her to a doctor?"

"Of course not," Mr. Linton said, outraged.

Mrs. Linton gave him a warning look that silenced him again. "We couldn't allow Grace to be examined by a man. She's a very sensitive girl, and if . . . if she is with child, that means someone . . . someone . . ."

"It means some man violated my little girl," Mr. Linton cried, near tears himself.

Mrs. Linton pressed her handkerchief to her lips to stifle a sob, and Mr. Linton covered his face with both hands.

"Of course," Sarah said in her most professional voice, knowing full well that the least trace of sympathy would completely undo both of them. "You're absolutely right not to take her to a doctor. If you like, I can examine Grace and see if I can determine her condition. I may be able to put your minds at ease completely. Considering the circumstances, it does seem very unlikely that Grace could be with child." She didn't promise that they would have nothing to worry about. The symptoms still concerned Sarah, but perhaps it really was nothing, as Mr. Linton had insisted.

For the first time, Mrs. Linton smiled. It was a sad thing

to behold because it was so full of desperate hope, but Sarah smiled back. "Thank you, Mrs. Brandt. Mrs. Simpson spoke so highly of you and the care you gave her when her last child was born. I just knew you'd be the right one to help us. How would you like to proceed?"

"Why don't you introduce me to Grace and let us get acquainted a bit first. Then you can explain to her that I'm a nurse, and you've asked me to check her to make sure she's healthy or something. Will she believe that?"

"She'll believe most anything her mother tells her," Mr. Linton said unhappily.

"I've never lied to her," Mrs. Linton said. "She'll trust me."

"Good," Sarah said. "May I meet Grace?"

DETECTIVE SERGEANT FRANK MALLOY THANKED THE elevator operator when he opened the door to let him out on the seventh floor of the office building on Fifth Avenue. He'd been here before, and the only thing that would have brought him back was a summons from one of the most powerful men in the city.

Nothing had changed here in the months since his last visit. The same middle-aged man, sitting behind the same desk, looked up when the elevator door opened, and he said, "Detective Sergeant Malloy, Mr. Decker is expecting you. Please have a seat while I see if he's available."

As the secretary disappeared into the inner office, Frank sat down to wait. Ever since he'd received the summons from Decker yesterday at Police Headquarters, he'd been trying to decide why Decker wanted to see him. The last time he'd been here, Decker had given him information that helped him solve the murder of one of Decker's oldest friends. He'd also made it clear at that visit that he didn't approve of Frank's friendship with his daughter, Sarah Brandt. Of course, Frank had only seen her once since the case had been solved, when she'd brought that little girl from the mission over to visit his son Brian. Frank had been careful since then to avoid Mrs. Brandt, so he didn't think Decker had called him in to warn him about seeing her. But what else could it be? Unless he'd found out how his wife had helped Frank and Sarah investigate that murder. Frank winced at the thought.

To Frank's surprise, Decker didn't keep him waiting, although he didn't rise and offer to shake hands this time, either, when the secretary escorted him into the large, airy office. "Thank you for coming, Mr. Malloy," he said. "Please have a seat."

Frank chose one of the comfortably worn leather chairs that sat in front of Decker's large desk. Decker was an imposing man, tall and handsome with the blond hair and blue eyes of his Dutch ancestors who had settled New York City. His expression said he was used to being obeyed and expected his will to be done. Frank hoped he wouldn't have to disappoint him.

"You're probably wondering why I sent for you," Decker said and didn't wait for an answer. "First of all, I want to tell you how much I appreciate your discretion in handling the Van Dyke case."

This time Decker did pause, but Frank had nothing to say to this. He hadn't been discreet for Decker's benefit. He waited.

Something flickered in Decker's eyes but was gone before Frank could identify the emotion. He allowed a few more seconds to tick off the clock before he said, "Are you still investigating Tom Brandt's death?"

This wasn't what Frank had expected, and he wasn't sure

what answer Decker was looking for. "As you pointed out the last time I was here, it's an old case, and there isn't too much evidence." Sarah's husband had been murdered nearly four years ago. Frank had once imagined he could find Dr. Brandt's killer and bring Sarah some peace, but what he'd learned since had given him second thoughts.

"You said you had a witness, someone who saw the killer," Decker reminded him.

"He saw a well-dressed, middle-aged man," Frank reminded him. "That isn't much to go on."

"You said the man mentioned my name that night," Decker reminded him. "He must be someone who knows me."

"Lots of people know you, Mr. Decker. That doesn't mean you know him."

"But what if I do? What if I can help you find him and bring him to justice?"

Frank didn't trust him. The last time they'd discussed Brandt's murder, Decker had been adamant he didn't want it solved. "If you know who the killer is, why don't you tell your friend Mr. Roosevelt?" Teddy Roosevelt was, for the time being at least, one of the Police Commissioners, although rumors swirled that newly elected President McKinley was going to appoint him to some federal government job as soon as he was inaugurated in March.

"Because I *don't* know who the killer is, not yet anyway. I have some information that might help you find him, though."

"I thought you didn't want to find him," Frank said. "You were afraid it would hurt your daughter if she knew what kind of a man her husband was."

Decker's finely boned face darkened with an emotion that might have been anger, and Frank expected him to unleash it on him. He probably wasn't used to being thwarted.

Instead, Decker simply waited a moment until he had full control of himself again. "Hurting her might also free her from the memory of a man who wasn't worthy of her."

Frank felt the sting of the silent rebuke. Decker wouldn't think Frank worthy of Sarah, either. That was at least one thing they could agree on, although Frank wasn't going to admit it. "Brandt has been dead a long time. She seems pretty free of his memory already."

"She still feels obligated to continue his *work*," Decker said with distaste. "As long as she regards him as a saintly figure who was ministering to the poor, she'll continue in this ridiculous quest of hers to save the world."

"What do you expect her to do if she finds out he wasn't a saint?"

Plainly, Decker considered this none of his business, but he needed Frank's help. "She will leave this midwife nonsense and take her rightful place in society again."

Frank doubted that Sarah would do any such thing, no matter what she found out about Tom Brandt, but he also knew he wasn't going to convince Decker. "Why are you telling me all this?"

"I want Brandt's killer found and the truth of his death revealed. I'm prepared to tell you everything I know about him. Combined with the information you already have, you may be able to solve his murder. I'm also prepared to pay you handsomely . . . to cover your expenses," he added tactfully when Frank visibly flinched.

They both knew the police only solved cases that involved "rewards," mostly because they needed the money, so this was a logical offer. Frank resented it all the same. He could feel his face burning with a combination of fury and shame. "It wasn't my case."

"I could ask Commissioner Roosevelt to assign it to you."

"Mr. Decker," Frank said, gritting his teeth to keep from raising his voice, "the last time I was here, I wanted to solve Dr. Brandt's murder because I thought it would give his widow some peace. You didn't want it solved because she would find out he wasn't the man she thought he was. It looks like we've both changed our minds, and now you're willing to hurt her, but I won't."

Decker raised his fair eyebrows in feigned surprise. "But Mr. Malloy, freeing Sarah from Tom Brandt's memory will surely be to your advantage."

Frank felt the rage boiling up inside of him, but he could hold his temper as well as Felix Decker. "Why would you *want* to give me an advantage with her?"

"I don't, of course, but I assumed you would."

Frank stared at Decker, trying in vain to read the expression in his eyes. He was very good indeed. "Hire a Pinkerton detective and give him your information, Mr. Decker. He'll have a much better chance at finding the killer than I would, because he'll have a lot more time to work on it."

"But you have the witness," Decker reminded him.

"He only saw the man once, and that was four years ago." Frank didn't mention that his witness might also be difficult to locate and reluctant to cooperate if they did find him.

"But if I find the man who did it?"

"I'll see if the witness can identify him. The police are always willing to help solve a crime," he added acidly.

"That's good to know," Decker replied with just a hint of sarcasm.

SARAH AND MRS. LINTON FOUND GRACE IN THE NURSery, a large room that had served as her playroom for her entire life. She sat on the floor having a tea party for several dolls that were seated in chairs around a small table. The dolls had obviously been well-loved for many years, and their relatively new dresses could not disguise their worn condition. Grace was serving them tea in miniature china cups from a miniature china pot. She looked up and smiled when the two women entered.

"Mama," she said with pleasure and scrambled to her feet. She was delicately made, like her mother, and slender as a reed except for a small bulge in her belly and the budding breasts stretching the fabric of her dress. She wasn't strikingly pretty, but her bright blue eyes glowed with a guileless joy that made her a delight to behold. She wore her corn-silk hair down in curls and her skirts short, as if she were still young enough to play with dolls, and Sarah would have guessed her age at closer to twelve than seventeen.

"We have a visitor, Grace," Mrs. Linton explained. "Mrs. Brandt, this is my daughter Grace."

"I'm pleased to meet you, Mrs. Brandt," Grace said brightly, proud of her good manners.

"I'm pleased to meet you, too, Grace. Would you let me join your tea party?"

"Do you really want to?" the girl asked in delight. "That would be fun!"

Grace led her over to the table. "You'll have to sit on the floor," she explained very seriously, "because you're too big to sit on the chairs. I tried it once, and the chair broke. Papa had to fix it."

"I'll be happy to sit on the floor," Sarah said, gathering her skirts and settling down near the table.

Grace took another cup and saucer from a box nearby and placed them on the table. Then she carefully poured some water from the pot into the cup, concentrating intently, her tongue sticking out from between her teeth from the effort, so she wouldn't spill a drop. "It's not really tea," Grace confided when she'd finished. "Tea can stain your clothes, so we just pretend."

"I like to pretend," Sarah said, taking the offered cup and pretending to drink. "What are your dolls' names?"

Grace introduced her to the group and added, "I'm glad you came today. You're very nice."

"Mrs. Brandt is a nurse," Mrs. Linton said. She'd taken a seat nearby to observe them.

"I had a nurse when I was little," Grace informed her. "Do you take care of a little girl, too?"

"No, I'm a different kind of nurse," Sarah said.

"Mrs. Brandt takes care of sick people. She's the kind of nurse who helps doctors," Mrs. Linton explained patiently. "Do you remember when Mrs. York was sick?"

"Oh, yes," Grace said proudly. "She's my friend Percy's mother," she explained to Sarah. "When her husband died, she got sick, and the doctor had to come and give her medicine, and then a lady took care of her for a while."

"That lady was a nurse, Grace," her mother said.

Grace looked at Sarah, then turned to her mother with a worried frown. "Are you sick, Mama?"

"Oh, no, dear. Mrs. Brandt is here to see you."

Now Grace was more confused. "I'm not sick. Why do I need a nurse?"

Mrs. Linton opened her mouth, but she couldn't think of a logical explanation, and quickly closed it again, casting Sarah a desperate glance.

"Sometimes nurses visit people who aren't sick," Sarah said. "One thing I do is help people keep from getting sick. Your parents asked me to visit you, to make sure you stay healthy."

"I don't want to be sick," Grace said. "I don't like it."

"I know you don't, dear, so I know you'll talk to Mrs.

Brandt and answer her questions and let her examine you."

"What does 'examine' mean?" she asked suspiciously.

"I'll look in your eyes and your ears and your mouth and listen to your heart and . . . Well, why don't I just show you?"

"Will it hurt?"

"Absolutely not." Sarah glanced at the dolls sitting primly in their tiny chairs. "You can even bring one of your babies along. I'll show you what I'm going to do on the baby first, before I do it to you."

"Can Mama be there?"

"Of course."

"We can do it in my bedroom," Mrs. Linton said. "You like being in there, don't you, Grace?"

"Yes, I do. Mama's room is very pretty," Grace told Sarah as she rose. "It's my very favorite place."

A short time later, Sarah had looked in Grace's eyes and ears and throat, taken her pulse, and demonstrated the stethoscope with which she would listen to Grace's heart.

"Would you unbutton your bodice for me, Grace?" Sarah asked. She could've listened through Grace's clothing, but she wanted to see the girl's breasts. Changes in them would tell her almost certainly if Grace were pregnant.

"Mama says it isn't proper to take your clothes off in front of other people," Grace said. "Except Barbara, of course, because she helps me get dressed."

"Your mother is right," Sarah said. "But sometimes you need to when a nurse examines you."

"It's all right this time," Mrs. Linton said.

Grace undid her buttons with the same intense concentration she'd used when pouring the tea. Sarah could see how tightly her dress was stretched across the front. Her breasts had definitely gotten larger since the dress had been fitted. After she'd listened to the girl's heart, she said, "Has your chest been sore, Grace?"

"Yes," she said with a frown. "It hurts just like it did when I first got my bosom. Barbara said they're just growing some more."

"May I look? Just to make sure nothing is wrong?"

After Mrs. Linton nodded her approval, Grace allowed Sarah to examine her breasts.

"Your mother said your tummy has gotten bigger, too," Sarah said as Grace buttoned her bodice.

Grace turned to her mother with a disgruntled frown. "Is this because I don't bleed anymore?" she demanded. "Because I don't want to bleed anymore. I don't like it. It makes my tummy hurt, and I don't care if I never do it again." She turned back to Sarah. "If that's why you came, you can just go home."

"Grace, it isn't nice to speak to guests like that," Mrs. Linton said sharply.

Grace looked ashamed, but the color still burned hotly in her cheeks. "You don't really have to go home," she said apologetically. She gave her mother a sidelong glance, and added, "But I still don't want to."

"Do you remember when you bled the last time?" Sarah asked.

Grace shook her head.

Sarah tried a different tack. "What was happening at the time? Maybe that will help you remember."

Grace frowned with the effort of recalling. "I think . . . we were having the church bazaar. Mama had to take me home because my tummy was hurting so much." She smiled with satisfaction at having given the correct answer.

"That was late July," Mrs. Linton said in dismay. "Almost six months ago."

"May I look at your tummy, Grace?" Sarah asked, holding her kindly smile with difficulty as her apprehension increased. "I'd like to listen to it with the stethoscope, too."

"Do I have to take my clothes off? It's not nice to take your clothes off unless you're going to bed, you know."

"Could you just lift your skirts? I can listen through your drawers."

When Grace obliged, Sarah could see that the girl's stomach was larger than it had appeared to be, just the right size for the sixth month of pregnancy. Many conditions could simulate pregnancy, of course, but those conditions would not produce the one thing Sarah was searching for with the bell of her stethoscope.

And then she found it: a tiny, fetal heartbeat.

2

As Frank climbed the stairs to the second floor of the tenement building, he could hear the door to his flat opening and then the clatter of a child's footsteps as his son ran down the hallway to the top of the stairs. His own step quickened as he hurried to meet the boy at the top of the steps. The instant Brian saw him, he launched himself into Frank's arms. Frank enclosed him in a bear hug, savoring the feel of his small, warm body.

The boy was making inarticulate sounds of joy, but Frank didn't bother to respond. Brian wouldn't hear him. Brian couldn't hear anything at all.

As Frank carried him up the last few steps, Brian pulled back and began making signs with his hands. He wanted to show Frank what he'd learned in deaf school. Frank recognized the sign for "father," but the others were a mystery to him. Brian wasn't quite four years old, but he was learning the signs for words as quickly as a hearing boy would learn the words themselves.

Frank's mother stood in the doorway of their flat, a small, round woman with a face like a dried-up potato. "I'll never understand how he knows when you're coming, but he always does. Runs to the window, he does, and starts dancing around and pulls me over to see," she reported sourly. Nothing, it seemed, ever gave his mother pleasure, and as far as he could tell, she disapproved of everything. Her only redeeming quality was that she adored Brian and would have given her life to keep him safe.

"How about it, boy," Frank said to his son. "Do you have the second sight?"

Brian grinned, having no idea what Frank had said but happy for his attention.

"Bite your tongue," his mother said, crossing herself. "And put him down. He can walk as well as you can, you know."

Not long ago, Brian hadn't been able to walk at all, until a surgeon Sarah Brandt knew had operated on his club foot. *Sarah Brandt*. He owed her so much. How could he stand by and let her father destroy her husband's reputation?

"What did you learn in school today, Ma?" Frank asked slyly as he carried Brian into their flat. "Tell me what he's saying."

Mrs. Malloy scowled at him as she closed the door behind them, but when Frank set his son down so he could take off his overcoat, he noticed she was doing something with her hands that looked suspiciously like signing. She put her palms together, as if she were praying, then opened them up to lie flat beside each other. Whatever she'd said sent the boy scurrying off to his bedroom. "He's got a book to show you," she said.

Frank hung his coat up on a rack. "What kind of book? Where did he get a book?"

"At school. He got it for you."

Before Frank could ask more, Brian came clomping back into the room, his specially built-up shoe making his steps sound slightly uneven. He carried a book which he proudly presented to his father.

Frank looked at the title, *Sign Language for the Deaf.* His heart felt odd in his chest, as if it had swelled or something. He opened the book and fanned through the pages. Inside were drawings of a person making signs, all kinds of signs, and the words for each were written underneath. "What's this?" he asked, his voice sounding thick because of the emotions clogging his throat.

"What's it look like?" his mother asked him impatiently. "It's a book so you can learn to make the signs and talk to Brian, too."

Frank had to swallow a couple of times. "How did he get it?" he asked in amazement. Frank had never purchased a book before. He had no idea how much it would cost, but he knew it would be a lot. "Where would he get the money? Where would *you* get the money?" he added, since she would have had to give it to him.

She made a derisive noise. "They wanted to pay me at that school. Can you imagine? All I do is look after the boy. He's too young to leave there alone all day, no matter what you think."

Brian was pulling on his pant leg, demanding attention. Frank handed him the book, and he immediately plopped down on the floor and began looking through it. "I told you, you don't have to stay there with him all day," Frank said in exasperation. "There's teachers there to look after him."

"And they've got a roomful of children to look after, too. What if Brian was to slip out? Who'd notice?"

They'd had this argument before, so Frank gave up. He'd known his mother would have to accompany Brian to and from the school, since neither of them wanted him to board there. Frank had imagined she might enjoy having her days free while he was in school, but he'd been wrong.

"What are you doing that made them want to pay you?" Frank asked suspiciously. He'd figured she'd been making a nuisance of herself, or at best, just sitting on a bench watching Brian all day.

She shrugged. "Nothing to speak of, helping out here and there. Supper's ready." She turned away and went into the kitchen. He followed her.

"You aren't cleaning or anything, are you? Because I pay good money for Brian to go there, and you don't have to—"

"I don't *clean*," she snapped over her shoulder as she began dishing up some stew from the pot on the stove.

He let a minute of silence go by while she finished filling the bowl she held. "Ma," he said in warning.

She gave him a glare that would've stopped a hardened criminal in his tracks. Many a rookie policeman would've envied her ability, but Frank was used to it. He waited patiently.

She set the bowl down on the table with a bang. "I told you, I help out."

"With the children?" he asked.

"Where do you think they need the help?" she replied, turning to fill another bowl.

"Is that how you're learning the signs, too?"

This time she gave him a disparaging look, as if she were disappointed in having given him life. "Somebody needs to be able to talk to the boy," she reminded him. "What's the use of him learning if he's got no one to sign to?"

For the second time today, Frank felt the sting of rebuke. "Ma, I don't have time to go to school to learn all that."

"Of course you don't," she agreed. "That's why we got you that book."

"Which brings us back to where we started. How did you pay for it?"

"I told you, they wanted to pay me for helping, but I told them my son provides for us, and I didn't need any money," she informed him. Frank took small pride in the back-handed compliment, the only kind she ever gave. "But I did say I'd like to have one of those books the teachers have, so they gave it to me."

Brian was tugging on his pant leg again. He wanted Frank to look at the book with him, and he was looking up at him with huge brown eyes that were so like his poor, lost mother's. Frank's heart swelled again, so full of love that he could hardly breathe. For the first three years of Brian's life, they had thought Brian was just a simpleminded cripple, but Sarah Brandt had changed all that. She'd been the one to realize that his mind was perfectly fine, just trapped in a body that couldn't hear. She'd also been the one to suggest a surgeon who could fix Brian's crippled foot, when other doctors had told him there was no hope.

He wanted—no, he *needed*—to repay her. Once he'd thought finding her husband's killer would do that, but now he knew differently. Now he knew that her father was determined to make her face a truth she'd never suspected and which might well destroy her soul. Frank couldn't stop him. No one could stop a man like Felix Decker. Frank didn't want to be a part of hurting Sarah.

But . . .

The truth was like a knife in his heart. If he was involved in the investigation, he would at least be able to control what Decker found out and, therefore, what he told Sarah. He might even be able to protect her from the worst of it.

This wasn't what he'd envisioned when he'd set out to re-pay her, but it was all he could do. He'd have to tell Decker he'd changed his mind.

Brian was making demanding squeaks and squeals and banging the book against his leg. "Ma," he asked, "what's the sign for 'supper'?"

"No, it's impossible," Mr. Linton insisted. This time Sarah heard panic in his voice.

She was back in the parlor with both of Grace's parents. Mrs. Linton was sobbing softly into her handkerchief, but Mr. Linton had chosen to shield himself behind anger.

"How can you be sure?" Linton demanded furiously. "You're just a nurse!"

"Wilfred!" his wife cried in dismay.

"Well, she's not a doctor," he reminded her indignantly.

"No, I'm not," Sarah agreed tactfully, "but I am a mid-wife, and I know how to judge if a woman is expecting a child. She's actually pretty far along, about six months, I'd guess from what she told me."

"She told you how it happened?" Linton cried. "Who did it? Who is responsible? I'll see him hanged!"

"Please, Wilfred, this is difficult enough," his wife pleaded. "And no, Grace didn't tell us anything about what happened. Mrs. Brandt didn't ask her, but she *was* able to remember when she last had her monthly cycle."

"And I can tell by how large her stomach is," Sarah added.

"But couldn't it be something else? Some illness? Per-haps a doctor could . . . could *do* something . . ." He ges-tured helplessly.

"Mr. Linton, you're right, Grace's symptoms could have been caused by an illness. In fact, at first I was afraid that she might have a tumor or some other growth that would explain the changes in her body."

Mrs. Linton made a horrified sound, her eyes large and bright with terror.

"Yes," Sarah confirmed, "it could have been something fatal, but thank heaven, it was not. She has all the signs of being with child, and most important, I was able to hear the baby's heartbeat."

This made Mrs. Linton start sobbing all over again, and Mr. Linton completely despaired, sinking into his chair as if his very bones had withered inside of him.

"But how? . . ." he wondered in despair. "Who could have done this to her? And when?"

"She mentioned a friend named Percy," Sarah recalled.

"Percy York?" Linton scoffed. "He's just a boy."

"He's much younger than Grace," Mrs. Linton said. "Young enough that he doesn't seem to notice Grace is . . . is different. At least not yet. So they're friends."

"They only see each other at church anyway," Mr. Linton said. He rubbed his hand over his bald head and sighed. "I don't understand. It's just not possible."

Sarah waited, giving them time to come to terms with the reality of their situation. After a few minutes, Mr. Linton looked up. "Mrs. Brandt, please forgive me for my rudeness—"

"I'm not easily offended, Mr. Linton," she assured him. "And you have every reason to be upset."

"You are very gracious, and I hope I won't offend you further by asking this, but I'm a man of the world, and I know that there are certain women who . . ." He glanced at his wife who was staring at him warily, not certain she wanted to hear what he would say next. He cleared his throat. "Women who can take care of girls in Grace's situation."

"I won't send Grace away," Mrs. Linton said, outraged. "She's going to endure a horrible experience. I won't frighten her by making her think we don't love her, too."

"I'm not talking about sending her away, Mother," Mr. Linton said gently. "I believe Mrs. Brandt understands me, though."

Sarah did, indeed. "It's a very dangerous procedure, but in Grace's case, it doesn't matter. She's too far along to have it done."

"What are you talking about?" Mrs. Linton demanded.

"An operation," Mr. Linton said wearily. "To remove the baby."

She stared at him in horror, unable to comprehend such a thing.

Sarah decided it was time to help them start thinking about realities and options. "Grace is young and healthy, and there's every reason to believe her baby will be, too. You'll need to explain to her what is happening and what is going to happen. And then, of course, you'll have to decide what to do about the child."

"What do you mean?" Mrs. Linton asked, still stunned by the thought of the unimaginable operation.

"Will you keep the child and raise it yourself or make other arrangements? You might have a family member who would welcome a child, or perhaps you could find a home for it with a couple who have no children of their own."

"Why, we'll keep it, of course," Mrs. Linton said quite certainly.

"But Mother, the scandal," Mr. Linton reminded her. "What will people say about Grace? And the child, what kind of a life will *she* have?"

"A good life, raised by people who love her," Mrs. Linton said, her voice throbbing on the edge of hysteria.

"You shouldn't try to decide today," Sarah advised them. "This is something you'll need to think about and discuss. Perhaps you'll want to talk to your minister about it, too, or a trusted friend."

"You're right, we will have to tell Grace, of course. She needs to know," Mrs. Linton said. She turned her pleading glance on Sarah. "Will you help me tell her?"

"Certainly," Sarah said. "But I think you should wait a while. You're both very upset right now, and we don't want to frighten her."

"Could you come back tomorrow?" Mrs. Linton asked anxiously. "I mean, if it wouldn't be too much trouble."

"We'll pay you, of course," Mr. Linton added. "Whatever your normal fee is, and we'll want you to take care of Grace when . . . when the time comes." His voice nearly broke, and he pulled out a handkerchief and blew his nose.

"I'll come back tomorrow," Sarah promised. She would have done so even if they hadn't asked.

FRANK CERTAINLY HADN'T PLANNED TO RETURN TO FE-lix Decker's office so soon. In fact, he'd fully expected never to return at all. Felix Decker wasn't the kind of man to forgive the kind of snub Frank had handed him yesterday. Frank was clenching his teeth as he waited for Decker to find time to see him. He still detested the man and the way he planned to hurt his own daughter, but if Frank hoped to convince Decker to put him on the case, he'd have to conceal his own feelings.

He'd spent some sleepless hours last night trying to decide how to convince Decker he'd changed his mind and what reason he could give for it. As much as it galled him, he'd finally realized the best way would be to confirm

Decker's low opinion of him. Frank's pride would take a beating, but it wouldn't be the first time. He'd survive, and more important, he'd be in a position to protect Sarah from whatever he found out about her late husband.

This time Decker left him cooling his heels for over an hour. Frank wasn't too worried about getting in trouble at work for being gone so long. They knew about Decker's summons yesterday, and he hadn't even had to explain why he was returning today. Frank was allowing himself to wonder what it would be like to command the type of power that meant no one would question you, when Decker's secretary finally told him the great man would see him.

Decker's desktop was covered with papers today, and his fine eyes were suspicious and a bit impatient.

"I hope you aren't going to waste my time again today, Mr. Malloy," he said coldly.

"I hope not, Mr. Decker," Frank replied, trying to sound humble but not certain he was successful. He took a seat, even though Decker hadn't offered one. "I thought a lot about your proposition yesterday, and I decided I should've taken it."

"Why?"

The word hung in the air like a challenge, holding more meanings than Frank could even guess. He cleared his throat and told his lie. "I could use the reward you offered." The words came more easily than he'd expected, but he couldn't stop the hot wave of shame that poured over him as he held his face rigidly expressionless.

Decker considered his claim for a long moment. "For your son, I suppose," he said finally.

This time the hot wave was fury, but Frank managed to hold his temper as tightly as he held Decker's gaze. "Yes," he managed through stiff lips.

"He's a cripple, I believe," Decker said, pausing to see if Frank would react. He didn't, although the effort cost him dearly. "Or he was," Decker continued. "Didn't David Newton operate on him? David's father and I were at school together."

Frank saw no reason to reply. Decker obviously knew everything about Brian. Had Sarah told him? No, he couldn't imagine her discussing the Malloys with her family. Decker must have had him investigated. How ironic to investigate a man you wanted to investigate someone else, but he supposed men like Decker did things like that all the time. He'd take nothing for granted and trust no one.

When Frank didn't reply, Decker said, "But he's still deaf, isn't he? Your boy, I mean."

Who else could he have meant? Frank simply sat, his fury like gall in his throat, waiting for Decker to finish demonstrating his superiority.

"So you want the money to take care of your boy," Decker concluded for him.

Frank swallowed down the bitterness. "Yes."

Decker studied him for a long moment. "Mr. Malloy, I know you wouldn't do this for money. I saw your reaction yesterday when I made you the offer. What really made you change your mind?"

Frank saw his error instantly. He'd underestimated Felix Decker, so he'd only prepared one lie, and now he had nothing else to offer. But maybe the truth would serve him just as well, if he only told part of it. "I don't trust anyone else to get this right," he tried.

"You were the one who advised me to hire a Pinkerton," Decker reminded him. "Don't you believe a professional detective could uncover the truth as well as you could?"

"I think he'd be willing to tell you what you want to

hear, whether it was the truth or not," Frank said. "I'm not interested in pleasing you, just in solving Brandt's murder."

"Even if that means proving Tom Brandt wasn't what he seemed? Even if that means my daughter may learn things she won't want to know about him?"

"Yes," Frank lied again.

"Yesterday you didn't want to hurt my daughter. What happened to change your mind about *that*?"

There it was, the perfect explanation, the one even Decker would believe. Frank should've thought of it himself. "I realized I want her to forget him. You said it yourself, it would be to my advantage."

Decker studied him for what seemed a long time. He didn't look as if he believed this, either, but he would have no reason to doubt it. Frank was sure of that. Decker himself had provided the reason.

"All right," Decker said suddenly, as if he'd come to some conclusion. Then he pushed himself up out of his chair and walked over to the far corner of the room where a small safe sat. He bent over and spun the dial with practiced ease. The handle made a soft, well-oiled thump when Decker twisted it, and the door swung open. He rummaged inside for a moment and pulled out a folder. After closing the safe, he carried the folder back to his desk.

"A few months before Tom Brandt died, I received a letter." He pulled a piece of paper out of the folder and passed it across the desk to Frank.

The paper was good quality, the handwriting neat and precise. The writer had been an educated man. The text of the letter was short and to the point. "Dr. Tom Brandt is a seducer of young women. He has taken advantage of innocent females under his care and ruined them both in body and in mind. Someone must stop him."

"There's no signature," Frank noted. "How can you take something like this seriously?"

"I didn't, not at first," Decker said. "But I had the matter investigated, just to be sure. This is the report."

He handed Frank the folder which contained half a dozen sheets of a handwritten report from the Pinkerton Detective Agency.

"Don't bother to read it all now," Decker said. "It says Brandt had several young, female patients whose symptoms were very similar and who had all lost their minds as a result of some kind of assault."

"A *seduction*?" Frank asked skeptically.

"That's a polite word for it," Decker said. "The man responsible was their doctor."

"What did you do about this report?"

"Look at the date on it, Mr. Malloy. I only received it a few days before Brandt was murdered. I hadn't decided what, if anything, I was going to do, and when he died . . . Well, there was nothing left to do."

"Except destroy his widow's memory of him," Frank said.

"Which would be to your advantage," Decker reminded him brutally.

Not if Frank were the one to uncover a horrible scandal about Brandt, he thought, but he didn't say it. Decker had probably already considered all the possibilities and knew even better than Frank how Sarah would feel about the man who did such a thing. She'd hate him, and he wouldn't blame her, and that would play right into Decker's plans to free her completely from both Thomas Brandt and Frank Malloy. On the other hand, Frank might be able to protect her from ever learning the truth at all, or at least the worst of it. Or even . . . Well, he hardly allowed himself to think of such a thing, but he might be able to prove these charges against Dr. Brandt were false. That wasn't something a hired detective would even consider, but Frank prided himself on having an open mind.

"WHY ARE YOU CRYING, MAMA?" GRACE ASKED. "I THINK it'll be fun to have a baby."

Mrs. Linton resolutely wiped the tears from her eyes and made herself smile. "I'm just worried because you're so young," she explained, looking to Sarah with a silent plea.

Sarah nodded, encouraging her to go on because she was doing fine. They were in the nursery, where Mrs. Linton felt Grace would be most comfortable to hear the news.

"Babies aren't like dolls," Mrs. Linton said. "You have to take care of them all day long. They cry, and they get hungry."

"We could get a nurse to take care of it," Grace said. "Like you did when I was little."

"Yes, we could," her mother said, dabbing at her eyes again.

This time Grace didn't notice. She was looking down at the mound of her stomach and rubbing it. "Why can't we get the baby right now? I want to play with it."

"It's not big enough yet, dear," Mrs. Linton said, her voice rough with tears. This time Sarah couldn't ignore the silent plea.

"The baby has to grow inside of you for about three more months, and then it will be born," Sarah said.

Grace turned her innocent gaze on Sarah. "How does it get out?"

Her mother made a small, distressed sound.

"Would you mind leaving me and Grace alone, Mrs. Linton? I would be happy to explain everything to her."

Mrs. Linton made some token protests, but Sarah easily persuaded her to leave this awkward task to a professional. Carefully and simply, Sarah explained the birth process to Grace and answered her questions as honestly as she could. Grace didn't ask the one question Sarah had dreaded the most, "Will it hurt?" Probably, she hadn't even considered the possibility. Sarah would save that explanation until much closer to the time. There was no use in frightening the girl now.

When Grace was satisfied that she knew enough, she went back to playing with her dolls. Sarah decided she would use this time to ask a few questions of her own.

"Grace, you seem to be a very happy girl," she began.

"Oh, I am. Mama and Papa want me to be happy. They're always telling me."

"Is there anyone in your life who doesn't make you happy? Maybe someone who hurt you?"

Grace's pretty face wrinkled in thought. "No one ever hurts me. Except Barbara sometimes, when she brushes my hair too hard. Is that what you mean?"

"No, I meant something much worse. Did a man ever hurt you? It would have been a long time ago, last summer. Can you remember back that far?"

"I already told you, I remember last summer," Grace reminded her. "I don't remember getting hurt, though."

"Maybe the man was someone you didn't know. Maybe he told you not to tell anyone what happened. Maybe he frightened you, or threatened to hurt your family if you told anyone. But it's all right to tell, Grace. What that man did was wrong. He shouldn't have hurt you."

Now Grace looked really puzzled. "Nobody hurt me or scared me. Why are you asking me these things, Mrs. Brandt?"

Sarah had fully expected the girl to at least become upset when Sarah mentioned the strange man and the possible threats. How else could Grace have become pregnant except by rape?

Then another, even more horrible thought occurred to her. She hadn't considered it before, but now . . .

"Grace, do you and your father have secrets? Things you don't tell your mother about?"

The girl considered this. "I don't think so."

"Does your father ever do things and tell you not to tell your mother?"

Grace tried hard to think of something, but then shook her head.

"Does he ever come into your bedroom?"

"Oh, no, that wouldn't be proper. I'm a big girl now, and it's not proper for a man to come into my bedroom. Mama explained it to me."

"So no men ever come into your bedroom?"

Grace gave Sarah an exasperated look. "I just told you, it's not proper."

"Does your father ever kiss you?" Sarah tried.

"He kisses me good night every night."

"Where does he kiss you?"

"Here," she said, pointing to her cheek.

"Do you kiss him?"

"Oh, yes. I like to kiss him. He smells good."

"Where do you kiss him?"

"On the cheek, but sometimes . . ." She covered her mouth and giggled.

"Sometimes you kiss him someplace else?" Sarah asked, not certain she wanted to know.

"It's a funny place. He likes it when I kiss him there, too."

Sarah's smile felt frozen on her face. "Where is this funny place?" she asked.

Grace giggled again, and looked around, as if checking to make sure no one could overhear. "I kiss him here," she whispered and touched the top of her head.

Sarah blinked. "You kiss him on the top of his head?"

"Where he doesn't have any hair," Grace confided. "His cheeks are scratchy, but the top of his head is really soft, and when I kiss him there, he always laughs. I like to make him laugh."

Sarah felt the tension drain from her body, leaving her limp with relief. Thank heaven Grace's situation hadn't been caused by incest. But it didn't appear that she had been raped, either, at least not that she could recall. Sometimes women didn't remember things like that, as if their minds were protecting them, but their shock was obvious. Their loved ones always knew something terrible had happened to them, even if the woman couldn't recall what. Surely Grace's family would have noticed if something awful had happened to her.

Sarah remembered Mr. Linton's reaction that it was impossible for Grace to be pregnant. Sarah was starting to feel the same way, and yet she was. There must be some logical explanation, and finding it was important. Someone had taken advantage of Grace, and he would probably do it again—if not to her, then to another unfortunate girl. He must be found and stopped.

But how, if his victim didn't even know what he had done to her?

3

Sarah trudged up her front steps wearily, emotionally exhausted from her encounter with the Linton family and their tragedy. Grace's parents were so overwhelmed by the prospect of her bearing a child that they didn't have the energy to consider the man who was responsible for that child. Perhaps they would later, when the shock wore off and they began to feel the anger that was natural in a situation like this.

But how could they bring the man responsible to justice? Grace could never testify in a court of law. Even if she'd been capable of understanding the legal process, her parents would never allow it. No parents would put their daughter through such a humiliating ordeal. Sarah was beginning to understand why the police sometimes took justice into their own hands.

As she stepped into her house, she heard the patter of Aggie's small feet running in from the kitchen.

"Be careful, dear! You shouldn't run in the house!" a familiar voice called, and Sarah smiled even before Aggie appeared from the hallway and flew into her arms. Sarah hoisted her up onto her hip.

"Is Mrs. Ellsworth helping you cook supper again?" she asked the child, who nodded vigorously.

"Mrs. Ellsworth is really showing us how to bake a cake," Maeve reported, having arrived at a more ladylike pace. "I didn't tell her that I already learned how at the mission," she added in a whisper.

"That's very nice of you," Sarah whispered back.

"I never knew how much fun it could be to have girls," Mrs. Ellsworth said as she emerged from the hallway into the front room. "My son never wanted to learn to cook or sew, of course, but *these* girls are so very clever, it's a joy to teach them."

"You're very kind to spend so much time with them," Sarah told her elderly next-door neighbor. Before Maeve and Aggie had moved in, Mrs. Ellsworth could most frequently be found sweeping her front stoop so she could keep track of everything that happened on Bank Street. Nowadays, however, she spent much of her time with Aggie and Maeve.

"I'm not a bit kind," Mrs. Ellsworth assured her. "It's my pleasure, although you were very right to bring Maeve to look after Aggie. I never could've kept up with her."

When Sarah had first considered bringing Aggie to live with her, Mrs. Ellsworth had volunteered to care for the child when Sarah had to work. Sarah could never have asked her to do such a thing, and she'd been relieved when a volunteer at the mission had suggested that one of the older girls would be an excellent nanny for Aggie. That decision had allowed Mrs. Ellsworth to play grandmother to the girls whenever she liked, a situation that suited all of them perfectly.

"What kind of a cake are you making?" she asked Aggie, as she set the girl back on the floor.

"Come and show Mrs. Brandt," Mrs. Ellsworth suggested, taking Aggie's hand to lead her back to the kitchen. Maeve followed, and Sarah did, too, after pausing a minute to remove her cape and boots.

"Oh, it's so warm in here," Sarah exulted, rubbing her stiff fingers and holding them over the comforting heat of the kitchen stove. "And something smells wonderful."

"It's just a simple, one-egg cake," Mrs. Ellsworth explained. "Do you want to finish mixing it, Aggie?"

The girl picked up the spoon that lay on the table, but she didn't get a good grip on it, and it fell from her hand, clattering back onto the tabletop.

"Oh, my, looks like we'll be having a visitor," Mrs. Ellsworth said.

"Is that what it means when you drop a spoon?" Maeve asked with great interest. In the weeks she'd been acquainted with Mrs. Ellsworth, she'd learned that the old woman knew a superstition for practically everything that happened.

"Only if the spoon falls on the table. If it falls on the floor, then it depends on how it lands. If the bowl is up, that means good fortune. If the bowl is down, that means disappointment."

"The bowl is up. Does that mean our visitor will bring us good fortune?" Maeve asked. Even Aggie was waiting eagerly for the answer.

Sarah wanted to groan. She didn't want the girls to become superstitious, but she also didn't want to hurt Mrs. Ellsworth's feelings. "We'll bring disappointment to our visitor if the cake isn't ready when she—or he—gets here," she said to distract them. "And as soon as you put the cake in the oven, you can lick the bowl."

That was enough to motivate Aggie to finish beating the batter. In another few minutes, they'd poured it into the pans and slipped them into the oven. The four of them made sure every drop of remaining batter was scraped clean from the mixing bowl and spoons. When they'd finished with that and had cleaned up the kitchen, Mrs. Ellsworth showed Aggie how to make the boiled icing while the layers cooled. When the cake was finally finished, they all had a piece, just to make sure it was suitable for the expected visitor. Then Mrs. Ellsworth went home to fix supper for her son Nelson, who would be home soon from his job at the bank, and the girls went upstairs to play.

Sarah took advantage of her solitude to savor the exquisite sensation of warmth and comfort in the peace of her own kitchen. Her life was very different from the one she had imagined when she and Tom were married almost seven years ago. She'd expected to raise a family and grow old with him, but Tom had died young, and now her family consisted of two misfit girls. Maeve would eventually be ready to take a job with someone who could pay her, and Sarah would select another girl from the mission to come live with them and train as a nanny.

Sarah wanted to legally adopt Aggie, so the girl would truly be hers, but her parents had convinced her to wait a while, to make sure Aggie could adjust to living with her. Perhaps they'd also hoped she would find having a child too much work and change her mind, although they hadn't actually tried to talk her out of it. In any case, having Aggie here had only served to convince her that she wanted the girl permanently. Soon she'd have to start the legal process.

Sarah sat for a few more minutes, savoring the thought of finally becoming a mother and feeling remarkably content and slightly drowsy when the sound of someone ringing her doorbell startled her back to the present. With a smile, Sarah rose from her chair, thinking it was probably Mrs. Ellsworth, returning to fulfill her own prophecy. Or perhaps it was a frantic father-to-be, summoning her to attend his wife. But the silhouette she saw through the frosted glass of her door wasn't Mrs. Ellsworth's, although it was familiar, and Sarah's smile broadened.

She was still smiling when she opened the door. "Malloy," she said by way of greeting. "Do you need some help on a case?"

Malloy's expression had been carefully neutral, but her question surprised him into almost smiling. She saw the flicker of it in his dark eyes before he caught himself. "No, I thought I'd stop by to see if you needed any help delivering babies," he replied, deadpan, delighting her.

"Then come inside so I can start your instructions," she said, more pleased than she cared to admit to see him on her doorstep. She'd forgotten how much she enjoyed his company.

Before he had even cleared the doorway, Aggie and Maeve were coming down the stairs to greet him. Both had fond memories of him from the mission.

"We knew you were coming, Mr. Malloy," Maeve announced. "Aggie dropped a spoon."

"A *spoon*?" Malloy repeated, giving Sarah a puzzled glance.

"Mrs. Ellsworth," she offered in explanation.

Malloy nodded in perfect understanding.

"Didn't you bring Brian?" Maeve asked. Sarah had once taken the girls to visit Malloy's son, which they had all enjoyed.

"Not today," Malloy said, and something in his tone warned Sarah he wasn't making a social call. Since he would probably cut off his own foot before willingly involving her in another murder investigation, what other business could have brought him here? She felt a small frisson of alarm.

Malloy was picking Aggie up in response to her silent demands. "How do you like living here with Mrs. Brandt, Aggie?" he asked.

Aggie didn't answer, of course, but she smiled hugely.

"Is Maeve taking good care of you?"

Aggie nodded.

"Maeve is an excellent helper," Sarah reported, making the girl blush.

She shrugged modestly. "I like it here. Would you like a piece of cake, Mr. Malloy? We made it just for you."

Malloy raised his eyebrows skeptically. "You shouldn't tell fibs," he teased her. "You didn't know I was coming."

"Yes, we did, because Aggie dropped the spoon," she reminded him smugly.

The girls induced Malloy to accompany them to the kitchen and sample the cake, which he declared delicious, and Sarah made some coffee. He wasn't used to socializing with young girls, but he managed to keep them amused. Sarah watched him in growing admiration. He truly was a remarkable man.

When everyone had eaten and thoroughly spoiled their suppers, Sarah sent the girls back upstairs so she could talk to Malloy in private. Or rather, so he could talk to her and tell her why he'd come.

When they were alone, neither spoke for several minutes. Sarah was surprised at this awkwardness between them, after all they'd been through together, but suddenly, his presence seemed somehow too real in the close confines of her kitchen. She couldn't stop herself from recalling some of the more intimate moments of their relationship, moments when it seemed they might pass that invisible barrier from friendship to something more. Yet here they sat, still friends and not even comfortable with that, if Sarah's tingling nerves and Malloy's unease were any indication.

"How have you been?" she said to break the silence.

"Fine," he said automatically.

"How is Brian doing in school?"

"He likes it a lot. My mother goes with him every day. She's learning sign language, too."

"She is?" Sarah exclaimed in surprise. "I thought she was against the whole idea."

"She was, but then she realized that if he learned sign language, nobody at home would be able to talk to him. She knew I wasn't going to learn it, so I guess she figured she'd have one up on me if she did."

"That's wonderful," Sarah said.

"Don't let her know you think so," Malloy warned. "She might stop, just for spite." Mrs. Malloy didn't approve of Sarah's friendship with her son, which reminded them both of the many barriers to any other kind of relationship.

The awkward silence fell again.

"I—"

"What did—" They both spoke at once, then stopped in embarrassment.

"You first," he said.

"I . . . I was just going to ask what brought you here today," she said. "Unless you saw some omen that told you we'd made you a cake."

His lips curved in a quick smile that vanished instantly. "I was wondering if you'd let me look at your husband's files again."

Now she was really surprised, and a knot of dread formed in her stomach, as it usually did when she thought of Tom's death. "I thought you hadn't found anything useful there." He'd spent quite a few hours examining all of Tom's medical files a few months back, when he'd thought he might find a clue to who had killed him.

"I came across an old investigator's report on his case, and it had some names in it. If those people were his patients, they might know something. It isn't much," he added hastily. "They might not even have been his patients, and if they were, they probably don't know who killed him. But I thought it was worth a look."

"Then you don't really have any new information about Tom's death?"

"Nothing important, like I said. Just a few names."

"Then certainly, you may check his files." Memories of her dead husband thankfully served to stifle her awareness of Malloy as a man. She led him into the front-room office where Tom's files were still located. "Do you need any help?"

"No, it shouldn't take more than a couple minutes." He pulled a folded paper out of his pocket and consulted it before opening a file drawer.

"I'll clean up the kitchen then," she said, for some reason not wanting to watch.

Clearing away the plates and cups took only a few minutes. She really should get started on supper, although she and the girls wouldn't be hungry for a while after eating all that cake. Sarah couldn't even begin to think of anything as mundane as supper while Malloy was in her front room, though. As if drawn by a magnet, she returned to the front office.

He was adding a file to a small pile of them on her desk. "That's all of them," he said.

"Then they *were* his patients," she said, not sure if she should be pleased or not. She wanted Tom's killer caught and punished. She'd wanted that for years, so why did she suddenly feel apprehensive? Maybe it was Malloy's manner. He didn't look the way he usually did when he was working on a case. He had no sense of eagerness or excitement, no feral gleam in his eye from the thrill of the hunt. Instead he seemed weary, almost sad.

"Don't get your hopes up," he warned gently. "It's probably nothing important. And don't even *offer* to help me," he added with a glimmer of his old spirit.

"I thought you were here to help *me*," she reminded him, feeling a glimmer of spirit herself. "Are you ready to begin your midwife training?"

"I don't think I'd be as good at it as you are at detective work," he said with a small smile. She loved that smile. "But if you ever have a crime with one of your babies, just let me know."

"Oh, my," Sarah said in surprise, "I *do* have a crime to deal with. How could I have forgotten?"

Malloy's face creased into a frown. She didn't love that frown. "It better not be a murder."

"Don't be silly, of course it's not a murder," she said. "If it was, you'd probably already know about it. But I could use your advice. Do you have a few more minutes?"

He was still frowning, but he followed her to the two overstuffed chairs that sat by the front window.

When they were seated, he said, "What kind of a crime is it?"

"A rape, I think," she said, making him wince. He didn't like to think of her even knowing about such things. That was one thing on which he and her family would agree. "It's a seventeen-year-old girl in Lenox Hill. She's expecting a child in about three months, and her parents just realized it. But as far as her parents can determine, she's never even been alone with a man."

"A seventeen-year-old girl can do a lot of things her parents don't know about," Malloy said. "Even one from Lenox Hill."

"Grace is seventeen physically, but mentally, she's more like a five-year-old, and she probably always will be. She still plays will dolls, and she has absolutely no understanding of what happened to her or what is going to happen."

"Even a simpleton would remember being attacked," Malloy said.

"I questioned her very carefully, but she insists no one ever hurt her in her entire life. I even . . ." Sarah hated to admit this, although she and Malloy had dealt with this very situation. "I even asked if her father had ever done anything to her, but all he's done is kiss her on the cheek."

"What about servants?"

"All female, and she only leaves the house to attend church and go on visits with her mother to other women."

"Do you think it's a miracle?" he asked with a hint of irony. "You'd need a priest for that, not a detective."

"Of course I don't think it's a miracle. Someone took advantage of this poor girl, and he shouldn't get away with it."

"And what if you do find him? Will her family charge him?"

"I doubt it," she admitted. "Even if they would, Grace would be a poor witness."

"Why try to find him, then?"

"There are other ways to punish someone besides putting him in jail," Sarah said. "I've been thinking about this, and I realized that gossip can be a powerful tool of punishment. No one would ever believe a girl like Grace was involved in a romance of any kind. The man must have forced her. Most people would consider that despicable, and the word would pass very quickly in society. He'd never be welcomed at any respectable home again."

Malloy stared at her as if he'd never seen her before. "You never cease to amaze me, Mrs. Brandt. I suppose you'd be willing to use your social connections to help ruin this man's reputation, too."

"Of course. What good is it being a member of one of the oldest families in New York if you can't stomp out evil now and then?"

"Just be sure you get the right man."

"What do you mean by that?"

"I mean don't jump to conclusions. And don't overlook the obvious."

"I haven't been able to find anyone obvious," she reminded him.

He shook his head and gave her a pitying look. "You already told me there's only one man who has contact with her."

"And I also told you her father isn't responsible."

"Why? Because he's a respectable man who lives in a respectable neighborhood and makes a good living? We both know incest can happen no matter how respectable the family is."

"I'd swear her father didn't do this. You didn't see him or talk to him, and you didn't hear what Grace said. I know how to find out these things, Malloy. I've delivered a lot of babies to unmarried girls, enough to tell when a girl is hiding something *from* her father and when she's hiding something *about* him, and enough to recognize when a father is outraged and when he's feeling guilty. Grace's father is outraged and heartbroken."

"If he didn't do it, who could have?" Malloy asked.

"I told you, nobody knows!"

"The girl knows. You just didn't ask her the right question."

Sarah wanted to smack him, but she knew he was right. "So what should I do now?"

"Why do you have to do anything?"

"What?"

"I said, why do you have to do anything?" he repeated patiently. "This isn't your daughter or your family, so you don't have to do *anything* about it. If her family wants to find the man and punish him, they can go to the police or . . ." He put up his hand to stop her when she would have sputtered in outrage over the unlikelihood of the police solving a crime like this. "*Or* they could hire a Pinkerton to investigate quietly. *They* can do whatever they want, but *you* don't have to do anything at all except take care of the girl and her baby."

She hated it when he was logical, and even more when he was right, so she fumed for a minute before she could say, "Would you go and talk to the parents?"

"About what?" he asked suspiciously.

"To encourage them to find out who attacked Grace. I'm afraid they'll be so interested in protecting her that they won't even try."

"Maybe they don't want to try. Maybe they don't want to know."

"But they should. Don't you see?"

"I see that *you* want this man punished, even if it's just execution by gossip, but they're probably more interested in protecting their daughter. And don't forget, her father may be protecting himself, no matter what you think about him. If he is, he'll never call in the police."

Sarah knew Mr. Linton was innocent, but she'd never

convince Malloy of it until he saw for himself. "Will you talk to them or not?" she challenged.

"Only if they ask to see me," he said stubbornly. "I can't just knock on their front door and tell them I heard their daughter had been attacked and I'm here to start investigating."

"But if I convince them to speak with you, you'll do it?" she said.

He gave a long-suffering sigh. "You know I will." Then his mouth quirked at one corner and his dark eyes gleamed. "At least it's not a murder."

FRANK TOOK TOM BRANDT'S PATIENT FILES HOME WITH him, and after Brian and his mother went to bed, he started reading them. He'd hoped that he wouldn't find the four women's files in Sarah's office, but Felix Decker's Pinkertons were the best money could buy. Of course they'd gotten that part right. They'd never seen the women's medical files, though, of that he was certain.

The four women seemed to have little in common except that they were all unmarried and all suffering from "hysteria." Frank had seen many hysterical women in his time, but in his experience, it was a temporary condition brought on by anger or terror or some other strong emotion.

One of the women also supposedly suffered from *dementia praecox*. Frank knew what dementia was. It meant she was crazy. She wasn't in the crazy house, though. Her family had kept her at home, like the rest of them, which meant they must not be dangerous.

Frank read through the reports carefully several times, struggling with Tom Brandt's handwriting in places, until he was sure he understood as much as he was capable of understanding without medical training. One woman was

thirty-four, one twenty-seven, another eighteen, and the de-
mented one was twenty-two. Only the thirty-four-year-old
had been Brandt's patient before she got sick. The others
were women with the same problem she'd had whom he'd
found through other doctors.

He'd obviously been seeking them out, too, visiting with
their families to win their confidence before beginning his
treatment of the "hysteric." Except Frank couldn't see that
he'd actually treated any of them, if that meant doing something to make them better.

The most disturbing part, however, was that the major
symptom of their disease was an unnatural interest in sex,
accompanied by a romantic devotion to an individual man.
They were consumed by passion for the man and obsessed
with him night and day, and from what he could make of it,
the women were all in love with Tom Brandt.

SARAH WAS CALLED OUT EARLY THE NEXT MORNING TO
deliver a baby, so she couldn't get to the Lintons' house until late that afternoon. She wasn't surprised to learn Mrs.
Linton had other visitors, since this was the proper time for
company to call. She only hoped she could outlast them for
a few private moments with the family at the end of the
visit.

The maid showed her into the parlor where Mrs. Linton
sat with two other ladies. When she saw Sarah, Mrs. Linton's welcoming smile dimmed to concern, but Sarah
smiled back reassuringly. "I was just in the neighborhood
and thought I'd stop in to say hello," she lied.

"I'm so glad you did," Mrs. Linton replied, still a bit uncertain of what to make of Sarah's presence. "Please join us,
Mrs. Brandt."

She introduced the other ladies as Mrs. Hazel York and her mother, Susannah Jessop Evans. Sarah remembered hearing Mrs. York's name mentioned when she'd been here before.

"Don't forget to introduce Percy, Mama," Grace's voice called from the far end of the room.

Sarah hadn't noticed her sitting there, and when she turned, she saw Grace sharing a window seat with a boy. The boy rose to his feet, remembering his manners. His dark hair had been pomaded firmly against his well-shaped head but was fighting to get loose here and there, and he wore his visiting clothes with the air of one who couldn't wait to throw them off in favor of knickers and a baseball bat. He sketched her a little bow.

"Pleased to meet you, Mrs. Brandt," he said in a voice that hadn't quite changed yet. Sarah guessed him to be several years younger than Grace, for all his gangling height.

"Mrs. Brandt is a nurse," Grace announced proudly. "The kind that takes care of sick people, not the kind that takes care of babies."

"I'm sure Mrs. Brandt can speak for herself, Grace," Mrs. Linton said uncomfortably. She was probably afraid Grace would say too much about Sarah's visit the other day. "Why don't you show Percy the sketches you did last week?"

Easily distracted, Grace jumped up and fetched a sketchbook from a nearby cabinet. Sarah took the opportunity to study Percy more closely. His fond gaze followed Grace as she flitted across the room. She was a pretty girl, and he a boy on the brink of manhood. It would be only natural for him to notice her. Perhaps he even lusted after her in the awkward way boys did when they knew nothing definite about the mysteries of sex except that girls were involved.

For an instant, Sarah tried to imagine him as the father of Grace's child, but just as quickly she rejected the idea. Percy might feel the first stirrings of desire, but he was too young to know what to do about it. Since Grace would have been even more innocent, whoever had impregnated her had to know exactly what he was doing.

"Would you care for some tea, Mrs. Brandt?" Mrs. Linton asked, distracting her from her troublesome thoughts.

Sarah joined the ladies and accepted a cup of tea and a cookie. Hazel York was a rather faded-looking woman in her mid-thirties. Sarah recalled Grace mentioning Mrs. York had been ill, and she didn't look as if she'd completely recovered her strength. Her dress was stylish but a bit loose, indicating she'd lost weight since having it made. She wore her brownish hair plainly, either because she'd lost interest in her appearance or perhaps because she didn't have the energy to deal with it.

Unlike her daughter, Mrs. Evans appeared full of life and energy, although her hair was mostly white and her face lined with age.

"Did Grace say you are a nurse, Mrs. Brandt?" Mrs. Evans asked, probably wondering why someone of such a low social status was paying a call on Mrs. Linton.

"Yes, I am, much to my parents' regret." Sarah rarely revealed her family background, but in this case, she knew she needed to make an exception.

"They didn't approve?" Mrs. Evans asked.

"No, they would have preferred to see me married to one of the Astor boys, I'm sure," Sarah said, shamelessly referring to the wealthiest of the many wealthy families in New York.

Mrs. Evans wasn't sure whether Sarah was simply bragging. "And who are your parents, Mrs. Brandt?"

"Felix and Elizabeth Decker," she replied.

Even Mrs. Linton's jaw dropped at this. She would have had no idea of Sarah's elite social connections.

Mrs. Evans needed a moment to absorb this information. "Well," she said before she could completely compose herself. And then, "May I ask how you know Mrs. Linton?"

Once again, Mrs. Linton's face registered alarm, but Sarah said, "We have mutual friends. Are you neighbors of the Lintons?" she added to turn the focus of the conversation away from herself.

"Yes, and we attend the same church," Mrs. Evans said.

"Percy seems to be good company for Grace," Sarah observed, glancing at the window seat where their heads were bent together over the sketchbook.

"They've been fast friends ever since he and Hazel came to the city," Mrs. Linton said with an affectionate glance at the two young people. "He was always kind to Grace, even when other children weren't."

"Where did you move here from?" Sarah asked Mrs. York.

The woman seemed to rouse herself with effort to reply. "We lived in Boston. That's where my husband's business was, but when he passed away, Percy and I came back home to live with Mother."

"And I've been blessed to have them," Mrs. Evans reported. "Watching Percy grow up has been one of the greatest pleasures of my life."

"He's growing into a fine young man, too," Mrs. Linton said. "I know it must have been hard to raise a boy without a man in the house, but you've done a marvelous job."

"Oh, we can't take all the credit for that," Mrs. Evans assured her. "We never could have managed without Reverend Upchurch. He's our minister," she explained to Sarah.

"He's so good with the children," Mrs. York offered, actually showing some enthusiasm for the first time. "Especially those who don't have fathers. He said he considered it his special calling, since he and his wife weren't blessed with children of their own."

"He's always got a group of boys in the churchyard, playing ball, or inside working on some project or another," Mrs. Linton added.

"He makes sure they do well in school and learn their manners, too," Mrs. Evans said. "He tells them they must be gentlemen fit for God's kingdom."

"You're very fortunate to have such a dedicated man as your pastor," Sarah said.

"We certainly are," Mrs. Evans agreed. "He also happens to be a spellbinding preacher, so we couldn't ask for more. You should visit our church sometime, Mrs. Brandt. I'm sure you'll find it an uplifting experience."

"Perhaps I will," Sarah said politely. She was thinking of all those boys in and out of the church, the only other place Grace went except to visit her mother's friends. "Do the girls in the church receive as much attention as the boys?" she asked.

"Girls don't need as much attention, now do they?" Mrs. Evans pointed out. "They're more easily satisfied with what they find at home."

"Of course, the girls are with the women whenever we're at the church," Mrs. Linton explained. "We have Bible studies and sewing circles, and we collect clothing for the poor and distribute it. The girls aren't neglected."

"And dear Grace is always right there with us," Mrs. Evans said with a glance at the girl. "I believe she's the best seamstress of any of us, too."

"That's kind of you to say, Mrs. Evans," Mrs. Linton said, obviously pleased by the compliment.

"Percy wants to play checkers, Mama," Grace called from the other side of the room.

"Then get the things out," Mrs. Linton replied. "You know where they are."

"But he always wins," Grace complained.

"I'll let you win this time," Percy offered generously.

Grace considered this for a moment and then happily agreed.

Sarah watched to see if the two young people would go into another room, but they set up their game on the table in the corner.

When Sarah turned her gaze back to the other ladies, she caught Mrs. Linton watching her. Mrs. Linton leaned over and whispered, "They're never alone. Not ever."

Perhaps not, Sarah thought, but what about all those other boys whom Reverend Upchurch shepherded?

4

"I DON'T KNOW, MRS. BRANDT," MRS. LINTON SAID DOUBT-fully. Her other visitors were gone, and Grace had returned to the nursery, leaving the two of them alone. "The *police?*" She said the word as if it left a bad taste in her mouth.

"I have a friend who is a detective," Sarah said, keeping her voice neutral and calm. She didn't want to seem too anxious or make Mrs. Linton feel she was being pressured to do something against her will. "I can assure you he'll be discreet. He'll also be kind and considerate of Grace."

Mrs. Linton looked as if she might weep. "It doesn't matter how kind he might be. There's no way to question her about this without upsetting her."

"I don't want to upset Grace, either," Sarah assured her. "But think about the man who did this. He could do it to another innocent girl, maybe more than one."

"Even if the police could find the man, Grace could never testify in court," Mrs. Linton said. "We would never permit it."

Sarah didn't point out that no court would accept testimony from someone like Grace, either. "There are other ways to punish a man like that," Sarah said. "And simply identifying him would help. People could spread the word that he was dangerous and not to be trusted around females. No one need ever know Grace was a victim."

"Gossip is an ugly thing," Mrs. Linton said, picking at an invisible piece of lint on her skirt. Sarah wasn't sure exactly what she meant—gossip could also hurt Grace—so she waited, giving the other woman time to consider the possibilities.

"I'll have to ask Mr. Linton," she finally said. "But I can't imagine he'd agree to anything involving the police."

"Perhaps you could ask him just to meet with Detective Sergeant Malloy. The two men might be able to come up with an idea for identifying this man and stopping him, at least, even if he can't be arrested and prosecuted."

Mrs. Linton's face twisted in pain. "Please don't think I don't want this man caught, Mrs. Brandt. I'd like to see him pitched over the side of the Brooklyn Bridge or thrown beneath the wheels of a speeding locomotive. I'd like him to suffer for what he did to my baby girl, and I'd certainly like to stop him from ever hurting another girl, but you must understand, I can't see Grace hurt any more in the process."

"I understand completely. If you decide not to investigate, Mr. Malloy will respect your wishes."

"I'll have to ask my husband," she repeated. "But I can't imagine he'll agree."

* * *

Frank had been waiting almost an hour, but he'd wait all day to see Dr. David Newton. Dr. Newton had operated on Brian's club foot, and he was the only doctor Frank trusted. They'd told him he'd have to wait until Dr. Newton was finished seeing patients for the day before he'd have time for Frank, and so he sat.

Finally, a nurse escorted him into the doctor's office. Newton rose from the chair behind his desk and put out his hand to greet him.

"Mr. Malloy, good to see you," he said with obvious sincerity. "How's Brian doing?"

"He's wearing out a pair of shoes a week from walking so much," Frank reported proudly, shaking the doctor's hand. "I can't tell you how much I appreciate what you did for him."

"I was happy to be able to help. Not all my operations turn out so well," he said modestly. "What can I do for you? My nurse said you needed some information for a case you're working on."

Newton motioned to a chair, and Frank sat down as the doctor took his seat behind his desk again.

"I came across a medical condition in some women, something I never heard of, and I was wondering if you could tell me anything about it."

"What kind of condition?"

Frank pulled a piece of paper from his pocket. On it he'd written the words used to describe the medical histories of the women involved. He handed it to Dr. Newton, not trusting his ability to pronounce the foreign words correctly.

Dr. Newton looked at the paper for a moment. "*Dementia praecox* is a tragic form of insanity that strikes otherwise healthy, normal young adults for no known reason. Some of them must be institutionalized because they are dangerous to themselves or others."

"Are they all violent?"

"Oh, no, only a few, but all of them are completely out of touch with reality. They hear voices and imagine all sorts of things that aren't true."

"Could a woman with this kind of insanity be kept at home by her family?"

"I'm sure it happens often, if the patient isn't violent, as I said. No one with the means to keep them would put a loved one into an asylum unless it was absolutely necessary."

Frank considered this a long moment. "What about 'hysteria.' What does that mean?"

"It can mean almost anything." Dr. Newton smiled sadly. "Sometimes it just means the doctor has no idea what's really wrong with the woman, so he calls it hysteria."

"Are the dementia and the hysteria the same thing?"

"I'm not sure. This isn't my area of study, but the symptoms can be similar, so they may be confused. Maybe the conditions even overlap sometimes. As I said, I don't know that much about insanity."

"All these women I'm investigating fell in love with a man they hardly knew, and they were convinced he was in love with them, too. They couldn't think or talk about anything else."

Dr. Newton's wise eyes lit with understanding. "I think I know what you're talking about. Many female patients fall in love with their doctors. It's mostly gratitude, and they usually get over it when they get well and their lives return to normal, but sometimes they don't. They actually continue to imagine themselves in love."

"What happens then?"

"Fortunately, I've never had this happen to me," he explained, "but some of my colleagues have. It's very awkward and embarrassing. The women often make a nuisance of themselves. One woman came to her doctor's office every day for weeks, bringing him gifts and leaving him love notes. Sometimes they even go to the man's home, imagining themselves to be married to him."

"Is this a real illness? Can you treat it like you treat a disease?" Frank asked, trying to determine if Tom Brandt had simply been performing his professional duty.

"I'm afraid I can't say. I operate on people's bodies. Their minds are beyond my field of expertise. I can give you the name of a doctor who might be able to answer your questions, though. He's recently returned from Vienna where he studied with Dr. Sigmund Freud."

"Freud?" Frank repeated with a frown. "Isn't he that foreign fellow with all those strange ideas they're always making fun of in the newspapers?"

Dr. Newton smiled. "People always ridicule what they don't understand. Dr. Freud has made some important discoveries in the treatment of insanity."

"Has he cured hysteria or *dementia praecox?*" Frank asked skeptically.

"No, not yet," Dr. Newton said graciously. "But he's the first to offer any real hope for eventual cures to all forms of insanity. Let me give you the name and address for my friend, Dr. Quinn. He'll be happy to answer your questions and will probably have much more information than I. Just tell him I sent you," he added as he picked up a pencil and began to write down the information.

The reference was more than Frank had expected and absolutely necessary if he was going to get this Dr. Quinn to see him. No one wanted to talk to the police unless they had to. He thanked Dr. Newton when he handed Frank the address.

"Glad to help," Newton assured him. "Tell me, what kind of a case are you trying to solve?"

"A murder," Frank said.

"Will you let me know when you solve it?"

Frank remembered that Newton had known Tom Brandt well. He and Sarah were still friends. "Yes," he said. "I'll let you know."

"Hurry, Missus, please," the young man begged Sarah the next morning as he led her through the crowded streets. "It is not far, only around the corner."

Sarah didn't bother to point out to the expectant father that babies rarely came as fast as most people feared. He wouldn't believe her. Men never did. So she quickened her pace as much as she could. The young man carried her medical bag for her, but even still, it was hard to keep up. As much as she dreaded being summoned to a delivery in the middle of the night, at least then she didn't have to worry about being delayed by the daytime traffic choking the streets and the pedestrians clogging the sidewalks, in spite of the winter cold.

All around her, street vendors shouted the virtues of their wares from the carts parked along both sides of every street. Whatever one might need was available for sale within a block or two, from the evening meal to shoes to ribbons to furniture. Little, save the food, was new, but no one on the Lower East Side could afford anything new anyway. Wagons and carts made their laborious way down the center of the streets, while people of all shapes, sizes, and nationalities shouldered their way through the throngs to wherever they were going. At least the low temperature kept the smell of decay to a minimum, but the noise of the crowds and the animals and the vehicles was intense.

Sarah and the young man had finally reached the corner, but he stopped in dismay when he saw what was going on in front of his tenement building. A horse had apparently dropped dead in the middle of the street, something that happened frequently in the city, particularly when the extremes of temperature made the animals' lot even more difficult than usual. This horse and another had been harnessed to an overloaded wagon, and the other horse was rearing and thrashing madly in an attempt to continue pulling or perhaps to break free of his dead partner. Whatever his wishes, he could not escape his harness, and the dead horse kept him from moving the wagon or even himself.

The driver was trying to calm the animal and not get killed by flying hooves at the same time. Everyone within earshot had come to watch and shout encouragement or advice, and the street was jammed with shouting people and backed-up traffic. Sarah and her guide couldn't possibly get through to his building.

The young man turned to her in desperation. "You can climb the fire escape, yes?"

"Oh, yes," Sarah assured him. She'd done it many times.

They retraced their steps to the alley that ran behind the row of tenements. Crisscrossed clotheslines filled the space between the back of the building and the back of the one that faced the next street. A few children played here among the refuse, out of the press of the crowds and sheltered a bit from the wind. A stray cat startled and dashed for cover as Sarah's companion let her medical bag bump an ash can. Across the back of all the buildings, a maze of black metal fire escapes reached from the ground to the sky, touching almost every window. The law that had mandated them had probably saved thousands of lives.

The young man reached up and pulled down the ladder

of one of them. Most of the ladders had been sprung so that they hung within easy reach at all times.

"I will go first," he said politely. If he let her go first, he'd be looking up her skirt.

He climbed with the ease of strength and youth, apparently not hindered at all by having to hold her heavy bag in one hand. Sarah hiked her skirt and began the one-story climb up the ladder to the first landing. Her companion had waited to help her to her feet on the metal grating.

"Only two more," he said, holding up two fingers.

From here the going was easier, because she had only to climb the metal steps. The hardest part was squeezing around the furniture and other belongings being stored on the landings. Residents used the fire escapes as extra rooms, sleeping on them in the heat of summer and storing bedding and extra possessions out there that might be in the way as the family lived their daily lives in the tiny tenement rooms.

When they'd reached the proper floor, the young man shoved open the window and helped Sarah climb over the sill into the back bedroom of his flat. There she found the bed had been stripped and covered with an oilcloth and a clean sheet. A very pregnant young woman stood in the doorway, looking calm but happy to see Sarah.

"My baby is coming," she reported, rubbing the mound of her stomach.

But not, Sarah thought with a sigh, for a long time.

BY THE TIME SARAH GOT HOME FROM DELIVERING THE baby, a strapping boy who had emerged screaming in outrage, her house was dark and the girls sound asleep. She'd purchased her supper from a street vendor and devoured it on the way home, so she only wanted to go to sleep herself, but on the way she stopped at her desk to glance at the mail.

She found an elegantly lettered envelope that was an invitation to some party her mother was giving. Elizabeth Decker never tired of trying to lure her daughter back into the elite social circle in which she and her husband moved. Sarah stuck the envelope on the bottom of the pile, to be opened tomorrow when she felt more able to deal with it. Another envelope bore the Lintons' return address, and Sarah ripped it open. A note from Mrs. Linton said that her husband had agreed to meet with her policeman friend, but that the meeting must be at his place of business. More than that, she could not promise.

Too weary to feel more than a sense of relief, Sarah gave a moment's thought to how she would notify Malloy of this. Tomorrow was Sunday. Perhaps she and the girls would pay a visit to Malloy's son Brian.

MAEVE BEGGED OFF THE VISIT. SUNDAY WAS HER DAY OFF, and she wanted to go to the mission and see her old friends, so Sarah and Aggie set out early in the afternoon for the neighborhood near Tompkins Square where the Malloy family lived.

Bundled against the cold, they walked through streets crowded with people celebrating their day of rest by attending church and visiting friends and relations. No elevated trains ran crosstown, and Hansom cabs were scarce, so Sarah tried to keep the pace slow and easy for Aggie's sake.

She wasn't having much luck, though. The prospect of visiting her friend Brian was enough to make Aggie want to run all the way.

"You remember that Brian can't hear, don't you?" Sarah asked when they were a block away from the Malloys' building.

Aggie nodded happily. She didn't mind a bit.

Sarah wasn't sure they'd find the Malloys at home, so she'd written a note to leave for Malloy just in case. She actually wasn't even certain if she *wanted* them to be home. Mrs. Malloy had made up her mind that Sarah was a desperate widow in search of a husband and that she had her sights set on Malloy, so she wasn't too pleased when Sarah came calling. In fact, she was frequently downright rude, but perhaps she'd be more charitable today since Aggie was along.

Aggie literally ran up the steps to the Malloys' second-floor flat, and she was banging on their front door before Sarah even reached the landing. The door opened, and Sarah could see Mrs. Malloy silhouetted.

"Who's this, now?" the old woman exclaimed, peering at the child in the dim hallway light. "Aggie, is it? You've not come here all by yourself, I hope!"

Before Sarah could reassure her, she heard Brian's cry of pleasure. Since he couldn't hear the sounds he made, they were often startlingly loud, and this one echoed in the hallway. He was dragging Aggie inside, almost knocking his grandmother over in the process.

"Good afternoon, Mrs. Malloy," Sarah said, having reached the doorway.

The old woman didn't look happy to see her. "I suppose you've come to see Francis."

"He invited me to bring Aggie over to play with Brian," Sarah lied pleasantly.

She made a humphing sound in her throat, but she stood aside and allowed Sarah to enter.

As always, the flat was spotlessly clean and tidy. Brian was showing Aggie some toys in the corner, but when he saw Sarah come in, he scrambled to his feet and ran to greet her.

"Easy there," Malloy cautioned when Brian threw his arms around Sarah's skirts, threatening her balance. He was coming out of the other room, shrugging into his jacket. Sarah figured he'd probably been sitting around in his shirt-sleeves and stocking feet on this Sabbath afternoon and had gone to make himself presentable.

"He can't hear you," Mrs. Malloy reminded him sourly.

"Then make some signs to tell him not to rough up our visitor," Malloy replied. "Ma knows all kinds of signs now that she's been going to deaf school with Brian," he added to Sarah.

Sarah had stooped down to return Brian's embrace. "I think it's wonderful that you've learned to talk to him, Mrs. Malloy," she said.

"Do you now?" Mrs. Malloy asked without much interest, but she tapped Brian on the shoulder, and when he looked up at her, she made a sign. He smiled sheepishly at Sarah and ran off to play with Aggie again.

"What did you say to him?" Sarah asked in fascination.

"Not to make a nuisance of himself," the old woman said, not even bothering to look at Sarah. "Let me have your coat, Miss Aggie, before you get overheated," she said to the child.

"And I'll take yours, Mrs. Brandt," Malloy said, his expression bland but his dark eyes sparkling with anger at his mother's rudeness.

"It's all right," she whispered as Malloy took her heavy cape.

"No, it isn't," he whispered back.

"What's that you're saying?" Mrs. Malloy asked. "I hope you didn't invite them to eat. I don't have a crumb in the house."

"What about that apple pie you made special?" Malloy asked. "I'll bet Aggie'd like some, wouldn't you, my girl?"

Aggie looked up and grinned and nodded her head. Delighted, Brian mimicked her, without having any idea of what he had just agreed to.

Mrs. Malloy grunted again, but she went off toward the kitchen with little grace.

"I'm sorry about that," Malloy said with a frown as soon as the old woman was gone.

"I don't blame her," Sarah assured him. "I probably wouldn't like me, either, if I were she."

"I don't even want to figure out what you just said," Malloy said. "Come on and sit down. Did you walk all the way over? You look half-froze."

"Actually, I ran most of the way. I had to keep up with Aggie."

Sarah took a seat on the sofa, and Malloy took the upholstered chair nearby. "All right, now," Malloy said as Sarah chafed the warmth back into her fingers, "which one of your friends has been murdered, because I'm thinking nothing less could've brought you out on a day like this."

"Your imagination is too grim, Malloy," Sarah informed him with a smile. "I just wanted to let you know that Mr. Linton has agreed to meet with you."

"Who?"

"The father of the girl I told you about." She reached into her purse and pulled out the note Mrs. Linton had sent her. "He wants to meet you at his business, not at the house. The address is in there."

"I'm sure he doesn't want me near his wife and daughter," Malloy said, taking the note. He put it into his coat pocket without looking at it.

"Aggie," Mrs. Malloy called from the kitchen. "Get Brian and come in here for some pie."

Both children eagerly raced into the kitchen.

"Mr. Linton is a good man," Sarah said when they'd gone. "And he loves his wife and daughter very much."

"Which is why he probably won't want the police involved," Malloy reminded her.

"But won't he want justice?"

Malloy just gave her a pitying look.

"Vengeance, then," she tried. "Wouldn't you want to punish someone who hurt Brian?"

"I'd want to kill him," Malloy admitted. "But I wouldn't chance the law taking care of it. Too many guilty people get off scot-free if they have money or influence."

"You'd take the law into your own hands?"

"You were the one who started talking about vengeance, Sarah," he reminded her.

"I can't see Mr. Linton killing anyone, no matter what they did."

"Then why are you bothering with this? He isn't going to let this become public, which is what he'd have to do if we arrested someone and put him on trial. If he isn't going to take revenge himself, what's left?"

"Just talk to him, Malloy. Please. You'll figure out something."

"Did you want some of this pie or not?" Mrs. Malloy asked them from the doorway before Malloy could think of an answer.

Malloy glared at her, but she'd already turned away and didn't see it.

"Pie sounds lovely," Sarah said as if she'd been graciously invited to partake and rose from her seat.

Malloy followed her into the kitchen, where Mrs. Malloy had set two additional pieces on the table for them.

"This looks delicious," Sarah said, taking her own seat before Malloy could pull out the chair for her. No sense giving Mrs. Malloy anything else to be annoyed about.

Malloy was still glaring at his mother, and she was staring defiantly back.

"Come on, Malloy," Sarah urged. "You know apple is your favorite."

Mrs. Malloy's head snapped around at that. "I suppose you've been baking pies for Francis, then, if you know his favorite kind."

"Oh, no," Sarah said sweetly. "And he should be glad I haven't. I'm not a very good cook, but my neighbor is, and she likes to please Mr. Malloy."

"She does, does she?" Mrs. Malloy asked, considering this new information with a worried frown. "I suppose she's a widow, too."

Sarah caught Malloy's eye. They both knew what his mother was thinking: another desperate widow out to catch herself a husband. "Oh, yes," Sarah informed her blithely. "And Mrs. Ellsworth is *extremely* fond of Mr. Malloy."

WILFRED LINTON'S BUSINESS WAS NEAR THE RIVER, a sturdy block building adjacent to a stretch of warehouses where merchandise arrived and departed in an orderly fashion, leaving behind a tidy profit for Mr. Linton.

Linton didn't keep him waiting, probably because he didn't want people wondering why a police detective was hanging around the building. The office Frank entered was crowded, the tabletops covered with stacks of papers. It seemed disorganized to Frank, but one look at Linton told him the man could probably put his hand on any necessary document in two seconds flat.

Linton rose to his feet, but he didn't offer to shake hands the way Dr. Newton had done, nor did he come around his desk. "Detective," he said. It was almost a question.

"Detective Sergeant Frank Malloy," he said. "Mrs. Brandt thought I might be of some help to you."

Frank could see the doubt in his eyes, but he said, "Please have a seat."

A single straight chair sat opposite Linton's desk, and Frank took it. Only then did Linton sit down himself.

"My daughter isn't strong," Linton began.

"Mrs. Brandt told me about her," Frank assured him.

"Then you know there's no question of us bringing charges. My wife would never put her through the ordeal of a trial, and we both know that no judge would even allow her to testify."

"You're probably right." Frank waited. It wasn't his job to convince Linton of anything.

After a moment, Linton said, "My wife . . . she's concerned that the man responsible might take advantage of another young girl."

"He probably will," Frank agreed. "In fact, your daughter might not even be the first."

Linton's eyes widened with horror at the thought. "You mean . . . someone else? . . ."

"Someone else's parents might've wanted to protect their daughter, too. They did nothing, and now if you do nothing . . ." He let the thought hang unspoken.

"Dear God," Linton said, rubbing a trembling hand over his bald head. "What can we do?"

"That depends on who the man is," Frank said. "And if we can even find him."

"I can't allow you to question Grace," Linton said. "She'd be terrified."

"Mrs. Brandt already asked her about it, and your daughter wasn't able to give her any information. I don't think I'd have any better luck."

"Then what can you do?"

"It's probably not that difficult. We just have to figure out which men had the opportunity. From what Mrs. Brandt says, there can't be many."

"There aren't *any*, and believe me, my wife and I have been thinking of little else for days." Frank could hear the strain in Linton's voice. Linton was a careful man, and things like this just didn't happen in his carefully organized world.

"You must have overlooked something," Frank pointed out, "or we wouldn't be here. What about at your house? Who lives there?"

"My family and three servants, all female."

"So you're the only man?"

"That's right."

Frank waited a moment to see if Linton would show a trace of guilt, but he saw none. "Mr. Linton, sometimes a man can become more than fond of his daughter."

"What do you mean?" He seemed genuinely puzzled.

"I mean *unnaturally* fond. Some men have even been known to have unnatural feelings for their daughters, feelings of desire."

Frank watched as the implication slowly dawned on Linton. His expression went from puzzled to horrified to furious in rapid succession. "That's obscene!" he cried, pounding his fist on his desk. "How dare you even suggest such a thing? Get out of my office this instant! I'll have your job for this!"

Frank didn't move. "I'm sorry, Mr. Linton, but I had to make sure. I didn't know what kind of a man you were, and it happens a lot more often than you can imagine. I couldn't take a chance of hunting down some poor innocent mug and ruining his life just to protect a father who'd do a thing like that to his own child."

Linton's face glowed crimson with fury. "I don't believe you! No man would do that to his own child, certainly no respectable man."

"I promise you, they can and they do, men who live on Fifth Avenue as well as those on the Bowery. But we don't need to think about that anymore. Your daughter must leave the house occasionally. Where does she go?"

Linton wasn't sure if he was ready to forgive Frank or not, but he grudgingly said, "She goes visiting with her mother and to church."

"Who do they visit?"

"Mrs. Linton's friends."

"Do any of them have husbands or sons?"

"Of course they do," Linton said in exasperation, "but Grace is never alone with them. In fact, she never leaves her mother's side. If you knew anything about social visits, you'd know that."

He'd meant to make Frank feel his inferiority, and he did, but only for an instant. "What about at church? She must see men there. What about the priest?"

"Our *minister* is a man, of course," Linton corrected him indignantly, "but you can't think a man of God would do something like this."

Frank had seen men—and women—of God do much worse things than rape a young girl, but he didn't say so. "If your daughter had been attacked by a stranger, she would've been upset and frightened. She would've told you or your wife. Even if the person had threatened her to keep her from telling, you would've known something was scaring her. Whoever did this could've been someone she trusted, someone who could convince her nothing bad had happened so she wouldn't tell anyone."

Linton rubbed his head again. "I hadn't thought of that."

"So what about the church? Would she meet men there?"

"Of course she would. We have a large congregation and many of them are men, but I'm telling you, Mr. Malloy, that can't be it. When Grace is at church, she's with me or her mother at all times. She is never alone. My wife and I have been over this and over it. The only time she's out of our sight for a moment is when she's in the safety of her own home!"

Frank sighed. Linton was wrong. She'd been out of someone's sight at least once, and she had a baby to prove it.

5

Frank waited until late that afternoon to visit the Lintons' church. He figured he'd catch the minister at the end of the day, when he was most likely to be alone. That's why he was surprised to find the building bustling with activity.

Half a dozen boys in their mid-teens, recently released from school, were attacking the sanctuary—Frank could think of no other word for it—with dust cloths and brooms. Two were using their bottoms to push dust cloths across the pews, racing each other to see who could slide from one end to the other the fastest. Others were polishing candlesticks or sweeping the floor, and one was up on a ladder, polishing a stained glass window. All of them were laughing and shouting.

Frank had never heard noises like that in a church, and he

found the irreverence disturbing, even though he himself had long ago lost all respect for organized religion. What kind of a minister would allow this kind of behavior?

One of the boys noticed Frank. "Hello, the cops is here, boys!" he cried.

Instantly, the room fell silent as every face turned toward Frank. Frank stared back blandly, looking for traces of guilt and seeing none. He did see worry and maybe a spark of fear here and there. The police were terrifying, after all, but these were middle-class boys whose biggest sins were probably sneaking a cigarette or stealing away to a pool hall when they should've been in school. If he'd been on the Lower East Side, boys this age would have run, just on general principles—some out of guilt from actually having done something worthy of arrest and the rest for fear of being blamed, innocent or not. If Grace's rapist was among these, he had no fear of having been discovered.

"What's going on here?" a booming voice demanded. "You boys are entirely too quiet all of a sudden!" The man who had appeared from a doorway in the front of the sanctuary planted his hands on his hips and looked around expectantly.

One of the boys jerked his chin in Frank's direction and said in a small voice, "He's a copper, Reverend Upchurch." Although Frank wore a suit not very different from the minister's, even boys from respectable families recognized his profession. Something about the way he carried himself always gave him away. Or maybe it was just his Irish face.

"He's a *policeman*, Mark," Reverend Upchurch corrected him gently. "A gentleman doesn't use slang."

Upchurch started down the aisle to where Frank stood. He wore a clerical collar with his black suit, but otherwise he didn't look the way Frank had expected the minister to look. Tall, broad-shouldered, and handsome, with a neatly trimmed beard, Upchurch strode toward Frank with strength and energy and confidence and a wide smile of greeting.

"Welcome to the Church of the Good Shepherd," he said, putting out his hand for Frank to shake. His grip was firm, his palm rougher than Frank had expected, as if he were no stranger to hard work.

"Detective Sergeant Frank Malloy," Frank said.

This only made Upchurch grin more broadly. "I suppose you're here for one of these boys," he said, glancing over his shoulder at them. "They're scalawags, every last one of them! You should take them all straight to The Tombs," he added, using the nickname for the city jail.

The boys smiled at that. They truly had nothing to fear from the police, and even Frank had to smile at the thought of rounding up these fresh-faced lads and marching them into the dismal old jail. "I don't have time to run them in today," Frank said, "but if you have a minute, I'd like to talk to you about an important matter."

"Anytime the police are involved, it's always important," Upchurch said, unruffled. "Isn't that right, boys?"

"Yes, sir," they agreed in voices that ranged from squeaky tenor to husky baritone.

"Let's talk in my office, Mr. Malloy," Upchurch said and started back toward the front of the church. "Isaiah, be careful on that ladder," he called to the boy polishing the window. "Good job on those candlesticks, Nathan," he said when they passed the boy working at the altar.

Frank couldn't help but notice how the boys all watched Upchurch, eager for his attention and thrilled to receive it. Plainly, they adored him, and from his attitude, he was equally fond of them. If one of these boys had a dark secret, Upchurch would know it.

The minister's office had been furnished long ago with
heavily carved pieces that matched the beauty and elegance
of the sanctuary, but Upchurch had shown little respect for
the stateliness of the décor. In one corner lay a jumble of
sporting equipment; baseball bats, balls of all descriptions,
a catcher's mask and glove, even a few hoops. On a small
table sat a checkerboard with a pile of checkers on one side
and a heap of chessmen on the other. His desk was covered
with papers, and not the organized chaos he'd seen at Mr.
Linton's office. This was simply chaos, piles of books here
and there, some open and turned face down to hold the
place and others on the floor where they had fallen and been
forgotten. A worn and moth-eaten sweater hung from a coat
tree, telling Frank what Upchurch probably wore when no
one was around, or when he was outside using some of the
sports equipment.

"That's for the boys," Upchurch said, seeing Frank's interest in the balls and bats. "The cleaning is for them, too.
We have a man who cleans the church, but the boys need
something to do to work off all that energy. I send them in
when the weather's too bad to play outside. If boys have too
much energy and nothing to do, they get in trouble. But
you probably know that better than I," he added with a
chuckle.

He indicated one of two chairs that sat near the pile of
equipment, facing each other. They matched the formality
of the other furniture, with intricately carved wooden arms
and legs, but the once-grand upholstery was worn and
faded. Frank figured this was where he counseled with
parishioners.

Frank sat down, finding the chair surprisingly comfortable. Upchurch took the other chair, leaning forward with
his elbows on his knees and growing serious, but even still

the energy radiated from him, as if he held himself still only with a great effort. "Now, what is it that brings you here, Detective? Nothing good, I'm sure."

"You're right, it isn't good. It's about a girl in your church," he began, having carefully considered exactly what to tell the minister while still protecting the Lintons' privacy.

Did he look surprised? Frank thought he saw a flash of it in those blue-gray eyes, but it was gone too quickly to be sure.

"Is she . . . in trouble?" he asked.

"Yes."

Reverend Upchurch considered for a moment. "I'm going to assume this is more than a simple seduction, or the police wouldn't be involved."

"The girl is very young, too young for a seduction. Someone took advantage of her, and she can't identify the man."

"Can't?" Upchurch frowned. "Or won't?"

"We aren't sure. Like I said, she's young. He may have threatened her, or maybe she doesn't want to get him in trouble, or maybe she just doesn't know who he is."

"Or maybe she knows him very well," Upchurch suggested. "Have you considered incest? It's a horrible thing, but it happens far more often than any of us would like to think."

"I did consider it, and I'm convinced that's not what happened."

Now Upchurch just looked puzzled. "I'm not sure why you've come here, then. You said it's a family in my church, and if you'll tell me who it is, I'll offer what comfort I can, but I'm not sure what else I can do."

"I came because I think the man responsible might be a member of your church."

Now Upchurch was concerned. "What makes you think that?"

"Because the girl is very protected. She doesn't go to school, and she only goes out in company with her parents, and here to church. She spends a great deal of time here, as a matter of fact."

"Many people do," he said with a trace of pride. "We have Bible study classes and sewing circles and missionary circles and auxiliary meetings here almost every day of the week. Oh, and committee meetings and trustee meetings . . . the list is very long."

"And do you have boys here every day of the week, too?"

Upchurch reared back at that, sitting up straight. All trace of kindness vanished from his pale eyes. "Are you insinuating that one of our boys would do a thing like that?"

"Somebody did," Frank reminded him.

"Not my boys," he said almost angrily.

"*Your* boys?" Frank echoed.

The color rose in his face, but he didn't look abashed at the odd claim. "I feel very protective of them. The boys you saw in the sanctuary are very special to me. They are all fatherless, and their mothers have entrusted me to provide them with the kind of attention their fathers would have. I've taught them all to behave like gentlemen toward females. They hold them in the highest regard, and not one of them would take advantage of an innocent young girl. I would stake my life on it."

Frank pitied anyone naïve enough to believe they could predict with certainty how another human being would act. "What about the rest of the boys in your church, the ones who do have fathers?"

Upchurch smiled with a touch of irony. "I'm afraid the rest of the boys, those with fathers and those without, only show their faces here on Sunday when their parents bring them. Believe me, the opportunities for taking advantage of a young girl during the Sunday morning worship service are very limited."

Frank heard the thread of anger in his voice. His patience was wearing thin, but Frank's was, too. "What about the men, then? In a case like this, it's more likely, anyway."

"The men in my congregation work for a living, Detective. Those who don't are elderly and unlikely to have the inclination, much less the strength, to force a young girl. Men are also unlikely to be here at a time when the ladies are. They hold their Bible studies and meetings in the evenings, and the ladies are here during the day."

"This is the only place she could've been assaulted."

"I'm going to have to take offense at the implication that this church is a haven for criminals." Upchurch was working himself up to full outrage. "And that this poor girl was assaulted here. This is a house of God, Mr. *Malloy*." He said Frank's name with more than a trace of contempt. "Perhaps things like that happen at *your* church, but I assure you, they do not happen here!"

Frank was used to prejudice, but somehow he hadn't expected it from this man. "Do you think Roman Catholics sacrifice virgins, Reverend Upchurch?" he asked mildly.

He squeezed his eyes shut and pinched the bridge of his nose between his finger and thumb. "Mr. Malloy," he said, having retaken control of his emotions, "Grace Linton was not attacked in this church."

For a second Frank wasn't sure he'd heard him right. "What did you say?" he asked.

"I said Grace Linton," he repeated impatiently. "That's the girl we're discussing, isn't it?"

"What makes you think so?" Frank challenged, beginning to think Upchurch must know more than he'd let on.

"You said she was a girl who didn't go to school. She's old enough to bear a child, but she couldn't tell who had attacked her. There's only one girl in the church who could fit that description."

So much for Frank's efforts to protect her identity. "Her parents don't want anyone else to know."

"Of course not. If they want to tell me, I'll pretend I had no idea. But she wasn't attacked here. As I said, the church is a busy place. Too many people are here at all times, or at least the times when Grace would have been here. Had she gone missing for any length of time, someone would have noticed, and had she cried out, someone would have heard."

"Maybe she didn't cry out. Maybe she was too frightened."

Reverend Upchurch sighed in exasperation. "And maybe it didn't happen here at all. Such an act requires a certain degree of privacy, the kind found in a private home, for example."

"Do you think she was attacked at her home?" Frank asked with genuine curiosity. "You know Mr. Linton. Do you think he's capable of violating his own child?"

Reverend Upchurch's face lost its robust color, and his expression grew hard and distant. "One cannot tell just by looking at a man of what he is really capable, Mr. Malloy. I'd expect you to know that."

He did, of course. He was just surprised Upchurch would so quickly assume the very worst about a man he must know well.

"Do you have any reason to believe Mr. Linton is responsible?"

Upchurch seemed to catch himself and consciously shake off his dark mood. "I certainly didn't mean to imply that.

Mr. Linton is a fine Christian man. I can't imagine him doing anything of the kind."

"You probably can't imagine anybody in your church doing it, because you only see people when they're in church and on their best behavior," Frank pointed out.

"Is that what you really think?" he asked in surprise. "Don't let this collar fool you, Mr. Malloy. Ministers know all about the darkness of the soul and the evil of which man is capable. We see it every day. We counsel some of its victims, and we bury a few, and we baptize its babies. Churches are full of sinners, not saints, and I know too many men who would think nothing of harming a girl like Grace."

"Maybe you could give me their names," Frank suggested.

"I wish I could. I wish I knew who the guilty man is. I'd tie the millstone around his neck myself."

"Millstone?"

"The Bible says a man who harms a child should have a millstone tied around his neck and be dropped into the sea."

Since Grace's rapist would probably never be punished under the law, Frank thought this sounded like an ideal alternative. "I hope you'd call me before taking the law into your own hands, Reverend Upchurch."

His handsome mouth quirked into a smile. "Don't worry. Millstones are hard to find in the city. Is there anything else I can do for you, Detective?"

"I'd like to talk to those boys in there," he said, nodding toward the sanctuary, from which they could still faintly hear the shouts and laughter.

"Whatever for?" Upchurch asked, instantly protective.

"Since they're at the church a lot, they might've seen something."

"I told you—"

"I know, you don't think it happened here, but the man

might've seen her here first. Maybe he's been paying particular attention to her or watching her."

"And you think those boys would've noticed?" Upchurch
scoffed. "They're *boys*, Detective. They don't notice anything.
Besides, I can't give you permission to speak to them. You'd
have to ask their mothers, and then you'd have to explain to
them why you wanted to speak with them, and soon rumors
would be flying, and someone would guess about Grace, just
as I did. I wouldn't want to be responsible for that."

Frank wouldn't, either. He rose from his chair, knowing
when he was defeated. "Thank you for your time, Reverend
Upchurch."

The minister shook his hand, and once again Frank was
impressed by his grip. "I wish I could've been more help."

"If you think of anything or remember someone who
paid Grace particular attention, please let me know." He
gave the minister one of his cards and left, exiting back out
into the sanctuary.

The moment Frank emerged into the sanctuary, the boys
stopped their work and fell silent. They watched him warily
as he moved down the aisle, six pairs of eyes full of mistrust,
until he passed through the large double doors into the street.

He shouldn't feel like a failure. He'd known finding
Grace Linton's attacker would be nearly impossible. He
wouldn't even really be disappointed if he didn't have to tell
Sarah Brandt.

FOR ONCE SARAH HAD ENJOYED A GOOD NIGHT'S SLEEP,
uninterrupted by a late night delivery. She was enjoying a
leisurely second cup of coffee when her doorbell rang. Maeve
and Aggie beat her to it, admitting a red-cheeked Frank
Malloy.

"No, Brian's in school today," he was explaining to the girls as Sarah came into the front room. "I'll bring him next time."

Aggie pushed out her lower lip in a pout, but Malloy reached down and tickled her tummy until she giggled.

"Good morning, Malloy," Sarah said, inexplicably happy just to see him.

"Good morning," he replied, apparently pleased to see her, too.

"Maeve, take Mr. Malloy's coat, will you?" Sarah asked, and waited until he'd shed the coat and hat and muffler he'd worn against the winter chill.

"Come on upstairs, Aggie," Maeve said when she'd taken care of his things. "Mrs. Brandt and Mr. Malloy will want to talk in private."

Aggie lingered just a moment, making eyes at Malloy and inching closer and closer until he took the bait and gave her tummy another tickle. With a shriek of laughter, she turned and ran for the steps. Maeve followed, shaking her head at the child's antics.

"She likes you," Sarah said. "And she's not afraid of you. Whatever happened to her, it didn't make her afraid of men." They both knew only too well the horrors that could befall a small child in this vast city, and something had made Aggie mute with terror.

"Don't try to figure it out," Malloy warned her. "Whatever it was, you're better off not knowing."

"That's cowardly," she argued.

"And safe," he argued right back. "I visited the Lintons' church yesterday," he added to change the subject.

"Oh, good. Come into the kitchen. The coffee is hot, although I'm afraid I don't have any pie to offer."

"Maybe Mrs. Ellsworth saw me coming down the street and will bring some over," he said with a sly grin.

This time Sarah shook her head and led him into the kitchen.

He was chafing his hands and rubbing the warmth back into his face while she poured him a cup of the coffee.

"Did you learn anything interesting?" she asked, taking her seat opposite him at the table.

"Their minister is interesting," he said. "He's got a pack of boys who spend a lot of time at the church with him."

"Boys without fathers," Sarah remembered. "Mrs. Linton told me that. He doesn't have children of his own, apparently, so he looks after those who need a male influence."

"Too bad more men in this city don't do the same thing," Malloy said, probably thinking of the hundreds of homeless children running the streets of New York.

"What did you think of the boys? Could one of them have attacked Grace?"

"According to Upchurch, the minister, nothing like that could've happened at the church."

"Upchurch? What an appropriate name," she observed. "How can he be so sure?"

"Mainly, I think he just doesn't want to believe anyone in his church could do a thing like that, but he's right that an attack would take some time and some privacy, neither of which would be easy to find at the church."

"I'd think there'd be lots of secret places at a church where it could happen," Sarah said.

"But someone would notice if Grace went missing for any length of time, and if she cried for help, someone would've heard her."

Sarah frowned, considering this possibility. "I suppose she'd have been upset and frightened afterwards, too. And her clothes would've been in disarray. Someone would have noticed that, at least, even if she hadn't been gone long and had been too scared to cry out."

"Upchurch thinks it must've happened in a private home."

Sarah considered this possibility. "But that would be the same situation. Grace only goes visiting with her mother, and she would have to disappear for a while and return disheveled and upset. Surely, her mother would have noticed if that had happened."

"Unless it was her own home."

"Are we back to Mr. Linton, because I can't believe—"

"I don't believe it, either," he assured her. "But you may have to accept the fact that you might never find out."

"And a rapist is free to hurt how many other girls?" she asked angrily

"Now you know what it's like to be a policeman, Mrs. Brandt," he informed her. "You don't always solve the crime."

"Does that mean you're giving up?"

"That means I don't have any other places to look. Linton won't let me talk to Grace, and Upchurch told me that if I wanted to talk to the boys at the church, I'd have to get permission from their mothers, but then I'd have to explain that I think their sons might've raped a young girl, so I doubt they'd be too cooperative. I wouldn't get a very warm welcome if I showed up at church on Sunday morning and started questioning people in the pews, and it's probably not a good idea to go knocking on the doors of all Mrs. Linton's lady friends, either. Without a suspect, there's not much else I can do without upsetting a lot of respectable people and letting everybody know what happened to Grace in the bargain."

Sarah sighed. He was right, of course. If they were deal-ing with criminals on the Lower East Side, Malloy's position as a detective would serve him well. On the *Upper* East Side, things were very different, though.

Malloy's brows lowered over his dark eyes. "What are you thinking?" he asked suspiciously.

"Just that . . . Well, what we need is someone who can min-gle with these people without causing alarm," she said. "Some-one who could ask questions without having to get permission and who could quite properly visit Mrs. Linton's lady friends."

"Someone like you," he said. He didn't sound pleased.

"You know I'm right, Malloy."

"Sarah," he said, and she felt a small thrill, as she always did when he used her given name. "This doesn't have any-thing to do with you. Just take care of Grace Linton and de-liver her baby."

"And how many more babies will there be before this man is stopped? And how many young girls' lives ruined? I can't just sit by and do nothing."

His expression was troubled, but she saw no trace of his usual anger. In fact, he almost looked resigned. Almost.

"It could be dangerous," he warned. "A man like that won't give up without a fight. If he realizes what you're doing—"

"Malloy," she said with a smile. "Be reasonable. I don't really have a chance of finding him, and you know it as well as I do, so how dangerous could it possibly be?"

He ran a hand over his face in exasperation, but she thought she glimpsed a trace of a smile before he caught himself. "I never thought I'd hear you admit that."

"I'm not stupid, Malloy. I know the chances of finding this man are very small, but I can't just sit by and do noth-ing. I couldn't live with myself if I didn't at least try."

"All right, then. Go visit Mrs. Linton's friends and their

church and make a pest of yourself, but if you find out any-thing important—anything at all!—promise you'll send for me."

"Of course I will," she promised. "And Malloy, don't worry. Remember, this isn't a murder."

He muttered something that sounded like, "Thank God for that."

AFTER LUNCH, SARAH TOOK THE NINTH AVENUE ELE-vated train uptown and walked past the lower edge of Cen-tral Park into the Lenox Hill neighborhood. There she easily found the Church of the Good Shepherd, just as Malloy had described it. She'd timed her visit near the end of the school day, so she could meet the minister and explain her purpose and still be there when the boys Malloy had told her about arrived.

The sanctuary was empty, so Sarah located the stairs and went down to the church basement where experience told her she'd find some activity. She followed the sound of voices to a room where a group of women sat rolling ban-dages. To Sarah's relief, Mrs. Linton and Grace were not among them, but she did see a familiar face.

"Mrs. Brandt, is that you?" Susannah Evans asked, rising from her chair to welcome her. "What brings you here?"

"You spoke so highly of your church that I thought I'd pay a visit to see what made it so special," Sarah explained to Percy's grandmother.

Mrs. Evans introduced Sarah to the other women, mostly matrons like herself who probably enjoyed the opportunity to visit and gossip while their hands were busy with a char-itable task.

"We're rolling bandages for the lepers. We send them to

the missionaries in Africa," she explained. "But I'm sure that's not what you came to see. In fact, I'm surprised you didn't choose to visit us on a Sunday morning."

"Oh, I will," Sarah said, quite certain she would try. "But I was interested in the activities you have to keep young people occupied. You see, I do volunteer work at a mission downtown. We minister to destitute young women, and when you told me how good your pastor is with young people, I wanted to meet him."

"Oh, my, that must be challenging work. I do so admire those who've been called to serve the poor. I'm sure Reverend Upchurch would be happy to give whatever assistance he can. Let's see if we can find him, shall we?"

Mrs. Evans showed Sarah where to hang her coat, and on the way to find the minister, Mrs. Evans gave Sarah a cursory tour of the building. The basement was divided into several large rooms that would allow different groups to meet at the same time and not disturb each other. Mrs. Evans explained that Sunday School classes met there, and during the week, the rooms provided space for Bible study classes and other meetings. Sarah looked around carefully for a place a young girl might be taken against her will, but she saw no place that would put her out of earshot of others in the building.

Mrs. Evans took Sarah back upstairs in search of the minister.

"You certainly have a beautiful sanctuary," she observed as they walked down the aisle toward the altar.

"We're very grateful for it," Mrs. Evans said. "Many people gave generously to build it."

Sarah could see small brass plaques beneath each of the stained glass windows, inscribed with the names of those who had purchased them for the church. Each pew also bore a small brass plate with a donor's name. She could almost feel the love and devotion that had motivated people to give in order to create this majestic house of worship.

Near the front of the sanctuary, Mrs. Evans led Sarah through a door into a short hallway. Mrs. Evans knocked on the first door and was invited to enter.

"Reverend Upchurch, you have a visitor," Mrs. Evans reported when she'd stepped into what was apparently the minister's office.

Malloy had described the room to her, but she was still surprised at the air of informality compared to the rest of the building. Reverend Upchurch had created a haven here where boys would feel comfortable. She made a mental note to look at the mission through the eyes of the girls to see what could be done to make it just as inviting as this office.

Mrs. Evans was introducing her to the minister who had stood up when they entered. Sarah felt a shock of surprise at how handsome he was. Somehow she hadn't expected that, and Malloy certainly hadn't mentioned it. "We've been bragging about our church, I'm afraid," Mrs. Evans was saying. "And Mrs. Brandt had to see for herself what we've accomplished."

"I hope we won't disappoint you, Mrs. Brandt," Reverend Upchurch said with a smile, coming from around his desk. He had a charming smile, and Sarah felt herself easily falling under its spell. Seeing no reason to resist, she smiled back.

"I'm sure you won't," she said. "As I told Mrs. Evans, I do volunteer work down at the Prodigal Son Mission on Mulberry Street. I heard how much you'd influenced Mrs. Evans's grandson and some of the other boys in your church, and I thought I'd see if what you're doing here could help us reach more girls on the Lower East Side."

"We aren't doing anything special." Plainly, he was uncomfortable taking any credit. "I just give the boys a place to come to stay out of trouble and have a little fun."

"Nonsense," Mrs. Evans scolded him good-naturedly. "He gives them much more than that," she told Sarah. "They adore him. He's like a father to every one of them, and he's never too busy to spend time with them."

"That's hardly the virtue Mrs. Evans makes it out to be," Reverend Upchurch said with an embarrassed grin. "Given the choice of sitting here writing a sermon or going out and playing baseball, what would you choose?"

Sarah thought about the other ministers she knew and couldn't imagine any of them playing baseball. "You must do more than play baseball with the boys," Sarah said with a meaningful glance at the pile of athletic equipment and the chess game that appeared to be in progress.

"Oh, he does," Mrs. Evans assured her. "In the summer, he even takes them on trips to the shore or to the country. As I told you, he's like a father to them, and whenever we have a problem with Percy, we simply call for Reverend Upchurch, and he comes immediately."

Sarah wondered what kinds of problems Mrs. Evans and her daughter had with Percy. He'd seemed well-behaved, but she supposed even a normally active boy might sometimes be too much for two women.

"Boys need a strong hand to guide them," Reverend Upchurch was saying.

"And a man to look up to," Mrs. Evans added, beaming at Upchurch.

Upchurch certainly looked like the kind of man every woman wanted her son to become, too. Tall and broad-shouldered, he practically radiated vitality.

Before Sarah could think of something else to ask, they

heard the front door of the church open and the sound of running feet in the sanctuary.

"Sounds like school is out," Upchurch said with a tolerant grin.

"The boys come here straight from school most days," Mrs. Evans explained, which Sarah already knew. "Maybe they could tell you what it is about our ministry here that appeals to them."

"Oh, I'm sure Mrs. Brandt doesn't have time for that," Upchurch said quickly, obviously wanting to spare her the ordeal of making the acquaintance of a pack of rowdy boys.

"I'd love to meet them, at least," Sarah said.

She got a fleeting impression that Upchurch wasn't pleased at the prospect, but it was gone so quickly, she thought she must have imagined it.

Mrs. Evans was already heading back to the sanctuary. "I'm sure they'd be delighted to meet you, too."

Sarah followed her, with the minister bringing up the rear. When Sarah stepped back into the sanctuary, she saw two boys scuffling at the back of the room, and about halfway down the aisle, another stood talking to a girl whose back was to them. He was older than the others, probably sixteen or so, and tall. He hadn't quite grown comfortable with his changing body, and he didn't seem to know what to do with his hands, but his young face betrayed his avid interest in this fascinating creature of the opposite sex.

Sarah's nerves tingled in alarm. Was this the boy who had seduced Grace? Was this girl to become his next victim? As the questions formed in her mind, the girl reached out and playfully plucked a piece of lint from the boy's jacket, then smoothed the lapel. It was a blatantly flirtatious gesture, and the boy responded with a flirtatious smile of his own.

"Rachel," Reverend Upchurch called sharply.

The girl turned toward the sound, and Sarah saw to her surprise that she wasn't a girl at all but a woman who was probably in her thirties. She was small and slender, almost birdlike, giving the illusion of youth, and she wore her dark hair in a cascade of curls, pinned up just high enough to be respectable. Her sharp-featured face was plain, almost boyish, but her dark eyes caught and held Sarah's attention. They seemed to hold a depth of emotion no mortal could contain. The impression was only momentary, but Sarah found it infinitely disturbing.

"Oliver," Rachel replied coolly. "Mrs. Evans, how nice to see you."

Susannah Evans didn't reply. She frowned in stern disapproval, as the boy flushed scarlet.

They all stood for a long moment in awkward silence until Upchurch remembered his manners. "Mrs. Brandt, may I introduce my wife?"

6

"I'M PLEASED TO MEET YOU, MRS. BRANDT," RACHEL UP-church said with a strange smile. "Are you a new church member?"

"Mrs. Brandt is interested in our work here," Upchurch informed his wife. Sarah thought she heard an edge of warning in his voice.

"And what work is that?" Rachel asked, never taking her dark eyes off Sarah.

"I'm interested in how Reverend Upchurch provides activities for boys to keep them out of trouble," Sarah said before anyone could reply for her.

Mrs. Upchurch considered that for a few seconds before lifting her strange gaze to her husband. "Is that what you do, Oliver? Keep them out of trouble?"

Upchurch ignored the question. "Isaiah," he said to the

boy with whom his wife had been flirting moments ago, "why don't you take the other boys downstairs and set up a game of dominoes?"

Apparently grateful for the excuse to escape this uncomfortable situation, the boy mumbled, "Yes, sir," and practically fled, gathering up the others as he left.

"We've been rolling bandages all afternoon, Mrs. Upchurch," Mrs. Evans told her with a trace of disapproval. "We're sorry you couldn't join us."

"So am I," Mrs. Upchurch replied without a shred of sincerity. "I do so enjoy rolling bandages. Mrs. Brandt, are you a widow?"

"Why, yes, I am," Sarah said, too surprised by the bluntness of the question to think of not answering.

"And why are you so interested in my husband's young playmates? Do you have a son of your own?"

"Oh, no, I—"

"That's good," Mrs. Upchurch said, cutting her off. "We already have enough fatherless boys around here, don't we, Mrs. Evans?"

"I . . . Why . . . whatever do you mean, Mrs. Upchurch?" Mrs. Evans stammered, not certain if she should be offended or outraged.

"I mean exactly what I said. I always do." Mrs. Upchurch gave her husband what could only be called a silent challenge.

"Rachel, don't you have something you should be doing?" Upchurch asked in an agony of embarrassment at her odd behavior.

"What could I have to do?" she replied, then turned back to Sarah. "Those are fatherless boys," she explained confidentially, indicating the direction the boys had gone. "I'm a boyless mother. And a girlless one, too."

"Many women aren't blessed with children," Mrs. Evans

reminded her sternly. "They still manage to find many worthwhile things to fill their time."

"What a quaint expression," Mrs. Upchurch observed. "*Blessed* with children. If only a blessing were all it took."

"I believe you wanted to meet some of the boys, Mrs. Brandt," Reverend Upchurch said in an obvious attempt to end this encounter with his wife. "I'd be happy to introduce you."

"Thank you," Sarah said, although she had a feeling this odd woman might be the only one in the church who could really help in her quest to find Grace's attacker. "So nice meeting you," she said to Mrs. Upchurch.

"Was it really?" she replied with a trace of a smile.

Reverend Upchurch indicated Sarah should precede him down the aisle toward the stairs, and as they passed his wife, Mrs. Upchurch turned to Mrs. Evans.

"Did you say you were rolling bandages? May I join you?" Without waiting for an answer, she fell in behind her husband, and the four of them made their way down to the church basement.

The sound of boys' voices led them to the room where Isaiah was organizing a game of dominoes on a center table. The voices fell silent the instant Reverend Upchurch led the ladies into the room.

"I'd like you to meet Mrs. Brandt," he told them. Their young eyes watched her with guarded interest, and she smiled in an effort to reassure them. "She came to see what our church is like."

"I didn't mean to interrupt your game," Sarah said.

The boys just stared, not hostile but not friendly either. She realized that they would see her as just another boring adult, keeping them from their fun. She wanted to ask them questions. She wanted to know if they'd noticed anything or anyone suspicious around the church or if they knew what might have happened to Grace Linton. She also understood in this one moment of confrontation that even if she could find a reason to ask them such questions, they'd never answer her honestly. They had no reason to trust her or even to take her seriously. If they did know something about Grace's attack, they'd never tell her.

"What's the matter, Isaiah?" Mrs. Underwood asked playfully. "Cat got your tongue?"

Isaiah blushed even more furiously than he had upstairs. "No, ma'am. You didn't interrupt our game, Mrs. Brandt," he added politely. "We didn't start yet."

"Did you want to ask the boys some questions?" Reverend Upchurch asked Sarah, but before she could reply two more boys came into the room. One of them was Percy York.

Mrs. Evans greeted her grandson, who managed to return the greeting in a manly enough way that his friends wouldn't tease him. "You remember Mrs. Brandt, don't you?" she added. "You met her at Mrs. Linton's house."

"Nice to see you, Mrs. Brandt," he said politely. "What are you doing here?"

"*Percy*," his grandmother scolded him for his bluntness, but Sarah only laughed.

"That's a good question," she told him, grateful for the opening she'd despaired of finding. "I came to find out why you boys would rather be here than out on the streets getting into trouble."

She wasn't sure what she had expected, but not the sudden wariness she felt crackle through the room. The boys all looked at Upchurch who had stiffened slightly, although his expression was still friendly and open.

"They're good boys, Mrs. Brandt," he said with just a

trace of defensiveness. "They wouldn't be getting into trouble even if they weren't here, would you, boys?"

"No, sir," they all agreed, almost in unison.

"But you *are* here, instead of many other places you could be," Sarah said, not sure exactly how to phrase a question so she'd get the answer she needed. "I'm interested in helping children in the Lower East Side stay out of trouble, so I'm wondering what you find at the church that you don't find anywhere else."

Now they all seemed uncomfortable, and once again they looked to Upchurch for something. Perhaps they needed a clue from him on how to answer. Or perhaps he himself was the answer.

"Don't be so bashful," Mrs. Upchurch ordered them with an odd glint in her dark eyes. "Tell Mrs. Brandt what it is that draws you here, fellows. You aren't ashamed, are you?"

Behind Sarah, Mrs. Evans made a disapproving sound, but the youngest boy in the group, the one who had come in with Percy just now, piped up. "We come for Mr. Upchurch. He teaches us things."

One of the older boys gave him an elbow to silence him, earning a black look, and Mrs. Evans decided she had had enough. "Of course they come because of Reverend Upchurch," she said in exasperation. "He cares about them, and he takes care *of* them. You should be proud to have such a fine man as your husband," she informed Mrs. Upchurch.

" 'Pride goeth before a fall,' " Mrs. Upchurch quoted, taking great delight in turning away the implied criticism with a scripture verse. "I'm sure my husband wouldn't want me to sin, would you, Oliver?"

Oliver didn't have time to say, because she turned with a swish of her skirts and left the room, leaving everyone gaping.

Reverend Upchurch was the first to recover. "Well, boys,

we'll let you get back to your game now." He touched Sarah lightly on the elbow, to indicate she should leave. She was only too happy to oblige. Mrs. Evans remained behind a moment to speak to Percy and the other boys.

"I'm terribly sorry, Mrs. Brandt," Upchurch was saying softly. "My wife is a very troubled woman."

Sarah looked around, half-expecting Mrs. Upchurch to be lying in wait to confront her husband and challenge his assessment of her character, but she didn't see the minister's wife. "I'm sorry to hear that," she said as neutrally as she could.

"Some women can accept not having children, but Rachel isn't one of them. I think she's angry at God, and she takes it out on me."

Sarah found this a rather personal observation to make to a virtual stranger, especially from a man whose profession demanded discretion. She could only conclude that he wanted her to know this about his wife. What she couldn't figure out was why.

"Thank you for your time, Reverend Upchurch," Sarah said, not wanting to invite any more intimate revelations. "You seem to be having great success, at least with those particular boys."

"We do what we can, Mrs. Brandt, and hope for the best. With children, you can never be certain how they'll turn out, though, can you?"

"No, I suppose you can't," she had to agree, a little disappointed that he didn't have more confidence in his efforts.

Mercifully, Mrs. Evans caught up with them then. Sarah thanked her for her help, and Upchurch fetched Sarah's cape. In a few moments she was standing on the sidewalk outside the church, trying to decide if she had accomplished anything at all with her visit.

"Mrs. Brandt!" a voice called, and Sarah looked up to see Rachel Upchurch walking toward her. Her cheeks were rosy, in spite of the thick wool cape she wore with its hood pulled tightly around her face. She must have been waiting out here in the cold for Sarah to emerge.

"Hello again," Sarah said.

"Is it true, what you said? Are you really interested in Oliver's work with those boys?" she asked, startling Sarah with her frankness. She hadn't been exaggerating when she said she always spoke the truth.

"Yes, I am."

Mrs. Upchurch's thin lips turned up in a sly smile. "Then call on me some afternoon, and I'll be glad to tell you more about it." She reached into her coat pocket and pulled out a calling card with her address printed on it. "I just live around the corner, and don't worry about privacy. No one ever calls on me. They find it too disturbing, but I think you may be made of sterner stuff than most. Are you, Mrs. Brandt?"

"I believe I am," Sarah replied, thoroughly intrigued. She took the extended card.

"Then I shall look forward to seeing you very soon." With that, Rachel Upchurch turned and strolled away.

FRANK HAD HEARD ABOUT SIGMUND FREUD. HE WAS some quack doctor over in Europe who thought he'd figured out why people go insane. He also thought he could talk them back into their right minds again. That was the part that didn't make any sense. Frank had always believed that too much talk was what drove people crazy in the first place. He knew that's how his mother sometimes made him feel.

Frank didn't believe for a moment that anyone could cure a person from insanity, but he did want to know more about

Tom Brandt's four female patients. From what Sarah had said about her late husband, he wasn't the type of man who'd take advantage of deluded women for his own pleasure. On the other hand, the wife was usually the last person to know if her husband had a sexual perversion he purposely kept secret.

Dr. Quinn's office was located on a quiet side street on the Upper West Side, identified only by a discreet brass plaque bearing his name. The door was locked, so Frank tried ringing the bell. After a minute or two, he rang it again and was just about to give up and come back another time when he heard footsteps inside. A disheveled young man answered the door. Frank guessed he hadn't seen thirty yet. He'd buttoned his collar too hastily, and his tie was crooked. He was still straightening his suit coat, and his hair looked like he'd been running his fingers through it.

"Did you have an appointment?" he asked Frank with a puzzled frown. Apparently, Frank didn't look like his usual clients.

"No, I'm Detective Sergeant Frank Malloy, with the police. I'd like to ask you a few questions about a case I'm working on."

"Does it involve one of my patients?" he asked in alarm.

"No, or not that I know of, anyway," Frank assured him. "Dr. Newton sent me. He said you'd be able to explain some things I need to understand about *dementia praecox* and hysteria."

Quinn blinked a few times in surprise. "Dr. Newton, you say? Well, I'll help you if I can. Come in, come in."

The doctor let him into the foyer of a modest house. The doors along the hallway were all closed, and Frank figured the good doctor lived here and saw his patients here, too. Quinn pushed open the first door on the right and motioned Frank inside.

The room was small and simply furnished, with a desk and a glass-fronted bookcase at one end. At the other sat a few comfortable chairs and a reclining couch of some kind.

"Would you like to lie down?" Dr. Quinn asked, leading Frank toward the couch.

"Why would I want to lay down?"

"Well, because . . . that is, some people feel more comfortable that way, especially when they are talking about difficult things."

"I'm usually fine sitting up, no matter what I'm talking about," Frank informed him.

Dr. Quinn smiled magnanimously. "Very well, then, please have a seat."

Frank took the chair he indicated, and Quinn sat in another one, facing him.

"Did you say Dr. Newton sent you?" he asked.

"Yes. He doesn't know much about insanity, but he said you could answer my questions. He said you'd studied with Freud."

"That's right," Quinn said proudly. "Dr. Freud is a genius. The things he's discovered about the human mind are astonishing."

Frank figured he knew a few astonishing things about the human mind that could curl Dr. Quinn's messy hair, but he refrained from saying so. "What can you tell me about *dementia praecox* and hysteria?" he asked to move the conversation along.

"Quite a bit, so perhaps you should tell me exactly why you need to know. Then I'll be better able to judge what information you need."

"A doctor had four patients, all women. They were all in love with him, and they all thought he was in love with them, too. They even said he'd seduced them."

"Have these women accused him of rape? Is that why you're investigating?"

"No, he's dead. Somebody killed him, and I think it was because of this."

"Oh, my," Dr. Quinn said in dismay. "You think one of the women? . . ."

"No, the killer was a man, probably a father."

"But not a husband. I'm guessing none of them is married."

"That's right," Frank said. "How did you know?"

"The condition you're describing is sometimes called 'Old Maid's disease,' because the women who suffer from it are usually unmarried."

"And it's also called hysteria?"

"Sometimes doctors use the term *hysteria* to describe a condition in a female they don't understand. It isn't exactly an accurate diagnosis."

"Then what can you tell me about this 'Old Maid's disease'?"

"It's been recognized for centuries. A Frenchman wrote a treatise about it in the early sixteen hundreds, and even Hippocrates referred to it in his writings." Frank wasn't sure who that was, but he nodded wisely as if he did. "Simply, it's a form of mental disease in which the sufferer imagines herself in a love affair with a man who has no feelings for her at all and may hardly even know her. Usually the man is someone prominent or sometimes just someone who has been kind to her. You said the murdered man was a doctor. Because of the nature of their work, doctors are often the love objects for these women."

"So it happens a lot?"

"More frequently than anyone would like, especially the unfortunate gentlemen who are the objects of this misplaced devotion. The woman will often make a nuisance of herself, paying inappropriate attention to the man, giving him gifts, following him, and sometimes even sneaking into his home because she imagines she is his wife and that she lives there with him."

"And sooner or later, the man takes advantage of her," Frank guessed.

"You mean because of the accusations of seduction?" Dr. Quinn asked. "No. Actually, the men involved are usually repulsed by the woman's attentions, but nothing they say or do can discourage her. She interprets a simple tip of the hat or an impersonal greeting as a declaration of undying devotion, and sometimes the man is someone famous who has never even met the woman or had any contact with her at all. The seductions are almost always in the woman's imagination. Even virgins will describe erotic encounters with the man they love, but rarely have these encounters actually happened."

"But why would a woman make up something like that? What would make her throw herself at a man who didn't want her?"

"We don't know, Mr. Malloy, at least not yet. People do many things that the rest of us consider irrational and will never understand. This is what Dr. Freud's work is all about. We're trying to find out what makes some people's minds malfunction to the point that they behave in a manner society calls insane."

"So what you're talking about is *dementia praecox*?"

"Oh, no, at least not always. *Dementia praecox* is a much more serious condition, and it afflicts men as well. The sufferers often hallucinate—see and hear things that aren't there," he explained. "They may develop an attachment to an individual as part of the illness, but they are seriously ill and unable to function normally. They must be confined for their own safety, while women suffering from Old Maid's disease are usually normal in every other way."

"How do you cure a woman of this?"

Dr. Quinn didn't like the question. "Since the woman is irrational, at least on this one subject, it's almost impossible to convince her anything is even wrong with her, so she isn't likely to seek a cure. Sometimes the attachment simply fades with time. Other times the families succeed in controlling the woman so she cannot continue to humiliate herself. Rarely is the woman 'cured' the way you mean it, though."

Frank considered all of this information and tried to decide how it applied to Tom Brandt.

"Have I helped you with your case, Mr. Malloy?"

"I'm not sure. If a doctor had a patient who fell in love with him like this, why would he go out and try to find more women who had this illness and get them to fall in love with him, too?"

Dr. Quinn's young face creased into a frown. "I . . . I wouldn't want to offer a conjecture without more information," he hedged.

"Oh, I think you could if you tried," Frank replied, leaning forward in a slightly threatening manner. "From what you said, most men don't like being pursued by these crazy women."

"We don't use the word 'crazy.' "

"Whatever word you use, that's what they are. So why would a man purposely go out looking for more of them?"

"I can't think of any logical reason," Quinn tried.

"Then how about one that isn't logical?"

Quinn swallowed. "I know what you're trying to make me say, and I assure you, no reputable doctor would engage in that sort of behavior."

"But one that wasn't reputable might," Frank said. "A man with certain sexual appetites might. And he might decide he liked having a woman who was willing to do anything he wanted. He might like it so much that he went looking for more of them."

Dr. Quinn's face went slack in despair. "I'm afraid I can't think of any other explanation, either."

SARAH HAD LITTLE TIME IN THE NEXT THIRTY-SIX HOURS to think about what she had learned at the Church of the Good Shepherd. She arrived back home only to be summoned to a delivery, and afterwards she was able to get just a few hours sleep before being called to another. When she finally returned home early the following morning, she found a note from Mrs. Linton, asking her to call that afternoon.

The note was brief, revealing nothing about the reason for the request, and for a moment Sarah worried something might be wrong with Grace. But then she realized that an emergency would have been worded much differently and not asked for a formal call. Deciding she was too weary to wonder about it, she finally made her way to bed.

By afternoon, Sarah was restored enough to spend some time with Aggie before setting out for Lenox Hill. The maid took her into the parlor to see Mrs. Linton at once.

Claire Linton had been sitting alone, sewing, but she set her project aside when Sarah came in. Her expression was guarded as she greeted her visitor.

"Is Grace all right?" Sarah asked as she took the offered seat.

"She's fine," Mrs. Linton said stiffly. "Would you like some tea?"

Sarah agreed, and Mrs. Linton sent the maid to fetch it.

A few moments of silence followed the maid's departure, and from the way Mrs. Linton was looking at her, Sarah began to feel like a schoolgirl who'd been caught cheating on a test.

Finally, she could stand it no longer. "Is something wrong?" she asked.

Mrs. Linton winced a bit, as if it pained her to speak. "Mrs. Brandt, I understand . . . that is, I've been told that . . . Well, that you went to our church the other day."

Sarah felt a pang of guilt, but only a small one. She hadn't really been investigating Grace's attack, and even if she had been, she hadn't learned anything useful. "I was so impressed by what you'd said about your pastor and how much he's done for the boys in your church, that I wanted to see for myself what he does. I'm not sure if I mentioned it or not, but I do some volunteer work down at a mission on the Lower East Side. We try to help homeless girls by giving them a safe place to live. I thought perhaps I might get some pointers from your minister that would help us in that work."

Mrs. Linton blinked a few times as she took in Sarah's explanation. "Oh," she said after a moment. "I didn't . . . I mean, you hadn't said . . . I thought . . . ." Her hands fluttered in embarrassment.

Sarah managed to look innocent and asked, "What did you think?"

"Well, I . . . that is, I feel foolish now, but I was afraid . . . I know you were concerned about who might have . . . have hurt Grace," she said, her voice showing the strain of her predicament. "I thought you might have gone there to ask questions or . . ."

"I would never betray your confidence, Mrs. Linton," Sarah assured her quite honestly. "I suppose you did mention that the church is one of the few places Grace goes, but I assure you, I never even mentioned her name. I did see your friend, Mrs. Evans, there, and she was kind enough to introduce me to your minister when I told her why I had come."

"Yes, I know. She was the one who . . . who mentioned she'd seen you there. I couldn't imagine what else might have brought you." Mrs. Linton lifted a trembling hand to her cheek. "We're just so worried about Grace . . ."

Sarah felt a rush of relief that she hadn't really done anything to cause this poor woman more concern. "I'm sure you are. Have you thought about what you will do when the baby comes?"

Mrs. Linton covered her eyes for a moment and shook her head. "If we were younger," she began and had to clear the tears out of her voice. "If we were younger, we would try to pass the child off as our own. I could go away to the country for a while with Grace and come back with it. People might suspect, but . . . but we're not young enough for that." She sighed.

"Do you have family who could take the baby?"

She shook her head. "Even if we did, who would want the child of a simpleton and a rapist?" Her voice broke on that, but the maid's knock distracted her before she could dissolve into tears. Snatching a handkerchief from her sleeve, she dabbed at her tears and cleared her throat again. "Come in," she called.

If the maid noticed her mistress was on the verge of tears, she gave no indication of it. She set down the tea tray and discreetly disappeared.

Sarah allowed Mrs. Linton to use the time she spent pouring tea for them to compose herself. She only wished she had some words of comfort to offer, but she was afraid Mrs. Linton was right about no one wanting the child.

Sarah took the cup of tea Mrs. Linton offered her and stirred some sugar into it. The familiar ritual gave them both something to do while they tried to think of a safe topic. Finally Sarah came up with one.

"I met Mrs. Upchurch while I was at the church," she said, watching closely for Mrs. Linton's reaction.

She looked up, startled. "You did? That's odd. She's hardly ever at the church. Except on Sunday, of course," she added quickly. "What I meant was, she seems to have her own interests."

Sarah remembered that one of those interests seemed to be the young boys, but she didn't say so. "She's very different than I imagined she would be," she tried, hoping Mrs. Linton would take the bait.

She did. "She's very different than she should be, if you'll excuse my saying so," she said with a disapproving frown. "I don't like to gossip, but in this case, well, she's certainly a trial to Reverend Upchurch."

"She is very outspoken," Sarah said, recalling Mrs. Upchurch's boast that she always spoke the truth.

"I think she actually *tries* to embarrass him. He makes excuses for her, but everyone knows that she's simply wicked."

"*Wicked?*" Sarah repeated, remembering the way Mrs. Upchurch was flirting with that boy Isaiah.

"Oh, I don't mean that she's . . . immoral or anything like that," Mrs. Linton hastily explained. "It's just that she seems to go out of her way to be cruel to Reverend Upchurch or to embarrass him with her rude behavior. Can you imagine? A woman should be grateful to have such a man for a husband."

Mrs. Evans had said the same thing, and most people would share that opinion, but Sarah knew from going into countless homes to deliver children, both wanted and unwanted, that you could never truly know what went on between two people in private from the way they acted in public. "I'm sure it's difficult being a minister's wife," Sarah offered. "And Reverend Upchurch said she misses not having children of her own."

"Perhaps she does," Mrs. Linton allowed, and then she sighed again. "How odd that God withholds the gift of children from someone who wants them so much and then gives one to poor Grace." For a moment Sarah was afraid she was going to weep again, but she pinched the bridge of her nose and drew herself up, the way a well-bred female was trained to do, and controlled her emotions. "Would you like to see Grace?" she asked suddenly. "She speaks of you often. I'm sure she would be pleased to see you."

Without waiting for a reply, she stood and went to summon the maid. While they waited for the girl to fetch Grace, Mrs. Linton made small talk about the weather, and Sarah made the required responses, respecting her need to speak of inconsequential things.

After a few minutes, Grace came in. She was rubbing her eye with a fist, the way a small child would, as if she'd just awakened.

"Grace, dear, you remember Mrs. Brandt, don't you?" her mother prompted.

"Hello, Mrs. Brandt," Grace said obediently, slumping down onto the sofa beside her mother and reaching for a cookie from the tea tray, but before she could lift it to her mouth, she yawned hugely.

"Cover you mouth, dear," her mother chided with a worried frown. "Are you tired?"

"No, I just woke up. I fell asleep," she reported in amazement.

Mrs. Linton's gaze lifted questioningly to Sarah's. "What do you mean, you fell asleep?" she asked the girl, silently asking Sarah if this was a matter of concern.

Grace's lovely face wrinkled as she concentrated, trying to remember. "I was sitting by the window, watching the birds. Barbara put some crumbs out on the fire escape for them." She turned to Sarah. "Birds like to eat bread crumbs, and they'll land on the fire escape and eat them. If you sit really still, you can watch them, but if you move, even just a little bit, they get scared and fly away."

Mrs. Linton reached out to stroke Grace's mussed hair. "So you were watching the birds, and you fell asleep?" she asked with a worried frown.

"I guess so. I tried not to move, because I didn't want to scare the birds away, but I just had to put my head down on the windowsill because it felt so heavy, and the next thing I know, Barbara is waking me up just now." She shook her head in amazement. "That's so silly. You're not supposed to sleep in the daytime!"

"No, you're not," Mrs. Linton said, a question in her voice as she turned back to Sarah.

"Sometimes it's all right to sleep in the daytime, if you're really tired," Sarah said. "You might be getting tired in the daytime from now on, Grace, and if you are, you should lie down and take a nap."

"Is this because I'm growing up?" Grace asked suspiciously.

"In a way," Sarah replied with a smile.

"Mama doesn't take naps," Grace argued.

"I do if I feel tired," Mrs. Linton said determinedly. "Mrs. Brandt is right, if you're tired, you should sleep."

Grace considered this advice. "I don't think I'll sleep on the windowsill anymore, though. It's not very comfortable."

Both Sarah and Mrs. Linton laughed at this, Sarah politely and Mrs. Linton with a trace of relief. "That's a very sensible idea, Grace," her mother said.

"I visited your church the other day," Sarah told Grace. "I

met your minister, and I saw your friend Percy. He was with some of the other boys."

"Those boys are mean," Grace informed her. "I don't like them."

Sarah saw Mrs. Linton tense, and she had to bite her tongue to keep from asking the question Malloy would have asked, if he was here. Fortunately, Mrs. Linton asked it for her.

"Why don't you like them?" Her voice was a little strained, but Grace didn't notice. "They seem like very nice boys."

"They make fun of me. They call me stupid. Except Percy, he doesn't. But the others do, even when he tells them to stop."

Mrs. Linton couldn't help the small cry of outrage. "That's awful. You should have told me. I'll speak to Reverend Upchurch about it."

"I don't care," Grace said airily. "I think *they're* stupid. Sticks and stones may break my bones, but words will never hurt me. That's what Barbara always tells me."

"Barbara is very right," Sarah said, even though she knew words could do far more damage than broken bones. "And if any of those boys ever did hurt you, you'd tell your mother, wouldn't you?"

"They never would," Grace said confidently. "Reverend Upchurch would get mad at them if they did, because he likes me. He told me I was a very special girl."

"Reverend Upchurch is right, you are a very special girl," her mother confirmed, stroking her hair lovingly. "Now why don't you take a few cookies upstairs to share with your baby dolls?"

When Grace had gone, Mrs. Linton turned to Sarah with a worried frown. "I know she would have told me if one of the boys had . . . had done anything."

"I'm sure she would have," Sarah said. "I shouldn't have said what I did. Please forgive me for meddling. It's just that I'm concerned about Grace, too."

"I know you are, and I'm very grateful." She twisted her hands in her lap. "I'm sorry I thought that you went to the church to . . . Well, I should have known you wouldn't do anything to hurt Grace."

"Thank you," Sarah said, knowing she didn't really deserve the compliment. "I may visit your church again, though, if you don't mind. I'm still very interested in Reverend Upchurch's success with those boys."

"Oh, please do visit," Mrs. Linton said. "We'd love to have you. You must come on Sunday morning. Our choir is excellent."

After a few more minutes of polite conversation, Sarah took her leave. She was turning to go when she recalled one more thing. "Mrs. Upchurch has invited me to visit her."

"She did?" Mrs. Linton asked in surprise. "She's hardly ever at home to anyone," she added. Being 'at home' meant you were receiving visitors. A lady could be at home but not receiving, which oddly enough meant she wasn't at home.

"You've made me very curious about her. I think I will go to see her," Sarah said.

Mrs. Linton frowned. "Well, if you do, just remember that you can't always trust what she says," she warned.

"Do you mean she tells lies?" Sarah asked, remembering Mrs. Upchurch's boast that she always told the truth.

"Not lies exactly, but . . . Oh, I shouldn't be gossiping about her at all, but you must understand that sometimes she says things just to be hurtful. You'll understand what I mean when you've met with her."

Sarah certainly hoped so, and she intended to meet with her as soon as possible.

7

FRANK FOUND THE ADDRESS EASILY ENOUGH, A MODEST house on a side street in Greenwich Village. A middle-aged woman answered the bell and stared at him suspiciously.

He identified himself and added, "I'm here to see Miss Edna White."

"What about?" the woman asked, still suspicious.

"About the murder of Dr. Thomas Brandt."

Her eyes widened, and she leaned out the door, looking up and down the street. "Come in, quickly," she said, clutching at the fabric of his coat sleeve and fairly pulling him inside when she was satisfied no one was watching. "I knew you'd come," she informed him. "I knew someone would come. I'm Edna White. I'll tell you everything you need to know about Dr. Brandt."

She took his coat and hung it on the hall tree, then led

him into the front parlor. "I'm so glad you came during the day. If my brother was home, he wouldn't let me speak with you. He keeps me a prisoner here, I'm afraid. Please, sit down."

Frank took a seat on the worn sofa, and she sat in a wing chair opposite. The furniture was good quality, but shabby. Miss White folded her hands in her lap tightly, as if to keep from fidgeting. She did seem very excited. Frank knew she was only in her late thirties, but she looked older. She seemed worn, too, like the furniture. Her face was plain and pale, even paler than most ladies he knew, as if her very blood were white. She'd never been attractive, not even in her youth. Her simple dress was faded and soft from many washings, although someone had made a new collar and cuffs for it recently. Her hair was the color of oatmeal, faded like everything else about her, and she wore it pulled carelessly into a bun. The only things not faded were her eyes. They sparkled with an intensity that made Frank uneasy.

"Are you here alone?" he asked, realizing this could be awkward for him if she was as insane as her file had indicated. She might accuse him of rape the way she had Tom Brandt.

"Oh, no. Miss Holly is here. She's always here," Miss White reported with disdain. "She's my hired keeper, but she drinks, you see. My brother doesn't know, of course, or he'd dismiss her at once, and I don't tell him, because it suits my purpose to have her drunk. If she wasn't asleep just now, I wouldn't have been able to see you, Detective." She smiled delightedly.

Frank had to clear his throat. "Maybe you'd like to wake her up and have her sit with us," he suggested. Few people, especially ladies, wanted to be questioned by the police about a murder. They usually wanted someone with them for support.

"Oh, no, she'd just make you leave or send for my brother, and he'd make you leave. Please go right ahead and tell me what you need to know."

Having no other choice, he did. "When did you first meet Dr. Brandt?"

"Oh, my, it was January twenty-second, 1892. I'll never forget that day. He came here to the house. I was very ill with the grippe. He saved my life. He's a wonderful doctor. But then, you must know that already."

"Uh, yes," Frank said. "That's what I've heard. So he treated you, and you got better."

"Yes, indeed I did. It took a long time to recover my strength, but Dr. Brandt returned again and again. He said he was going to make sure I was completely well. Then one day he brought me a flower, to cheer me up. A perfect red rose. That's when I knew." Her dark eyes seemed to glow as she looked at something far away, something only she could see.

"Knew what?" Frank prodded.

She looked at him in surprise. "Why, I knew that he loved me." She glanced at the open parlor door, as if checking to see if anyone had overheard. "They don't like for me to talk about it," she explained, lowering her voice. "My brother and Miss Holly. You wouldn't believe the things they've done to keep us apart."

"Did they tell you Dr. Brandt was married?" Frank asked carefully, not certain what effect this information would have on her.

"I know all about his wife. She's a spoiled rich girl, and she only married him to shock her family. She never really loved him. Theirs is a marriage in name only. He never knew what true love was until he met me."

Frank looked at this dried-up stick of a woman. He'd

once considered the possibility that Tom Brandt had found his patient attractive enough to seduce and thus cause her romantic attachment to him, but now that he'd met her, he knew that was impossible. No husband of Sarah's could feel the slightest attraction to Edna White. "He told you he loved you?" Frank asked, nearly choking on the words.

"Many times. I know a lady should never admit such things, Mr . . . Malloy, was it? . . . but Dr. Brandt and I are lovers. It's a sin, of course, because we aren't married, but we're married in our hearts. I'm sure God doesn't judge lovers too harshly, aren't you, Detective?"

Frank had no idea, so he said, "Where did you . . . meet? To be together, I mean," he asked as tactfully as he could.

"He has a flat in Chinatown. They know how to keep secrets in Chinatown, Mr. Malloy. We meet there in the afternoons. He wants to divorce his wife, but it's difficult. Her family is very wealthy, and they don't want the scandal, but he's going to win, and then we'll be married. Meanwhile, I must be patient, as difficult as that is."

Frank hardly heard the lies about Sarah. "You *still* meet him?" he asked incredulously.

"Oh, yes. It's not easy for me to get away, of course, but Miss Holly drinks, as I said. When she falls asleep, I sneak out. I must, you see. Dr. Brandt couldn't endure his miserable marriage if he couldn't see me from time to time. Most women would have given up hope by now, but my love is stronger than that. I'll wait forever if I must."

"Miss White," Frank began, not quite trusting his own senses. She seemed so reasonable, but the words she was saying were totally insane. He was even starting to wonder if they were talking about the same man. "Did they tell you that Dr. Brandt is dead?"

She straightened her spine and sniffed in outrage. "Of

course they did. They've been telling me that for years. I
don't suppose I blame them very much. Albert can't bear
the thought of his beloved sister having a married lover. He
simply doesn't understand, so he made up that lie. He must
have thought if I believed Dr. Brandt was dead then I would
forget about him, so he told me that awful story about him
being murdered. But I knew it wasn't true, and now you've
come here to prove it!"

As Mrs. Upchurch had said, her home was just
around the corner from the church. The manse had been
built of the same material as the church and sat at the rear of
the property. Sarah wasn't certain what she had expected,
but the house looked no grander than the others on the
street. All were comfortable abodes for families with comfortable incomes who could afford to keep several servants.

The maid seemed startled when Sarah presented her card
and asked to see Mrs. Upchurch. Apparently, Mrs. Linton
had been correct in assuming Mrs. Upchurch rarely enter-
tained visitors. The girl showed Sarah inside and asked her
to wait in the front parlor. The room was chilly, the grate
cold, but Sarah couldn't help admiring the elegant furnish-
ings. Although the modern trend was to clutter every available surface with knickknacks and to fill the room with as
many pieces of oversized furniture as possible, Mrs. Upchurch had defied convention. She'd chosen delicately
carved piecrust and marble-topped tables to accent the
graceful sofas and chairs upholstered in gold velvet. A magnificent jade dragon adorned the mantelpiece, and a few
other exquisite jade figurines sat on the tabletops. An oriental rug woven in golds and greens covered part of the highly
polished floor. Lace curtains shielded the windows beneath

gold velvet draperies. Sarah even imagined she caught an Oriental scent in the air.

"Millie is such a fool to put you in here," Mrs. Upchurch announced, entering the room like a small tornado. "We haven't lit the fire in this room in weeks. But perhaps she's hoping I'll freeze to death. Oh, yes, good afternoon, Mrs. Brandt. How kind of you to come," she added politely, with just the slightest irony.

Sarah couldn't help a smile. "Good afternoon, Mrs. Upchurch. I was just admiring the room." She gestured toward the jade dragon. "Have you been to China?"

"I grew up there. My parents were missionaries," she said. "Come back to my lair, and I'll show you some really interesting pieces. You'll also be much warmer."

Without waiting for Sarah to agree, Mrs. Upchurch turned away, leaving her no choice but to follow. Walking down the hallway behind her, Sarah had an opportunity to notice her gown. Made of deep maroon silk, its simple lines clung to her small frame in the absence of adequate petticoats, accentuating her lack of female curves. Today she'd tied her hair at the back of her neck with a ribbon, and Sarah could see the curls were natural and a bit wild when she didn't bother to tame them. Once again she was struck by how young and girlish she looked from behind.

As Sarah had suspected, the "lair" was the less-formal back parlor where a cozy fire burned.

"I see that idiot Millie didn't even take your cape. Give it to me, and then sit down. That chair is the most comfortable," she added, indicating the one nearest the fire.

Mrs. Upchurch called the maid by shouting in an undignified manner. The girl came at a run. "Hang this up," Mrs. Upchurch said, handing her Sarah's cape, "and bring us something hot. Tea or coffee, Mrs. Brandt?"

"Either is fine," Sarah said.

"Coffee then. And I said *hot*."

The girl scurried away, and Mrs. Upchurch closed the door behind her. "I can't keep good help," she explained. "I'm too difficult to please. Sit," she added, pointing to the chair again. As Sarah did as she'd been bidden, Mrs. Upchurch took the chair across from it. Oddly, it didn't look comfortable at all, although it was obviously where she usually sat, because her workbasket was on the small table beside it. The chair was straight-backed with bare wooden arms. A thinly cushioned seat was the only effort at comfort, and it was well-worn. A small and equally worn footstool sat in front of it.

"You see," Mrs. Upchurch said, indicating the mantel. "I told you the pieces in here were better."

This room had been decorated in shades of red, to match the reddish material of the many carved figurines adorning the mantel and the tabletops. "What are they made of?" Sarah asked, marveling at the intricate patterns someone highly skilled had spent months creating.

"Jade. Jade comes in many colors, not just green."

"They're all so beautiful. The Chinese are very artistic. You said your parents were missionaries. Are they still working there?"

"No, they're dead," she said coolly. "They were killed by the Chinese in one of their many uprisings against the foreign devils."

"I'm so sorry," Sarah said automatically.

"Don't be. I'm sure they were thrilled to become martyrs. They would have considered it their ultimate accomplishment."

Sarah needed a few seconds to absorb this information. She wasn't used to people being quite so brutally frank. "You managed to . . . escape," she tried.

"I was away at school when it happened," she said. "I was almost always away at school, come to that. I hardly ever saw them from the time I was five years old. They said it wasn't safe for me in the interior, but I think they just didn't want to be bothered with me. They had their work, and that was more important."

Sarah recalled Mrs. Linton's warning that Mrs. Upchurch often said things just to be hurtful. She wondered whom she might be trying to hurt with this conversation. Her parents were beyond such things, and it couldn't be pleasant for her to remember them herself. But maybe she was just trying to shock her visitor. "You must have some happy memories of China, though, or you wouldn't keep all these beautiful things around you."

"I hated China. I hated everything about it. No one in China ever says what they think. No one here does, either, of course, particularly if it's unpleasant. That's why I keep these things around me, to remind me to always tell the truth. The trouble is, no one wants to hear the truth, so people avoid me, which means I have no one to whom to speak the truth. That's why I have to stand in the street and invite perfect strangers to visit me." She grinned then, a huge, ingenuous, delightful grin that startled Sarah into grinning back.

"Do you do that often?" she couldn't resist asking.

"Only when I find someone interesting. I found you *very* interesting, Mrs. Brandt."

"Why is that?" she asked, more than curious.

"Because you're different from the other women at the church."

"In what way?"

"You think for yourself, for one thing. I could tell from the questions you were asking. Everyone who comes to the church wants something, but usually they want something for themselves. You wanted to help someone else."

"That's what Christians are supposed to do."

She grinned again. She looked like a mischievous little boy. "Which is why it hardly ever happens. Tell me why you're different, Mrs. Brandt."

"I have no idea," Sarah said quite honestly.

"Then I suppose I shall have to figure it out for myself," she replied, obviously delighted by the prospect. "You said you are a widow. Who was your husband?"

"He was a doctor, but not a wealthy one. He treated anyone who came to him, whether they could pay or not."

"How very foolish of him, or at least that's what most people would think," she added to soften the criticism. "I suppose he was happy, though, because he was working to please himself."

"Yes, he was," Sarah answered in surprise. She'd never thought of Tom's life in those terms before. "We were both very happy."

"How did he die?"

Sarah braced herself for the pang she always felt when she thought of Tom's death. Time had dulled the sharp edges of the pain, but it still hurt.

Mrs. Upchurch misunderstood her hesitation. "Oh, dear, I've been offensive, haven't I? I'm afraid I'm not always sensitive to what others find offensive. You see, I'll be quite delighted to answer that question someday, because it will mean that my dear Oliver has gone to his eternal reward, and I shall be free of him at last."

FRANK STARED AT MISS WHITE IN AMAZEMENT. "BUT DR. Brandt really is dead. He was murdered almost four years ago."

Miss White's face crumbled, and for a moment Frank thought she was going to cry, but she just shook her head in despair. "He sent you, didn't he?"

"Who?" Frank asked, thinking of Tom Brandt sending messages from the grave.

"My brother, Albert." She shook her head again. "I try to remember that he loves me, too. He only wants what's best for me, or so he says. He just won't understand that Dr. Brandt *is* what's best for me. I can't live without him. Do you think I would have waited all this time if I didn't love him beyond all reason?"

Frank felt certain this was true. "Your brother didn't send me," he tried. "I told you, I'm investigating Dr. Brandt's murder. He really is dead."

She gave him a pitying look. "This is very cruel, and you should be ashamed of yourself. I guess you must need money very badly to have hired yourself out to do a thing like this. Are you an actor?"

"No, I'm not an actor," Frank said in exasperation. Why hadn't anyone ever sat this woman down and made her see reason? How could her brother have let her believe this fairy tale all these years?

"You should be," Miss White said. "You fooled me completely. I thought I could trust you."

Just then the front door burst open, and a man came rushing into the front hallway, looking around frantically. "Edna, where are you?" he cried.

Miss White rose regally to her feet. Frank had already jumped up when the door slammed open. "I'm right here, Albert, speaking with this gentleman you sent here to tell me more lies."

Albert White turned to Frank. He was a gangly man with little grace, his plain face flushed from running through the windy streets and creased with concern. His clothes were well made but not elegant. He resembled his sister, but a lack of beauty doesn't matter so much in a man. "Who are you?" he demanded breathlessly.

"Detective Sergeant Frank Malloy with the New York City Police. I'm investigating the murder of Doctor Thomas Brandt."

"Enough," Edna said imperiously. "This deceit has gone far enough. I know what you've done, Albert, and you wasted your time and your money. Mr. Malloy was no more successful at convincing me Dr. Brandt is dead than you have been."

White's baffled gaze darted from his sister back to Frank.

"She thinks you hired me to convince her he's dead," he explained.

White ran a trembling hand over his face and belatedly thought to remove his hat. "I've told you never to let anyone in the house, Edna," he said, as if speaking to a disobedient child. "Where is Miss Holly?"

"She wasn't feeling well, so I told her to lie down. And what are you doing home at this hour? Have you been dismissed from your job?"

Frank thought he detected a spark of annoyance in White, but he managed to control it. "Mrs. Abernathy saw you letting a strange man into the house. She telephoned my office."

"Mrs. Abernathy should mind her own business."

Frank figured Mrs. Abernathy was the same kind of neighbor as Mrs. Ellsworth.

White sighed. "Please go to your room, Edna. I'll talk to you about this later."

"And apologize, too, I hope," she said. "Good day, Mr. Malloy, and I encourage you to find a more honest way to make your living."

She marched out, leaving Frank staring after her in amazement. When she was gone, he turned to White. "Does she really believe Dr. Brandt is still alive?"

"Yes, just as she believes he was in love with her. What are you doing here, Mr. Malloy?" he asked wearily.

"Like I said, I'm investigating Dr. Brandt's murder."

"And you think Edna killed him?" he asked sarcastically.

"No, I know a man killed him, a man who thought Dr. Brandt had harmed his daughter."

White sighed wearily. "Then you've wasted your time here. Our father died years before Edna met Dr. Brandt, so he couldn't be the killer. If that's all you need to know, I should get back to my office before I really do get dismissed."

"Could I ask you a couple more questions, Mr. White? I'm trying to understand what happened with your sister and the doctor."

"I've been trying to understand it for years, Mr. Malloy. What makes you think a few questions would be enough?"

"I'm sure you're right, but can you at least tell me what you do know? It might help me find Dr. Brandt's killer."

"Old Maid's disease," he said bitterly. "That's what they called it. I took her to another doctor when she made a fool of herself over Dr. Brandt. He said it happens when a woman is lonely. She misinterprets the simplest kindness as an expression of affection, and then she begins to imagine all kinds of things that aren't true and refuses to see what really is true."

"She thinks Dr. Brandt is still alive, and that she still meets him."

"I know, even though she never leaves the house. Believe me, if she did, my neighbors or her companion, Miss Holly, would tell me."

"By the way, Miss Holly drinks. That's why she's laying down."

White ran a hand over his face again. "I know that, too. It's been hard to find a companion for Edna since my wife . . ."

His voice caught, and Frank felt a wash of pity for him. "Your wife passed away?"

"No," he said, suddenly angry. "She's very much alive, but she left me. She wouldn't live here with Edna, so she moved back to her parents' house. She wants me to put Edna in an asylum, but I can't put her in a place like that. She's my only living relative. She spent her youth nursing our mother who was an invalid. She was the sweetest, most loving sister you could imagine, and she still is, except for this one thing. I can't abandon her."

"Can't you talk to her? Can't someone reason with her?" Frank asked.

"Don't you think I've tried?" he cried, his composure broken at last. "Nothing will convince her. Even when Dr. Brandt himself told her he didn't love her, she decided he was only being gallant, that he didn't want her to waste her life waiting for him when he might never get a divorce. She won't even believe he's dead!"

"Do you think Brandt ever encouraged her? Or that he took advantage of her?"

"At first I thought he must have. Edna was so certain he loved her. I just couldn't believe she'd imagined something like that, but when I confronted him . . . Well, it was obvious he'd done nothing of the kind. Then he did everything he could to discourage her, but that only seemed to make it worse."

"You said you took her to another doctor," Frank prodded.

"Yes. He's the one who explained it to me. It happens more often than you'd imagine, and often to doctors. There's nothing to be done for it except to keep Edna locked away where she won't embarrass herself or anyone else."

"Did Dr. Brandt ever try to cure her?"

"Except for trying to reason with her, no. He didn't know what else to do, but he told me he was going to try to find out everything he could about this . . . this problem. He wanted to help Edna. I think he felt guilty, as if he'd somehow brought it on. But then I read in the paper that he'd been killed." He laughed mirthlessly. "I thought that would end it. I thought Edna would be cured then." He shook his head. "I've really got to go back to my office now, Mr. Malloy."

Frank thanked White for his help and took his leave. As he turned up his collar against the wintry wind, he thought about the depth of loneliness necessary to drive a woman to lose touch with reality. Edna White seemed the perfect candidate. Even if she'd attracted suitors when she was young, which she probably hadn't, she'd been too busy taking care of her sick mother. Then a handsome man comes into her life and is kind to her when she's sick and frightened. Any woman could be excused for developing tender feelings for him. She might even daydream about what it would be like if he returned her feelings.

But Edna White wasn't just any woman. Her loneliness was greater, and her needs enormous. Only an ardent and devoted lover could satisfy her, so she made one up and gave him Tom Brandt's face. How would the good doctor have felt to be the object of so much passion from such a pathetic creature?

Frank tried to imagine Brandt's consternation and frustration. No wonder he had determined to find a way to free Edna White from this spell of her own creation. Of course, Frank couldn't be sure that's what he had done, but from what Albert White had said, it seemed likely. Frank might even be able to confirm it if he could speak with the other

three women or their families. At least it would explain why
he'd sought out the other women in the first place.

Now Frank would, too.

Sarah couldn't quite believe she'd just heard Mrs.
Upchurch declare that she'd be happy when her husband
was dead. She'd known many women who probably had
such feelings, but none of them would ever dare speak them
aloud, especially to a total stranger. "My husband was murdered," Sarah said to answer Mrs. Upchurch's original question about how her husband had died. Usually, she didn't
mention the cause of Tom's death, but it seemed no topic
was too outrageous for this encounter.

"Murdered?" Mrs. Upchurch echoed in amazement.
"How awful! I'm so sorry. I had no idea."

"Of course you didn't," Sarah agreed. "He was on a call
one evening, and someone killed him in an alley."

"That's dreadful," Mrs. Upchurch exclaimed. "And terribly unfair. He sounds like the kind of man who should have
lived so his work could continue. Why do people like him
die young while men like—" For once, she caught herself
before she said something even more outrageous.

Sarah knew instinctively that Mrs. Upchurch would
have named her own husband, but why would she be so
happy to see him dead that she would say so out loud to a
stranger?

Before she could decide, the intimidated maid returned
with a tray of steaming coffee and small cakes. When she
had fled, Mrs. Upchurch served them both. By then Sarah
had regained her composure. Surrendering to an ignoble curiosity, she chose her next words carefully. "Your husband
seems to have a successful ministry at the church."

"Oh, yes, he's been very successful," she agreed readily enough. "The church membership has tripled since he came, and the offerings have increased more than that."

"I meant the work he does with those young boys who have no fathers."

"Are you really interested in that, Mrs. Brandt?" she asked with genuine curiosity.

"Yes. I told you, I'm hoping to learn something I can use at the mission where I volunteer."

"Don't bother. Nothing that Oliver does here will help you there," Mrs. Upchurch said.

Perhaps she'd been involved with too many murder investigations, but Sarah decided not to allow conventional manners to stop her from finding out what she wanted to know. "You don't seem to have much respect for your husband's work, Mrs. Upchurch. Some people might think you're jealous."

Instead of being offended, as most people would, Mrs. Upchurch brightened. "That's what they told you, isn't it? They think I'm jealous of those boys because I don't have children of my own. Do you have children, Mrs. Brandt? You said you had no son, but do you—"

"My husband and I had no children," Sarah confirmed, too uncertain yet to speak of Aggie as her own.

"I wanted children, Mrs. Brandt. I wanted a houseful. I hated being an only child with no parents. I wanted a huge family so I'd never be alone again. That's why I married Oliver. Oh, I suppose I loved him, too, in the beginning at least. It's hard to remember now. But I needed a husband to father my children, so I married him, but he denied me those children I wanted so desperately."

"You can't be certain why you haven't been blessed," Sarah said, wincing inwardly when she remembered how

Mrs. Upchurch had mocked that particular word. "It's not really anyone's fault."

"You don't understand," she insisted. "He didn't even *try* to give me a child. You were married. You must know what I mean."

"I'm also a midwife," Sarah said, not certain she believed her hostess. It was a shocking claim, so she wanted Mrs. Upchurch to know that she wouldn't be easily convinced.

Amazingly, Mrs. Upchurch grinned again, showing all of her small, even teeth. "Then you know. You understand. You *do* understand what I'm saying, don't you? My husband has never known me, not that way, not the way a man knows his wife."

"Mrs. Upchurch, are you sure you want to tell me this? You hardly know me and—"

"That's the very reason I *can* tell you. Don't you see? I could hardly say these things to any of the ladies I meet at church. They'd never believe me, and they'd think I was crazy or lying to turn them against Oliver. He tells everyone I'm insane, so no one listens to me. That's what he told you, too, isn't it?" she challenged.

"He said you were . . . troubled," Sarah admitted.

"We both know what he meant, though, don't we? An hysterical woman whose mind is twisted because her womb is barren. That's something they can easily understand. They pity me, and they feel sorry for him because he's burdened with me."

She was right, of course, but Sarah couldn't judge Oliver Upchurch without a lot more information. "Some men are simply unable to fulfill their marital duties," she tried. "No matter how much they might want to—"

"Oliver *didn't* want to," she said, to Sarah's dismay. "Oh, he tried, but he found me . . . repulsive. He told me so. He prefers . . . *different* flesh. Younger and . . . and innocent." Her face twisted with an emotion Sarah could only imagine. Mrs. Upchurch hugged herself, rubbing her arms, her eyes dark and distant with some awful memory.

As Sarah watched, Mrs. Upchurch's words echoed in her mind as her heart ached in her chest. *Younger. Innocent.* She'd known men like Oliver Upchurch before, men whose sexual desire could only be slaked on children.

Sarah was very much afraid she had finally discovered Grace Linton's rapist.

8

Sarah was tucking Aggie into bed that evening when she heard someone ringing her doorbell.

"I'll answer it," Maeve said with a smile. "It'll be some poor man, frantic and wanting you to come right away. I'll make him wait until you're ready."

"Thank you, Maeve," Sarah said, smoothing the covers over Aggie and leaning down to kiss her petal-soft cheek as Maeve made her way downstairs. "I'll have to go out and help a lady with her baby tonight," she explained to Aggie. "Maeve will take care of you while I'm gone, like she always does, and if you need anything, Mrs. Ellsworth is next door."

Aggie pushed out her lower lip in an exaggerated pout.

"I'll miss you, too, but you know I have to go. That's how

I make the money we need to buy food and clothes. Remember, I explained it to you?"

Aggie's pout squeezed into a grimace. She understood. She just didn't like it.

"I love you, Aggie, and I'll be home again as soon as I can. Go to sleep now. I might even be home by the time you wake up tomorrow."

Aggie smiled at this, and when Sarah started to rise from where she sat beside her on the bed, the girl grabbed her hand and pulled her close, wrapping her small arms tightly around Sarah's neck. Sarah returned the hug, holding the child fiercely to her heart.

"I do love you," she whispered into the silky cloud of the girl's hair. "And I'm going to keep you safe here with me for as long as you live. You never have to be afraid again."

As always, Aggie made no sound, but her arms squeezed even more tightly for a moment in acknowledgment. When she released Sarah and sank back against her pillow, she was smiling. Sarah kissed her again, put out the light, and closed the bedroom door with a sigh. How she wished she didn't have to go out into the cold tonight. She wanted to be here in the morning to surprise Aggie with breakfast.

As she descended the stairs, she was surprised to hear Maeve's laughter drifting up from the foyer below. A few more steps and she saw why. Frank Malloy stood with her, still bundled against the winter winds. Sarah's smile was only partly because she wasn't being called out on a delivery.

"Malloy," she said when he saw her on the stairs. "What brings you out on a night like this?"

"I figured I better check in on you so you didn't have to leave me a message at Headquarters," he replied wryly. He was always teased unmercifully whenever she did.

"You made the right decision, because I do have some

news for you. I was trying to decide how to let you know discreetly."

"There's some soup left from supper, Mrs. Brandt," Maeve reminded her. "Potato," she informed Malloy. "Mrs. Ellsworth brought it over."

"Sounds delicious. I guess you'll never have to worry about starving to death with Mrs. Ellsworth as a neighbor," he observed.

"Maeve, would you build up the fire in the stove while I take Mr. Malloy's coat?" Sarah asked, and the girl hurried away after giving Malloy another grin.

"Is something wrong?" she asked when Maeve had gone.

"What makes you think something is wrong?" he asked right back, unwinding his muffler.

"Because it's a bit late for a social call. Is Brian all right?"

"He's fine." He unbuttoned his coat.

"Did you find out something about Grace Linton's case?"

"No."

"Well, I did."

He raised his eyebrows in silent disapproval, but he let her take his coat and hang it on one of the pegs nearby. He hung his hat and muffler beside it.

"Do the Lintons approve of your snooping around?" he asked.

"I'm not snooping," she said indignantly. "Can I help it if people just tell me things?"

He made a rude noise, which she ignored. She led him back to the kitchen. Maeve was setting the pot of soup back on the stove.

"Won't take a minute to heat up," she told them, wiping her hands on her apron.

"Thank you, Maeve. Now go take some time for yourself before you go to bed."

"Thank you, Mrs. Brandt. Good night, Mr. Malloy."

Malloy bid her good night, and when they were alone, he said, "She seems like a good girl."

"She is. She wasn't on the streets very long before she came to the mission. Sometimes the girls get so hardened that we just can't reach them anymore, so it's important to get them as quickly as possible. We'd like to spread the word so the girls know they can go straight to the mission when their families put them out."

"Good luck with that," Malloy said. He'd been warming his hands at the stove, and now he took a seat at the table while Sarah started making coffee. "So, what did you find out about the Linton girl?"

Sarah sighed. "I found out the minister likes young girls."

Malloy swore under his breath, and Sarah pretended not to hear. She wanted to swear herself. "How in God's name did you find out a thing like that?" he demanded.

"His wife told me."

"His *wife*?" he nearly shouted.

"Shhh, you'll wake Aggie," she warned him. "Yes, his wife. I think she's been wanting to tell someone for a long time, and I was the first person she thought would believe her."

Malloy squeezed the bridge of his nose between two fingers. "Do you have anything to put in that coffee? I think I'm going to need it."

Wordlessly, she reached under the sink and pulled out a bottle of whiskey she kept for medicinal purposes and poured some into a glass for him. He swallowed it in one gulp. "All right," he said. "Tell me the whole story."

"Only if you promise not to shout again."

He sighed with long-suffering. "I'll try."

She told him how she'd gone to the church, using the excuse of finding out what Reverend Upchurch was doing to be so successful with the boys, and how she'd met Mrs. Upchurch. "I had the distinct impression she was flirting with one of the boys."

"What do you mean by *flirting*?"

"Being overly friendly, making eyes at him. You know, Malloy, the way girls do when they're trying to get a boy to notice them."

"But she's a grown woman."

"Yes, which was why it shocked me. Her husband seemed embarrassed, too, and after I thought about it, I decided that she does it to make him angry, maybe even jealous."

"Jealous? Why would that make him jealous?"

"I wasn't sure until she told me about his preference for girls. Now I'm guessing that she might think that what's good for the goose is good for the gander or something. If he can chase after young girls, she can flirt with young boys."

"That's crazy," he protested.

"People do crazy things," she reminded him. "You should know that better than I."

She had him there, but he didn't admit it. "All right, you caught her flirting with some boy. How did you become her trusted friend so fast?"

"She invited me to visit her. Apparently, no one in the church ever visits her. She's a very strange woman, outspoken and bitter. Her husband also warns people about her. He told me she was 'troubled.'"

"Sounds like he's right."

"Then Mrs. Linton warned me about her, too. I started wondering about her, and I wanted to find out for myself what she was like, so I called on her."

"And she just told you about her husband's interest in little girls?"

"No, first she told me that the reason she doesn't have any children is because her husband is disgusted by grown women and has never exercised his marital rights."

Malloy's expression reminded her how uncomfortable he was talking about such things. "Is that something women usually talk about with somebody they just met?"

"No, of course not, but you have to understand her. She's been living with this secret for many years. Her husband tells people that she's unbalanced because she doesn't have children. I know he does, because that's what he told me. He actually said that he thought she was angry at God but took it out on him. Can you imagine? If a man said something like that about me, I'd strangle him!"

"Thank you for the warning," Malloy said dryly.

"You know what I mean," she said, checking the soup, which was beginning to steam. She ladled some into a bowl for him.

"Mmm, that smells good," he said when she set it in front of him.

"You knew it would be. Mrs. Ellsworth made it," she reminded him.

"All right," he continued. "We know you'd do violence to a man who made you mad, but do we know what Mrs. Upchurch would do?"

"What do you mean?" Sarah asked, checking to see if the coffee was ready. It wasn't, so she sat down across from him.

"I mean, would she lie? Would she make up a shocking story about him and tell it to someone who was likely to spread it around or even go to the authorities?"

"That's a terrible thing to make up about someone, especially your own husband. How would she even think of it?"

"Pretty easily, if she knows about Grace Linton. Somebody got Grace with child, and nobody knows who it could've been. Just about the only place Grace goes is to church, and one of the only men she knows well outside her family is the minister. It's even logical. Does she know about Grace?"

"I have no idea, but her family was determined to keep it a secret from everyone. You told Reverend Upchurch when you went to see him, didn't you?"

"I didn't plan to tell him it was Grace, but he guessed from what I said that she was the one."

"He might've mentioned it to his wife," Sarah said.

"He promised he wouldn't tell anyone, but I guess he could've been lying."

"He might've told her about it without revealing the girl's identity. She wouldn't have even needed to know who the girl was," Sarah realized. "If he mentioned to his wife that a girl was with child, she only has to accuse him of seducing young girls. Someone else will naturally make the connection."

"You're talking like you think she made it up to get even with her husband."

"You suggested it first," she reminded him. "I'm just trying to figure out if you could be right. I guess it's possible she made it all up, but if you'd seen her face . . ."

"Upchurch acted pretty innocent to me," Malloy said. "If he's not, he's a good liar."

Sarah got the coffee that was starting to boil over and poured them each a cup. Malloy had finished his soup, so she refilled his bowl without asking. He didn't protest.

"So what do we do now?" she asked, sitting down again.

"*You* should mind your own business," he said, digging into his soup.

"Then that leaves you. Are you going to question Reverend Upchurch again?"

He glowered at her, but she simply smiled sweetly and waited for his reply. "I suppose if I want any peace, I'll have to."

"You know you want to give him the third degree," she said, referring to the rough way the police questioned reluctant suspects.

"If he raped Grace Linton, I do," he replied. "But I can't go around beating up ministers, so I'll restrain myself, at least until I'm sure one way or the other."

"If he did it, I hope you put him in The Tombs and let the other prisoners take care of him."

"Does your mother know how bloodthirsty you've become?" he inquired.

Sarah thought of her genteel mother, raised in wealth and privilege, and knew she'd feel exactly the same way. "I just want to see justice done, and I don't think any punishment is severe enough for someone who seduces a girl like Grace. Don't pretend you don't agree with me, either."

"Oh, I agree with you. The trouble is, I've got to have proof before I lock up a respectable man. If I don't, I'll be out of a job. In fact, I could be out of a job just for bothering him too much. If I was a female, I suppose I could just strangle him, but I'm not, so I have to be careful."

He was trying to get a rise out of her, but she refused to take the bait. "You'll go back and question him again, won't you? We've got to be sure."

"I'll be sure. Do you have any more of this soup?"

She got up and refilled his bowl with the last of it. "Doesn't your mother feed you?"

"I haven't been home yet," he said. "And now she'll be mad at me because I already ate."

"Don't tell her I fed you, then," Sarah said. Mrs. Malloy already hated her enough.

"I won't," he promised.

They sat in silence for a few minutes while Malloy finished his soup. Finally, Sarah remembered something. "Why did you stop by this evening?"

He froze for a moment, with the spoon halfway to his mouth, then he lowered it back to the bowl and looked up at her thoughtfully. "Are you . . . ? Are you still interested in solving your husband's murder?"

"Of course I am!" she said, even though the thought of it sent a sharp pain through her heart. "Did you find out something from those files you took?"

He lifted his hand in a silent warning not to get too far ahead of herself. "I might have. Did your husband ever mention a patient named Edna White?"

Sarah tried to recall, but no memory responded. "The name doesn't sound familiar, but it's been a long time."

"She was very sick. This was back in 'ninety-two. She said he saved her life, and she developed a . . . a sort of affection for him. Even imagined she was in love with him."

"Oh, yes, I do remember that. I'd just forgotten her name. Tom was very disturbed about it. He didn't want to hurt the woman's feelings, but he found her attentions embarrassing."

"What did she do?"

Sarah tried to remember. "She came to the office a lot. She had a different complaint every time, but she was never really ill. She'd bring him a present when she came. A bit of candy or some socks or a scarf she'd knitted, sometimes a pie or cake. One time she tried to give him her dead father's gold pocket watch."

"Did he take it?"

"He had to. She wouldn't accept it back, so Tom returned

it to someone in her family . . . her brother, I think. She wrote him letters, too. I never saw them, and Tom burned them, but I gathered they were love letters. When Tom took the watch back, he told her brother about the letters. He didn't want the brother to find out some other way and think he'd been leading this poor woman on. After that, the letters stopped coming, and so did she."

"You think the brother had something to do with stopping it?"

"I'm sure he did. Tom said he was mortified when he found out." She waited a few moments while Malloy considered what she'd told him. "Does this have something to do with Tom's death?"

"Did he have other patients like this? Women who fell in love with him?" he asked.

"Not that I knew of. He did consult with his colleagues, and he found out it isn't unusual for female patients to develop an affection for their doctors. Several of them had had the same experience."

"What happened to those women?"

"I have no idea."

"Do you remember who the doctors were?"

"I don't . . . I'm not sure I ever knew. What's this all about? How is it connected to Tom's death?"

"I'm not sure it is. It's just a possibility."

"You think this woman killed Tom?"

"No. I'm pretty sure a man killed him, but he might've been related to one of his female patients."

"This woman had a brother," Sarah reminded him.

"I know, but he's not the killer, and he's her only male relative. That's why I'm trying to find out if there were other women like her."

"You took four files with you the other night," she re-

membered. "Could one of them be the woman you're looking for?"

"I don't know, but I'm going to find out."

Frank WASN'T SURE IF HE WAS ON OFFICIAL POLICE BUSI-
ness or not as he entered the Church of the Good Shepherd.
No crime had been reported, so he wasn't investigating, but
he did know a crime had been committed. If he didn't ask
questions, it might also go unpunished. Of course, even if
Reverend Upchurch proved to be Grace's rapist, he might
still go unpunished. So was it police business or a fool's errand? Frank was afraid to decide, but since it was Saturday,
he figured it didn't matter.

The hour was early enough that no one else was around,
and he found the minister in his office. The door stood open,
a silent invitation to anyone who might happen by, even
though Upchurch appeared to be busy, his pen scratching
away as he wrote something. Frank knocked on the open
door.

Upchurch looked up and started to smile in greeting until he recognized Frank. His expression froze, half-pleasant,
half-alarmed. "Detective," he said, probably not remembering Frank's name. "What brings you back?"

"I had a few more questions for you," he said. He walked in
and closed the door behind him, not waiting for an invitation.

This made him even more uncomfortable. "If this is
about poor Grace, I'm afraid I don't know any more than I
did the last time you were here."

"Don't you?" Frank asked.

"No, I don't," he insisted. Upchurch remained ensconced
behind his desk, as if looking for some degree of protection,
so Frank took one of the straight-backed chairs sitting in

front of it. The last time, they had conversed comfortably, as equals. This time Upchurch wanted the upper hand.

"I understand you don't have any children of your own," Frank began, watching the minister carefully for reaction.

His eyes widened in surprise. "What does that have to do with anything?"

"Why is that, I wonder, a big, strong man like you? You look like you could father a whole baseball team of boys."

Upchurch flushed crimson. "I don't question God's will," he tried.

"Are you sure it's God's will and not something else?"

"How dare you ask a question like that? Get out of my office."

Frank ignored the request. "The reason I'm asking is that I heard a rumor about you."

The color quickly receded from the minister's face. "Gossip, you mean. Surely, you know how accurate gossip is."

"Where there's smoke, I usually find some fire, Reverend, and the source of this . . . *gossip* was pretty reliable."

"You must understand that when someone is successful at something, certain people will always try to discredit them. You might not realize it, but even ministers can be jealous of one another. People in the church get angry, too. They want things to be as they were before. They don't like new people coming into the church, so they start making up stories about the minister."

Frank could see how agitated he was, a stark contrast to how cool and confident he'd been at their last meeting. "What kind of stories do they make up about you?"

"I have no idea!" he almost shouted. "They say that I'm . . . They say I waste too much time on the children in the church. They want me to visit the elderly members more. They want me to preach better sermons. They want me to preach shorter sermons or longer ones. No matter what I do, someone is displeased."

"Do *you* think you waste too much time on the children?" Frank asked mildly.

"What do you mean?" His composure was thoroughly broken now. Frank thought he might even be sweating beneath his clerical collar.

"What do you think about women, Reverend Upchurch?" he asked, ignoring the question.

He blinked in surprise. "I . . . they're God's blessing to mankind. They must be sheltered and protected."

"Protected from the lusts of men?"

"Yes! And if you're talking about Grace Linton—"

"I'm talking about your wife, Reverend Upchurch. Should she be protected from the lusts of men?"

"My wife? She . . . Of course! What are—"

"Should *she* be protected from *your* lusts, Reverend Upchurch?"

"Yes! I mean, no! What are you talking about?" he cried.

"I'm talking about why you don't have any children of your own, Reverend Upchurch. You protect your wife from your lusts because you don't like women at all, do you?"

"What? Of course I do. I have every respect—"

"But you don't lust after them, do you? In fact, they disgust you."

"No, I—"

"Grown women disgust you, don't they?" Frank insisted, leaning forward into Upchurch's sweating face. "You've got to have younger flesh, innocent flesh."

"That's insane! *You're* insane!"

"And that's why you seduced Grace Linton, because no one is more innocent than she is!" Frank concluded in triumph.

Upchurch's protest died on his lips, and he simply gaped

at Frank, his eyes wide with shock for a long moment until the meaning of his words finally registered. Then
slowly he closed his mouth and slowly the color returned
to his face as the confidence returned to his manner. "Is
that what you think? That I seduced Grace?" To Frank's
amazement, he threw back his head and laughed. Frank
recognized it as the laugh of an innocent man who had
nothing to fear from the police.

"What's so funny?" Frank demanded, furious that he'd
allowed Sarah to convince him without more proof.

"You are, Detective. Coming in here and accusing me of
something like that. Ask Grace if I've ever laid a hand on
her. You said she couldn't name her attacker, but if I were
he, she'd be able to identify me. She knows me as well as she
knows anyone. She and her mother are here four or five days
a week. But I have never even been alone with Grace, and
you will never prove that I was, no matter how many people
you try to intimidate. Grace herself will exonerate me."

"But your wife . . ." Frank said before he could catch
himself.

"My wife? Oh, yes. I should have told you when you were
here before that she cannot be trusted. As you pointed out,
we have no children, and I'm afraid it has affected her mind.
She imagines things that aren't true and delights in shocking people by telling them as fact. I try to keep her away
from people as much as I can, but short of putting her in an
asylum, it's impossible to confine her completely. Did she
tell you that I've never touched her? Of course she did. I can
see it on your face. She blames me for not giving her children, so she made up that horrible lie to punish me."

"You deny it, then?"

"I'll admit that I ceased having relations with my wife a
few years ago, as soon as I realized how fragile her mental

state is. I couldn't take a chance that we'd finally have a child to be raised by an incompetent mother."

"That must be difficult, living with your wife and not enjoying her."

"It is, but it is my duty to protect her from herself. Now, if you don't mind, I'd like to end this unpleasant discussion and get back to my work. I'm finishing my sermon for tomorrow, and I'd like to be done by the time people start coming in for Saturday activities."

Frank didn't want to leave. He knew Upchurch hadn't raped Grace Linton, but something else was wrong, very wrong, with Reverend Upchurch. It might not have anything to do with Grace, but it was there just the same. Trouble was, he didn't know what it was, so he didn't know what questions to ask or how to force it out of him. Even worse, if he tried without knowing, he wouldn't succeed in doing anything except irritating the minister enough to complain about him to his superiors. That would ensure Frank would be forbidden from speaking to him again and possibly even lose his job, in the bargain.

Left with no other choice, he rose to his feet. Before he could think of something to say, someone rapped on the office door and without waiting for a reply, pushed it open. A young boy about thirteen or fourteen burst into the room, halting abruptly when he saw Frank. His broad, expectant smile faded to uncertainty.

"I'm sorry, sir. I didn't know—"

"That's all right, Percy. The detective was just leaving," Reverend Upchurch said with a knowing smile at Frank.

Frank tried to think of something cutting to say, but nothing came to mind that didn't sound foolish. He turned and walked toward the door where the boy still stood. He stepped aside warily to let Frank pass. Frank noticed how clean he looked. He seldom saw a really clean boy. Boys in the Lower East Side rarely washed at all, and those in the better parts of the city managed to collect grime like a magnet the moment they left their mothers' sides.

Percy watched him, his large eyes wide with innocence and a touch of fear for the terrible policeman. Frank tried to remember ever being that young and innocent, but failed. He nodded politely at the boy, but Percy just kept staring back, mesmerized.

When Frank was in the hallway, Reverend Upchurch said, "Close the door, Percy, so we can have our private talk."

"Why is that policeman back?" the boy asked. "Is something wrong?"

"No, nothing's wrong," Upchurch said, just as the door closed.

No, nothing at all, Frank thought angrily. He'd done everything right. He'd asked the right questions, and he'd terrified Upchurch—right up until he'd mentioned Grace Linton. Frank was now certain that Upchurch hadn't harmed Grace Linton. He'd actually been relieved when he realized that's what Frank was talking about. But he was guilty of something else, something evil. Frank just had to figure out what.

Lost in thought as he walked through the sanctuary, he almost didn't see the boy sitting on the back pew. Frank remembered him from his last visit. He was the youngest of the group who had been cleaning the church. He stared up at Frank with the same frightened innocence as Percy.

"You here to see Reverend Upchurch?" Frank asked, ready to tell him the minister was in his office with Percy.

"No, sir. It's Percy's turn," he said, his voice showing no sign of being ready to change.

"Turn for what?"

The boy hesitated, not sure if he should answer but afraid not to. "We . . . we each have a turn with him. Private time, he calls it."

"Private time for what?"

The boy squirmed in his seat. "We talk. He . . . he teaches us stuff."

"What kind of stuff does he teach you?"

The boy shrugged. "Stuff our fathers would teach us. We don't have fathers, and our mothers don't know what a father would teach us."

"Mark!" a young voice called sharply.

Frank looked up to see another of the boys from the cleaning group coming toward them. He'd just come into the sanctuary, and now he was hurrying over to Frank and Mark.

"What's going on? What's he saying to you?" he asked Mark.

"Nothing," Mark said defensively.

"Is there something he shouldn't tell me?" Frank asked. "Something that's a secret?"

"No," the older boy said, then turned back to Mark. "What did you tell him?"

"Nothing, Isaiah," he said defensively. "I'm just waiting for Percy."

"He was telling me how Reverend Upchurch spends private time with each of you boys, teaching you things," Frank said, watching Isaiah's reaction.

The boy was already angry, and that made him angrier. "It's none of your business what Reverend Upchurch does. It ain't against the law or anything."

"He just likes us," Mark offered.

"Yeah, he likes us. You gonna arrest him for that?" Isaiah challenged.

"No," Frank admitted. "Not for that."

He looked down at Mark one last time. Another clean boy, neat and scrubbed and innocent. Frank walked away, aware of the boys watching suspiciously.

Out on the church steps, he stopped to button his coat and wrap his muffler more tightly, but even as he stared out at the crowds moving down the busy street, he saw the faces of the three boys. Young and innocent.

Something tugged at his consciousness, something important, but he couldn't figure out what it was. He was sure of one thing, though. Upchurch hadn't raped Grace Linton, and he'd have to tell Sarah Brandt she'd been wrong.

9

Sᴀʀᴀʜ ʀᴇᴀᴅ ᴛʜᴇ ʙʀɪᴇꜰ ɴᴏᴛᴇ ᴛʜʀᴇᴇ ᴛɪᴍᴇs ʙᴇꜰᴏʀᴇ ᴀʜᴇ was sure she understood Malloy's message. "He didn't do it." Apparently, Malloy had questioned Upchurch and somehow determined he hadn't raped Grace Linton. Sarah couldn't believe it. She'd been so sure Upchurch was guilty. Now she had to figure out what Mrs. Upchurch had meant or if Malloy was right, that she'd just been trying to blacken her husband's name. It was an ugly thought, but no uglier than anything else that had happened.

What now? Sarah wondered. Another visit to the Lintons? No, they had nothing more to tell her, and they'd certainly wonder why she was back nosing into their affairs. Call on Mrs. Upchurch again? If she had been lying before, she'd only lie again. But *had* she been lying? Had Upchurch somehow fooled Malloy? Not likely, but someone had raped

Grace, and the only place she encountered potential rapists was at that church.

From upstairs, Sarah could hear Maeve talking to Aggie. The girls were playing with Aggie's dolls. Sometimes Sarah thought Maeve enjoyed it as much as Aggie did. She'd had no dolls in the hovel where she grew up. Tomorrow was Sunday, Maeve's day off. She'd go to the mission for the Sunday services there and to visit with the other girls. The mission was the best home she'd known, and what was left of her family had disappeared into the teeming tenements, leaving no trace.

Sarah usually took Aggie to the mission services on Sunday, too, if she didn't have a delivery, but maybe she should try taking her to a real church for a change. She'd been invited to attend the Church of the Good Shepherd several times. Perhaps she'd accept those invitations. Malloy would probably disapprove, but he didn't have to know.

GRACE LINTON SAW THEM FIRST. SHE AND HER PARENTS were already seated in the sanctuary, but Grace was looking over her shoulder so she could watch who was coming in.

"Mrs. Brandt!" she cried, waving furiously.

Her mother shushed her, but she looked, too, and smiled a greeting.

"Would you like to sit with the Lintons?" the usher asked and escorted Sarah and Aggie down the aisle.

Mr. Linton rose politely, and Mrs. Linton said, "I'm so glad you decided to visit our church." All of them looked at Aggie curiously.

Sarah wished them all a good morning. "This is Aggie. She's recently come to live with me," she explained. "Aggie, this is Mr. and Mrs. Linton and their daughter, Grace."

Aggie smiled shyly.

"We're pleased to meet you, Aggie," Mrs. Linton said.

"Aggie is very quiet," Sarah added.

"That's good," Grace said, "because you have to be quiet in church or people look at you. Will you come sit next to me, Aggie?"

Aggie looked up at Sarah for permission, and Sarah nodded. The Lintons made room in the pew for Aggie and Sarah, who sat on Aggie's other side. When they were settled, Sarah took a moment to glance around.

Their arrival had caused a bit of a stir, and a few heads had turned their way. Strangers smiled and nodded in welcome. Across the aisle, she saw Mrs. Evans and her daughter, Mrs. York. Percy wasn't with them. He probably preferred to sit with his friends.

As she continued to look around, Sarah felt the hairs on the back of her neck rise. Instinctively, she looked to her right and there she saw Mrs. Upchurch. She stood at the other end of their aisle, staring directly at Sarah. She seemed to glow with fury, and her plain features had taken on a strange beauty. She held Sarah's gaze for a long moment, as if trying to send her a silent message. If she wanted to let Sarah know how angry she was, she succeeded. Beyond that, Sarah couldn't begin to guess what was wrong. Could Mrs. Upchurch be angry because Malloy had confronted her husband? If she didn't want her husband exposed, then why had she confided in Sarah in the first place?

"My goodness," Mrs. Linton said softly, noticing the minister's wife's scowl. That seemed to break the spell, and Mrs. Upchurch turned away, taking her place in one of the front pews.

"You've met Mrs. Upchurch, I assume?" Mrs. Linton said, speaking over Grace and Aggie.

"Yes, I . . . I called on her the other day."

Mrs. Linton's expression silently reminded her that she'd been warned.

"Maybe Mrs. Brandt will bring you to visit me sometime," Grace was saying to Aggie.

Aggie gave Sarah a pleading look. "I'm sure we'd both enjoy that," Sarah said diplomatically. Mrs. Linton would need to issue the true invitation.

Before she could, the organ began to play, and the soft conversations around them ceased abruptly. A few minutes later, two boys in robes came down the aisle carrying candle lighters. Sarah recognized both of them from her previous visit.

"That's Percy," Grace whispered to Aggie. "He's my beau." Sarah smiled, wondering if Percy had any idea Grace considered him her beau. He'd probably be mortified.

"Shhh," Mrs. Linton warned, lifting a finger to her lips.

Grace covered her mouth and gave Aggie a conspiratorial look that made her grin. They all watched as Percy and the other boy solemnly lit the candles in the twin candelabras at the front of the church. Then they extinguished their lighters and took seats on the front pew.

Sarah had to agree that the service was beautiful. The choir sang three soul-stirring songs, and when Reverend Upchurch ascended to the pulpit, every face in the room turned to him raptly.

As Sarah had expected, he was a magnificent speaker. His voice rang with conviction as he admonished his congregation to care for even the least of these, my brethren, for in doing so, they will have ministered to Christ himself. Knowing what she did of Upchurch's work with the fatherless boys, she thought this an appropriate topic. In spite of her suspicions about him, when he was finished, she felt a renewed commitment to the girls at the mission. Even Aggie seemed enthralled with the message, and she rose reluctantly for the closing hymn, as if she didn't want the service to end.

As people began to make their way out of the church, Mrs. Evans squeezed through the crowd to speak to Sarah.

"I'm so glad you came," she said, taking Sarah's hand in both of hers.

"Thank you for inviting me," Sarah said. "You were right about the choir being excellent, and Reverend Upchurch is a wonderful preacher," she had to admit.

"We're so very fortunate to have a man like him."

Sarah introduced Aggie to Mrs. Evans and Mrs. York, who had also come over. Slowly, they all began to move toward the exit. Grace had Aggie by the hand and was explaining something to her. Sarah was the last to leave the pew, and just as she was stepping out into the aisle, someone grabbed her arm from behind.

She turned in surprise to see Mrs. Upchurch's angry face. She'd come down the pew from the other end to catch Sarah.

"That policeman, did you send him?" she demanded.

"What?" Sarah asked in confusion.

"That policeman. He got it all wrong. I thought you understood what I told you. He doesn't like *girls*! It's boys he—"

"Mrs. Upchurch," Mrs. Evans said sharply, a strained smile on her face as she came to rescue Sarah from the crazy preacher's wife. "How nice to see you."

Mrs. Upchurch gave her an impatient glance, then turned back to Sarah. "Remember what I said. You know who he spends his time with." With that, she turned away and retraced her steps to the other end of the pew to make her escape down the opposite aisle.

"What was she saying to you?" Mrs. Evans asked. "She looked absolutely crazed."

"I . . . I really didn't understand her," Sarah lied, a little breathlessly. She felt as if someone had punched her in the stomach. Could she have possibly heard what she thought she'd heard? Could Reverend Upchurch really have done what his wife had implied?

"We've invited the Lintons over for Sunday dinner, and I was wondering if you and the little girl would join us," Mrs. Evans was saying.

Sarah had to pull her attention back from the abyss of horror to focus on the present. Mrs. Evans had invited her and Aggie to dinner. She thought how much Grace and Aggie would enjoy being together, but she had urgent business that wouldn't wait. She made her excuses and tried to ignore Grace and Aggie's disappointment. She had to promise them both a visit very soon before they could escape.

She and Aggie stopped at a coffee shop for a quick snack before taking the EL down to Malloy's neighborhood. She just hoped he'd be home.

Mrs. Malloy pretended not to notice Sarah was accompanying Aggie and almost closed the door in her face.

"Francis isn't here," she informed Sarah with a trace of satisfaction. By then Brian had run over to greet them. He was pulling Aggie over to his pile of toys, but he had to come back and give Sarah a hug when he saw her, too.

"Do you know when he'll be back?" Sarah asked. "I have something important to tell him. It's about a case he's working on."

"Are you working for the police now, Mrs. Brandt, that you know so much about Francis's business?"

Sarah ignored the sarcasm. "I'm sorry he's not here, but Aggie and I don't have anything else to do this afternoon, so we can wait as long as we have to for him to come home." She started to unbutton her cape.

As Sarah had expected, the prospect of being stuck here with her all afternoon proved too much.

"He's down at the beer garden with his friends," she reluctantly admitted. "If it's as important as you claim, I can send a neighbor boy for him."

"I'm sure he'll want to hear this news as soon as possible," Sarah said to encourage her.

She sniffed to indicate how put-upon she felt, but she said, "I'll be back in a minute," and walked down the stairs in search of an idle boy to send on the errand.

Sarah took off her cape and Aggie's coat and made herself at home. She was enjoying watching the children communicate in silence. Brian tried making signs, but he quickly realized Aggie didn't know what they were and gave up. Sarah found herself wishing she knew some. How nice it would be to speak to Brian and have him understand.

Mrs. Malloy was gone a long time. At first Sarah thought she must have had a hard time finding a willing boy, but then Sarah heard the heavy footsteps on the stairs coming up behind her. She'd obviously waited downstairs until Malloy had come so she wouldn't have to entertain Sarah alone.

"Thank you very much, Mrs. Malloy," she said when the older woman came back into the flat.

"I'll make some coffee," she said sourly and went into the kitchen.

Malloy came in behind her. "Mrs. Brandt, what a pleasant surprise," he said, with just a trace of his mother's sarcasm. At the sight of him, the children came running.

When they had been suitably greeted and returned to their play, Malloy took his coat off and hung it up.

"Didn't you get my note?" he asked.

"Yes, and I decided to go to the Church of the Good Shepherd this morning to see if I could figure out how I could've made such a mistake."

He glanced at the children playing nearby. "Let's go into the kitchen." Brian couldn't hear them, of course, but Aggie could, and this wasn't a subject for young ears to overhear.

Sarah preceded Malloy into the kitchen, earning another scowl from Mrs. Malloy, this time for invading her private kingdom without her permission.

"We don't want the kids to hear this," Malloy told her and then ignored her cluck of disapproval. He held out a chair for Sarah.

"I suppose you don't want me to hear it, either," Mrs. Malloy snapped.

"Suit yourself," Malloy said. "It's about a Protestant minister Mrs. Brandt suspects of raping one of the girls in his congregation."

Mrs. Malloy murmured something under her breath and crossed herself, but Sarah noticed she stayed right where she was.

Malloy took a seat at the kitchen table opposite her. "Did you find out something new this morning?"

"Not new, but I think I figured out what I'd misunderstood. I told you Reverend Upchurch liked little girls, but that's apparently not what his wife said."

They both ignored Mrs. Malloy's gasp.

"Do you remember exactly what she did say?"

"I've been trying all the way over here. She said her husband found her repulsive and that he liked other flesh, younger and more innocent."

Malloy stiffened as if she'd slapped him, and Mrs. Malloy gasped again.

"What is it?" Sarah asked him.

"Nothing, just something I was thinking yesterday when I was at the church. That's all she said?"

"Yes, and she must have known you questioned her husband yesterday, because she was furious."

"Why? I thought she wanted to get him in trouble."

"She was angry because I'd misunderstood her. We only had a moment together, but she specifically said, 'He doesn't like girls,' and told me to remember who he spends all his time with."

Malloy ran a hand over his face and sighed wearily. "Ma, you don't want to hear the rest of this."

"Aye, you're right there, but I ain't moving," the old woman declared, crossing her arms belligerently across her chest.

He looked at Sarah, his dark eyes full of disgust. "Do you know what she meant? Did you figure it out?"

Sarah closed her eyes. She'd known, of course, even though she'd been hoping Malloy would have another interpretation to offer. She'd been hoping the truth wasn't really as horrible as she knew it must be.

"Oh, dear heaven," she breathed. "It's the boys, isn't it?"

"That's why he spends so much time with them," Malloy said. "It has to be. When I went in to question him, he was nervous about something. He was actually relieved when he found out I was talking about Grace. He wasn't worried about some poor girl, because it's the boys he's involved with."

"Boys?" Mrs. Malloy asked. "What is this about boys, Francis? What are you saying?"

Malloy sighed with resignation. "That he uses young

boys for . . ." he searched for a word that he could use in front of his mother. "He uses them the way a man uses a woman."

"That's not possible," Mrs. Malloy insisted, her face flushed with outrage. "I won't believe it."

"It's better if you don't. Go on now. You've heard enough."

Mrs. Malloy fled back to the front room, and Sarah wished she could do the same.

"I didn't think it could be worse than if he'd raped Grace," Sarah said when she'd gone.

"I told you not to get involved with this," he reminded her.

Sarah sighed. "And now we know about *this*, and it doesn't even have anything to do with Grace."

"What do you want me to do now?"

Sarah stared at him in surprise for a moment. "What do you mean?"

"I mean, do you want me to go after him? Because if you do," he continued before she could reply, "remember that a lot of people will get hurt."

"Those boys are being hurt now!" she cried.

"And if I don't stop him, more boys will be hurt," he said. "But if I do, then everyone will find out what happened to the boys. They'll be humiliated, and their families will be furious. Some people will refuse to believe what happened and stand by Upchurch against them. They'll accuse the boys of lying, just because they can't believe something so horrible could really happen. Some of their own families will probably refuse to believe the boys."

"How can you be so sure?"

"Because I've seen it before. If we're really lucky, Upchurch will kill himself to avoid a scandal. If he doesn't, and it's not very likely he will, and if he decides to brazen it out and deny everything, then those boys' lives will be ruined, and he'll just keep on."

Horrified, Sarah could hardly make her mind absorb what he was saying. "Isn't there any way? . . . Can't we make him stop, at least? Could you frighten him enough to make him stop?"

"I doubt it. If he knows I want to keep it a secret, he'll know he doesn't have to be afraid of me. Besides, he'll just deny it. He'll say the boys are lying, and that's only if we can get the boys to admit what's going on in the first place."

"Oh, dear heaven," Sarah groaned, leaning her head on her hand. "What have I done?"

"You haven't done nothing yet," Mrs. Malloy informed her. Malloy and Sarah looked up in surprise to see her standing in the kitchen doorway. Apparently, she'd changed her mind about knowing more. "You haven't done nothing until you've put this fellow under lock and key so nobody else's boys will be defiled by him."

Malloy just looked at Sarah, waiting for her decision. She didn't want that responsibility. She didn't want to be the one to cause so much pain to so many people. She thought of Upchurch with his charming smiles and his pious sermons fooling so many people. No one knew from looking at him that inside he was rotten, like a festering sore on society. Mrs. Malloy was right, he did need to be put away. She remembered seeing surgeons amputating rotten flesh. Sometimes they had to cut away some healthy flesh, too, in order to save the patient.

That's what they would have to do now.

"Your mother is right. We have to stop him," she said.

"Nobody at Police Headquarters is going to be happy about going after a minister for something like this without a lot of proof, and all we have right now is suspicion."

"You'll have to talk to the boys," Sarah said.

"They might not admit anything, either. They'll be ashamed, and they won't want to get Upchurch in trouble, either."

"After what he's done to them?" Sarah cried in outrage.

"They love him, don't forget. He's like a father to them. And even if the boys will accuse him, that's not enough. We'll need at least one of the families to make a complaint, but *they* aren't going to want anyone to know what happened to their sons."

"Even if we can't get him arrested, we can let him know that he's been found out. That might frighten him."

Malloy didn't look convinced. "Before we start making accusations, I'll need to talk to the boys and their families. Can you find out their names and where they live?"

Sarah thought about going back to Mrs. Linton for that information. The poor woman couldn't think her any stranger than she already did, and Sarah could probably think of a logical reason for wanting to know that information. Or at least she hoped she could.

FRANK CONSULTED THE LIST SARAH HAD SENT HIM TO verify the house number of the first boy. As good as her word, she'd called on Mrs. Linton on Monday and somehow obtained the names and addresses of all of Upchurch's boys.

Since he wasn't officially assigned to investigate this case, he'd waited until the end of the day to start looking for them. They would've been in school all day, anyway, he'd reasoned. Now all he had to do was convince the mothers to let their boys talk to the police about something he couldn't explain to them.

Frank had chosen the oldest boy on the list first, Isaiah Wilkins. According to Sarah, he's the one Mrs. Upchurch had been flirting with. He was also the most likely to understand the situation and to make a credible witness if it came to that. He was also the most likely to understand the reasons for keeping Upchurch's sins a secret.

A wide-eyed maid admitted him, and after a few minutes escorted him into a fashionably furnished parlor to see Mrs. Wilkins and her son. Mrs. Wilkins was a plump partridge of a woman with a smooth, slightly stupid face. She looked bewildered and a bit frightened. She rose to her feet when Frank entered, clutching a handkerchief in one hand and pressing it to her bosom.

"You're from the police?" she asked apprehensively.

"Yes, Detective Sergeant Frank Malloy," he said. "Thank you for seeing me, Mrs. Wilkins."

"Is there something wrong in the neighborhood? Has there been a crime?" she asked.

"Yes, there has," Frank said, grateful she'd given him the perfect excuse. "I'm questioning some people we think might have seen something."

"I'm sure I haven't seen anything out of the ordinary," Mrs. Wilkins said. "I can't be of any help to you."

"I know. I need to talk to your son, though, and I wanted your permission," Frank said.

"Isaiah?" she asked, even more alarmed now. She glanced over at where he stood, staring sullenly at Frank, whom he recognized from seeing him at the church. "I'm sure Isaiah would have told me if he'd seen anything untoward, wouldn't you, dear?"

"Yes, Mother, I would have," he agreed with a defiant glare at Frank.

"He might not realize that what he saw was important,"

Frank said, relentlessly patient. "Would you mind if I asked him a few questions if it would help catch a criminal?"

"Well," she said, glancing at Isaiah and back to Frank again. "I suppose it would be all right, so long as he isn't in any danger."

"He won't be," Frank said, glad she hadn't mentioned his being in any trouble. Frank would have had to lie about that. "Just a few questions, that's all."

"Very well," she reluctantly agreed. "You don't mind, do you, Isaiah? If it will help?"

The boy didn't answer. He just kept glaring at Frank, as if he knew why he'd come and was daring him to proceed.

"Go ahead then, and ask your questions," she said, taking her seat again.

"If you don't mind, I'd like to see him alone," Frank said, still calm and patient.

"Alone? Whatever for?" She was alarmed again.

"Well," Frank said, giving Isaiah a meaningful glance, "You know how boys are. Even good boys don't always tell their mothers everything they do."

"You said Isaiah hadn't done anything wrong," she protested.

"I don't think he has, but he's more likely to be honest with me about what he saw if his mother isn't listening."

Frank waited, not stirring, not betraying any hint of the impatience he felt, knowing she would give in if he didn't press her.

She gave her son a questioning look.

"Go on, Mother. Don't worry about me," he said. Did he look worried himself? No, Frank decided. He was just angry.

After another protest or two and a warning to her son that he didn't have to say anything he didn't want to, she left them alone.

The door had hardly closed behind her when the boy said, "She sent you, didn't she?"

"Who?" Frank asked, wondering how he could have known about Sarah's involvement.

"Mrs. Upchurch. What did she say about me?"

"Nothing in particular," Frank said.

"She sent you, though, didn't she?"

"Yes, she did. I guess she doesn't like what's going on."

"I thought she liked it fine." His smirk set Frank's teeth on edge.

"What made you think that?" Frank asked, wondering if Upchurch could have told the boys that his wife knew about his perversion and approved.

He shrugged, still oddly cocky. "What are you going to do to me?"

"Nothing. I just need you to tell me the truth about Upchurch. I know all about your private times with him and what he does—what he does with all the boys. You know it's wrong, don't you?"

Isaiah's smirk vanished, and his face flushed crimson. "You don't know anything!"

"I want to stop him, Isaiah," Frank said. "When did he start with you? How old were you?"

"I don't have to tell you anything," he said. "My mother told me I didn't, and I'm not going to."

"Did he tell you he loved you, Isaiah?" Frank asked. "He says that to all the boys, but he doesn't really love you. If he did, he wouldn't make you do those things."

"I'm not going to talk about him, no matter what you do to me, so you might as well leave," Isaiah said, his voice rising.

"What did he tell you, Isaiah? Did he make you promise to keep it a secret? Why would he do that if it wasn't wrong?"

The boy's eyes grew wide. They held emotions Frank didn't even want to name. He was close, so close to breaking. What would push him over the edge?

"You missed having a father, didn't you? He pretended to be a father to you, but he wasn't. A father wouldn't do those things. A real man wouldn't use boys the way he used you."

"You don't know anything about it!" Isaiah challenged desperately.

"I've got a son of my own. I'd kill any man who did those things to him."

"Is that what you're going to do, kill Reverend Upchurch?" he scoffed.

"The law will punish him," Malloy promised rashly, knowing it was probably a lie.

"No, it won't. He told me. No one will believe me. No one will take my word over his, and people will laugh at me. You can't do anything to him."

"Then you admit that he—"

"I don't admit *nothing*," the boy insisted. "And you can't make me. If you try, I'll say you tried to force me to lie about him. They'll believe that, and you'll be the one in trouble."

He was right, of course, and Frank swore under his breath. "What about the other boys? And the ones he hasn't started with yet? He'll just keep finding new ones unless somebody stops him."

"Why should I care about the others? Nobody cared about me!" he cried.

"I care about you. I want to stop him."

Isaiah's eyes darkened with despair and his young face seemed to crumble. "You can't stop him. Nobody can. Now leave me alone."

Without waiting for Frank to respond, he darted for the

door and let himself out, leaving Frank staring after him impotently.

He swore again. He'd certainly messed that up. He wouldn't get another chance at young Mr. Wilkins, either. Even if the mother would agree, he'd never confide in Frank now. Mentally crossing Isaiah off his list, he showed himself out without waiting for the maid or the mother. At least he'd learned what not to say to win a boy's cooperation. Now if only he could figure out the magic words to make one cooperate.

By Thursday morning, Frank was ready to give up. The second and third boys' mothers had refused to have their sons involved with the police. Everyone knew no good could come of that. The fourth boy had been warned by Isaiah and refused to say a thing about Upchurch. That left only the two youngest, the ones least likely to be of help. They'd never be able to endure a trial, even if their mothers would allow it, and what mother would?

Knowing he'd failed, he felt an obligation to tell Sarah. She'd expected him to stop this monster, and he couldn't. He hated having to disappoint her almost as much as he hated what Upchurch had done to those boys, but he had no choice. He couldn't go on letting her hope.

He stopped by her house on his way to work the next morning, knowing he wasn't going to waste any more time on the case. He almost hoped she was out on a call, but he found all three females in the household enjoying breakfast together.

The girls insisted he have some coffee with them when he refused their offer of food, so he sat with them for a few minutes, until they were finished.

Sarah knew his news wasn't good. He'd never been able to fool her, but she kept up a cheerful front until she'd sent the girls upstairs.

"What is it, Malloy?" she demanded when they were finally alone.

He told her what had happened. "I don't see any reason to try the two younger boys. Their mothers won't trust a cop any more than the others did, and they'll be too afraid of Upchurch—or of me—to tell us anything."

She considered this for a few moments. "I don't think the boys are afraid of him," she mused. "They certainly don't seem to be. In fact, they want to be with him. Even Isaiah is just discouraged, because he's old enough to figure out it's wrong, and Upchurch has convinced him he's untouchable. But what if the other boys haven't figured it out yet?"

"What do you mean?"

"I mean, who knows what Upchurch tells them? They'd believe everything he said. What if you asked the younger ones about it but didn't let on that it was wrong or that Upchurch was in trouble? They might think it was all right to tell you."

Frank frowned at this unlikely result. "How do I explain why the police are interested in Upchurch then?" he challenged. Surely, even she couldn't figure out that one.

She tried, wrinkling her forehead with the effort. Frank decided that watching her think was a fascinating activity.

Suddenly, she brightened. "I know, we'll tell them the truth!"

"What truth?"

"That someone has accused Upchurch of something terrible, and you're investigating. Everyone will want to prove him innocent, so they'll be anxious to answer your questions."

"What if they won't let me in at all?" he asked skeptically.

"I know Percy York's mother and grandmother will let you in if I'm with you," she offered.

Frank never ceased to be amazed at the way her mind worked. "And just how will you explain helping the police?"

He had her there. No respectable lady would be involved with the police, who were for the most part as dishonest as the criminals they arrested. None except Sarah Brandt, that is.

"Oh, let's see," she said, thinking out loud. Her brow furrowed again. "I'll tell them that . . . that you were a friend of my husband's."

Frank almost snorted at that, but he let her continue, curious to see what fable she'd concoct.

"And you asked me if I knew anyone in this church who would speak with you, because no one would cooperate, and you were anxious to clear this up before a good man like Reverend Upchurch was ruined by rumors."

He did snort at that.

"It doesn't have to be true. It just has to be something they'll believe, and something that will compel them to help."

Malloy tried to glare at her, but it was a good idea, and she knew it. She simply grinned back.

"I'll have to go with you," she continued, "to make the introduction. I can even talk to Percy and tell him he should be honest with you because it will help Upchurch."

"You'd lie to that poor boy? How do you live with yourself?" he asked in mock amazement.

"It's not a lie," she argued. "It will help Upchurch reform. It's the Christian thing to do."

He shook his head in wonder at her logic. "And what if this boy tells us the truth about Upchurch? Do you think his mother will charge him? Do you think they'll let him testify in court? Do you even think anyone would believe him?"

"There are other ways to punish Upchurch. I've been thinking about that, too, and if we can prove he's guilty, I'll explain it to you. When can we go to see Percy York?"

10

Susannah Evans frowned suspiciously at Malloy. Plainly, she didn't like the idea of a policeman sitting in her parlor. Sarah just kept talking, hoping the flood of information would overwhelm her into cooperating.

"My husband was a doctor. He often worked on the Lower East Side, and he was able to help Mr. Malloy with some of his cases. He knew Mr. Malloy as a man of integrity, and I have the utmost respect for him."

Mrs. Evans looked more puzzled than ever. No man of integrity would ever be successful as a policeman. It simply wasn't possible, and Mrs. Evans knew it. "I see," she said, although she obviously didn't.

"Mr. Malloy is investigating some charges that have been made against Reverend Upchurch," Sarah continued relentlessly.

"Reverend Upchurch!" Now Sarah had her complete attention.

"Yes, and he naturally wants his inquiries to be discreet, because if the charges are false, even a breath of scandal could still ruin his ministry."

"Of course it could!" Mrs. Evans agreed, outraged at the very thought. "What on earth has he been accused of?"

She'd asked Sarah, but Malloy answered, which was just as well because Sarah hadn't thought up a lie for this. "I don't like to say, Mrs. Evans," he explained respectfully. "Like Mrs. Brandt said, even a rumor can ruin a man like Mr. Upchurch."

"Of course," she agreed quickly, seeing the truth of it. "How horrible. Who could have done such a thing?"

"I can't tell you that either, ma'am," Malloy said. Sarah marveled at how polite he could be when the occasion demanded.

Mrs. Evans sighed in disgust. "I don't suppose you can, but it's simply scandalous how anyone can accuse a man like Reverend Upchurch of something and then be protected himself."

"It is a terrible thing," Malloy agreed. "That's why I'd appreciate your help in getting this settled as quietly as possible."

Mrs. Evans seemed mollified, but then she turned back to Sarah. "I don't understand why you've come to me, though. Anyone in the church could vouch for Reverend Upchurch's character."

Sarah somehow resisted the urge to glance at Malloy. Instead, she leaned forward slightly, knowing she had to convince this woman to do an unthinkable thing. "Mr. Malloy would like to speak with Percy, Mrs. Evans."

"Percy?" she exclaimed in surprise. "Whatever for?"

This time Sarah did glance at Malloy, silently begging him to respond.

"I'm speaking to all of the boys Reverend Upchurch spends time with," he obliged her, still calm and reasonable, giving no hint of his true suspicions. "They are at the church a lot, and they're in a position to know what Reverend Upchurch does when other adults aren't around. If he's guilty of the accusations, they'd probably know about it, but what's more likely is that they can say they never saw him doing what he's been accused of."

Mrs. Evans laid a hand over her heart. "Oh, my, this is so dreadful. But why do the boys have to be involved? Isn't there someone else you could ask?"

Malloy gave her a smile Sarah had never seen before. It made him look positively humble. She tried not to let Mrs. Evans see her shock.

"I have to get the truth. I've found through experience that well-brought-up children will usually tell the truth, but adults will usually lie, especially if they think they're helping or protecting someone they respect. In this case, even a well-meaning lie could hurt Mr. Upchurch. Besides, if I question adults, they'll have to know Reverend Upchurch is being investigated by the police. If the boys can clear this up right away, no one else needs to find out."

"I just don't know," Mrs. Evans murmured, shaking her head in confusion.

"Would you like to talk to his mother about it first?" Malloy asked.

"Oh, no," Mrs. Evans said in alarm. "My daughter's health wouldn't . . . she's not strong enough to deal with something like this."

Sensing Mrs. Evans's inner struggle, Sarah started her barrage again. "I know how upsetting this must be for you, and how much you want to protect your grandson, but I wouldn't have brought Mr. Malloy here if it wasn't important. We want to protect your church, too."

"Oh, yes," she said, her face pale from the agony of indecision. She turned to Malloy and looked him directly in the eye. "I've heard how the police treat people. Percy is just a child, and he's very sensitive."

"The police aren't kind to criminals, Mrs. Evans, but Percy isn't a criminal. I have a boy of my own, and I'll treat your grandson the way I'd want someone to treat Brian."

"Can I be with him when you question him?" she asked.

Sarah held her breath as she waited for Malloy's reply.

"If you are, then you'll know what your minister has been accused of," he reminded her. "You might never be able to look at him the same way, even if he's innocent."

Sarah's jaw actually dropped open before she caught herself and snapped it shut. Mrs. Evans didn't close hers.

"Oh, my," she said again, as softly as a prayer this time. "Isn't there any other way?"

"No, ma'am, there isn't," Malloy told her.

Sarah felt a small pang of guilt over the way they were bullying this poor woman, especially because she knew the infinite pain Reverend Upchurch's betrayal would cause her whole family.

Sarah and Malloy waited, giving Mrs. Evans time to consider their request. Sarah needed all her will power not to fidget or demand that the woman give them Percy. What would they do if she refused? Tell her what they suspected? Frighten and disgust her until she agreed? And would anything they said convince her to allow her grandson to publicly accuse the minister?

"I'll get Percy," Mrs. Evans said, rising to her feet. "But you must promise not to frighten him," she added to Malloy.

"I'll be as gentle as I can," Malloy promised.

Mrs. Evans's brow wrinkled with doubt. Sarah might have doubted, too, if she hadn't seen Malloy with his own son.

"He'll be all right," Sarah added, not sure if she meant Percy or Malloy.

However Mrs. Evans interpreted it, she went to get her grandson.

When they were alone, Malloy turned to Sarah. "You'll need to sit with her while I'm with the boy. Keep her talking. We don't want her changing her mind and coming to get him before I'm finished."

Sarah understood. "You won't have to scare him, will you?"

The look he gave her made her heart sink. "I need to find out the truth about Upchurch. I'm going to do whatever I have to."

"I know," she said sadly. She pushed herself to her feet and began to pace, unable to sit still.

After what seemed an eternity, Mrs. Evans returned with Percy. Sarah couldn't begin to guess what she'd told him, but he came in with his eyes wide. Fortunately, he looked simply bewildered and not nervous or afraid.

"Percy, you remember Mrs. Brandt. You met her at the Lintons' house."

"Yes, ma'am," he said dutifully. "How are you, Mrs. Brandt?"

"Very well, thank you," Sarah lied. She really felt sick. The boy looked even younger than his years, standing there like a lamb being led to the slaughter.

"And this gentleman is Mr. Malloy," Mrs. Evans added.

"I saw you at church," Percy said. "You were with Reverend Upchurch. He said you're a policeman."

"That's right," Malloy confirmed, his voice gentle, the

way it was when he spoke to Brian, even though Brian couldn't hear it.

Percy gave his grandmother a questioning look.

"Mr. Malloy would like to ask you some questions, Percy," she said. Sarah could hear the anxiety in her voice, and she knew the boy could, too.

"About what?" he asked, a trace of youthful rebellion creeping into his tone.

"About a very important matter," she said. "He needs some information from you."

"Information about what?" he asked suspiciously.

"Don't worry, I'm not going to ask you to rat on your friends," Malloy said with a conspiratorial grin, using slang that Percy wouldn't have dared use in front of his grandmother. It made the boy grin back.

"That's good, 'cause I'm no squealer," he replied.

"What kind of talk is that?" Mrs. Evans demanded.

"It's the way coppers talk, Grandmother," Percy explained with a trace of pride that he knew.

"Well, you are not a copper, and you will not use cant, young man."

"Yes, ma'am," he said solemnly, although his eyes glinted with mischief.

"Now you be sure to answer all of Mr. Malloy's questions and tell him everything he wants to know. And if you . . . need me . . . for anything," she added uncertainly, plainly remembering what she'd heard about coppers giving people the third degree, "I'll be nearby. You just have to call."

He seemed surprised that she was going to leave him alone with a policeman, but he didn't protest.

"I'll go with you," Sarah said to Mrs. Evans. "I've been wanting to talk to you about the other activities at the church," she added, taking Mrs. Evans's arm and guiding her from the room. As she closed the door behind them, she glanced back to see Malloy and Percy sizing each other up. She breathed a silent prayer that Malloy would find a way to stop Upchurch.

As he looked at the boy standing in front of him, Frank felt a hot ball of rage eating through his insides. Part of him yearned to find out his suspicions about Upchurch were false, that the minister's wife was a wicked liar and he and Sarah had misunderstood everything. Nothing in his life's experience gave him any reason to expect it, though. As always, he expected the worst.

"Let's sit down, Percy," he said, indicating two chairs sitting side by side and turned slightly toward each other to make conversation easier.

Pleased to have been invited instead of ordered, Percy took a seat.

Frank had given a lot of thought to how to approach the boy, and he knew Sarah was right. He couldn't let on that what Upchurch had done was wrong or he'd never find out anything.

"Somebody's trying to get Reverend Upchurch in trouble, Percy," he began.

"Who would do that?" the boy asked, his eyes wide again.

"I can't tell you, but it's my job to find out the truth about it."

"What kind of trouble is he in?" the boy asked. "Are they saying he stole something?"

This was probably the worst crime he could imagine. "I can't tell you that, either. What I *can* tell you is that your answers will help me clear things up."

"I don't want Reverend Upchurch to get arrested," he protested.

"I don't blame you," Frank said, managing not to let his true feelings show. "When I'm investigating a case, I talk to all the people who know something about it. Sometimes they tell me things that prove the person is guilty, but sometimes they tell me things that prove he isn't. You want to help me prove Reverend Upchurch didn't do anything wrong, don't you?"

Percy nodded solemnly.

"I thought you would, but you'll have to tell me the truth, even if you're embarrassed or if Reverend Upchurch told you to keep it a secret. Do you understand?"

Percy nodded again. "Yes, sir. At least, I think so."

Frank drew a deep breath and began. He started with nonthreatening questions about when Upchurch had first taken an interest in Percy.

"Were your mother and grandmother happy that he started paying special attention to you?" he asked then.

Percy nodded. "They're always saying how sad it is that my father died. They think I need a male influence."

"Do you know what a male influence is?"

The boy shrugged. "Somebody to play ball with and to teach you things."

"Is that what Upchurch does? Teach you things?"

"Yes, sir. He teaches us the things our fathers would, if they were still alive."

"What kinds of things does he teach you?"

"Well, playing ball. He's really good at baseball."

"Besides sports, what does he talk to you about?"

Percy grinned sheepishly and kicked his heels against the chair a couple of times. "You know. The things we aren't supposed to talk about."

"Who told you not to talk about them?"

"Reverend Upchurch. He said we should never tell a female, of course, because they aren't supposed to think about those things. He said men don't talk about them to each other, either, because it's not gentlemanly. That's right, isn't it?"

"Upchurch thinks that's important, doesn't he? Being a gentleman?"

Percy's eyes grew very serious. "It's the most important thing a man can be."

"Do you know that gentlemen always tell the truth, no matter how hard it is?"

"I . . . I guess so," the boy allowed.

"Good, because I'm going to ask you to tell me about the things Upchurch told you gentlemen don't discuss, because he was wrong about that. Men talk about those things all the time, even gentlemen. They don't talk about it in front of women. That part was right. I think Upchurch just wanted to be sure you boys wouldn't embarrass anybody by talking about it."

"Are you sure? Do men really talk about it?" he asked doubtfully.

"Didn't you and the other boys talk about it?" Frank asked, taking a chance.

Percy's young face flushed scarlet. "Not . . . not very much," he hedged, confirming Frank's suspicion.

"It's really all right," Frank assured him, wishing that were true, wishing it really *was* going to be all right. "I need to make sure he did what I think he did."

"Oh, so he won't be in trouble," Percy guessed.

Frank somehow managed not to wince. "Tell me about the things he taught you that you're not supposed to talk about."

"Just the usual things," Percy said with another shrug. "What a father teaches his son so he'll know what to do when he loves a girl."

The ball of rage threatened to choke him, but Frank kept his voice calm. "Can you tell me exactly what he did?"

Percy looked a bit annoyed. "You should already know. Didn't you learn this stuff? Didn't anybody ever show you?"

Frank swallowed down hard. "Reverend Upchurch isn't your real father, Percy. I need to know that he . . . that he told you the right things."

Percy looked up at the ceiling. "It feels strange to talk about it."

"You don't have to look at me, if you don't want to."

The boy sighed. "I *know* he taught us the right things."

"I'm probably a better judge of that than you are. Go ahead."

"You won't laugh, will you? The older boys always teased me and Mark about it, because we're younger. They thought they knew more than us."

"I won't laugh, and I won't tease you," Frank promised, knowing he couldn't possibly find any humor in it at all.

Percy sighed. "All right. But Reverend Upchurch did say we should only do it with the girl we love. He said there's some girls that will do it for money, but we should never use *them*."

"He's right about that," Frank said, feeling the sweat breaking out under his shirt. "Did he just explain what you were supposed to do?"

"Oh, no," Percy assured him. "He showed us, and then we had to practice."

"With him?" Frank's throat felt like someone was tightening a noose around it.

Percy nodded. "Because we don't have fathers, he was doing what they would do."

Frank fought to keep his voice steady. "Just so I know for sure, can you tell me exactly what you did?"

Reluctantly, he did, speaking in a normal, almost bored voice, as if he were telling Frank about the way Upchurch had taught him how to throw a baseball. Sarah had been too right. Upchurch had used the fatherless boys' vulnerability to tell them the most horrible lies, convincing them he was only filling a father's role in their lives.

Frank thought about the boys he usually dealt with, boys whose families had turned them out when they'd been younger than Percy was now. Boys who'd lived on the street, scrounging for food and doing whatever they must to stay alive, knowing far too much about the evils of this world. Most people would say Percy was fortunate to have been raised in a good home with a loving family, but ironically, his good fortune had made him the perfect target for Upchurch's perversion. No guttersnipe would have fallen for his lies.

Eventually, Upchurch's victims would come to understand what he had done to them, of course, as Isaiah obviously had. They'd be too ashamed to expose him, though, and like Isaiah, too angry and bitter even to help the younger boys.

As instructed, Percy hadn't looked at Frank during his explanation. When he was finished, he turned to him, and he must have seen the horror Frank couldn't hide.

"What's wrong?" he asked anxiously.

Everything, Frank thought, but he said, "You didn't do anything wrong, Percy, but he lied to you. Upchurch lied to you about everything. Fathers don't make you do those things."

The boy's eyes were enormous and filled with incredulity. He didn't know Frank and couldn't trust him. "*You're* lying!" he cried. "Reverend Upchurch tells the truth! He's a preacher!"

"Sometimes even preachers can be bad men."

"Coppers are bad men!" Percy insisted. "I know all about it. My friends told me. You beat people up and take them to jail for no reason! You take bribes and let guilty people go!"

"I never did what Upchurch did. I never made a boy do anything he didn't want to do," Frank said, ignoring the accusations. "You didn't want to do those things with Upchurch, did you? You knew they were wrong, but you didn't want him to get mad at you, did you?"

The color drained from Percy's face, confirming Frank's theory. "He loves me!" he insisted.

"If he really loved you, he wouldn't have done those things to you," Frank said relentlessly. "He did what *he* wanted, not what you wanted."

"I don't believe you!" Percy cried, his eyes red from unshed tears, but Frank could see he was beginning to.

Slowly, gently, and at times awkwardly, Frank told him why Upchurch had lied to him and the other boys and betrayed their trust and used them. He described the proper relationship between a father and son, and watched as the boy began to understand. The horror in his young eyes gave way to pain and anguish and rage and finally to despair. Although he tried not to cry, the tears rolled down his young cheeks just the same, even as he scrubbed at them furiously with his sleeve.

Frank gave him a few minutes to collect himself, and when the boy could speak again, the first thing he said was, "Don't tell my mother. Females aren't supposed to know about these things, are they? And she's not very well. She'll get upset, and she might even die. They think I don't know

how sick she is, but I heard the doctor telling Grandmother.
I don't want her to die because of me."

The boy's pain was so raw, Frank felt the sting of tears in
his own eyes, even though he'd thought his heart had hardened beyond hope. He had to remind himself that he
couldn't let Percy's pain affect his judgment. "We'll have to
tell someone," he said reasonably, "So we can protect you
from Upchurch."

"What will he do to me?" Percy asked in alarm.

"Nothing," Frank assured him. "Not anymore. I mean
we need to make sure he can't use you like that anymore.
You don't want that, do you?"

"Oh, I didn't think . . . I mean . . . ," he stammered uncomfortably. "No, I guess not."

"You probably won't want to go to church there anymore. I don't think your grandmother and mother would,
either, if they knew, but if they don't know, how will you
explain why *you* don't want to go?"

He obviously hadn't thought about this either. "I . . . I'll
just say I don't feel good or something," he tried in despair.

"Every Sunday? And they'll want to know why you don't
go to the church after school anymore. They'll be mad at
you. They'll try to make you go because it's good for you.
They'll think you're being bad, and they'll punish you."

He knew Frank was right. His eyes filled with tears
again. "What can I do?"

"We can tell your grandmother."

"But . . . but females . . . they aren't supposed to know!"
he protested, his voice breaking again.

"That's another lie," Frank said as kindly as he could.
"Your grandmother will understand. She'll make sure you
never have to see Upchurch again."

He was crying now, as the reality became clear to him.

His whole world was crumbling, and nothing would ever be the same again. "My friends," he sobbed.

"What about them?" Frank asked.

"What . . . what will happen with them?" he asked brokenly.

"That's up to you."

He look up, his eyes wide with terror. "Why is it up to me?"

"Do you want to stop him from hurting your friends, too?"

"I . . . They'll be mad, 'cause I told. They'll hate me."

"Maybe they want it to stop, too, but they don't know what to do."

"They'll be mad," he insisted. "Isaiah, he'll be *real* mad. He doesn't like me anyway."

"Why not?" Frank asked with a frown.

"Because . . . because Reverend Upchurch likes us better than him."

"Who does he like better?"

"Me and Mark."

"Why is that?"

Percy shrugged. "Isaiah says because we're younger."

If Upchurch preferred *young* boys, eventually the boys would get too old for his taste. Frank remembered Isaiah's anger and bitterness, and he wondered if this was part of it. The whole thing made him sick, and the more he learned, the sicker he got. "I'll talk to your grandmother, if you like, so you don't have to. I can explain it to her."

"She'll be mad at me, too," he said sadly.

"No, she won't. I'll make sure she isn't. This isn't your fault, and she'll know it."

"She loves Reverend Upchurch. She won't want to hear anything bad about him."

"I'll bet she loves you more."

Percy didn't look convinced. "I could just stop going to the church after school. I could tell Reverend Upchurch I'm not allowed to anymore. Nobody has to know. My grandmother and my mother could keep going to church like always."

"What about the other boys?"

Percy winced. "They can do what they want, can't they?"

"Even if all of you decide to stop going to see Upchurch, he'll find other boys. He won't stop. He'll *never* stop unless you stop him, Percy. It's up to you."

Mrs. Evans looked as if she were carved in stone as Sarah and Malloy told her of the unspeakable horror that Upchurch had perpetrated on her family. She'd been shocked and incredulous at first, certain such a thing could never have happened, but they'd answered all of her questions as honestly and tactfully as they could, chipping away at her disbelief with the edges of their certainty. She'd endured the entire ordeal stoically. Sarah knew how many years of training and practice it had taken to allow her to sit, expressionless, as everything she'd once held sacred was ripped brutally from her.

"This is . . . difficult to believe," she said hoarsely when they had told her everything they could and answered all her questions.

Sarah imagined it was. "You must be wondering how Mr. Malloy came to suspect Reverend Upchurch in the first place. Believe me, this is the last thing I expected to discover when I visited your church."

"What did you expect to discover, Mrs. Brandt?" she asked, her eyes narrowed with quiet rage. "You obviously had some purpose when you came snooping around, and don't bother telling me that fairy tale about your work at some mission on the Lower East Side."

Stung, Sarah reminded herself that Mrs. Evans was extremely angry, and she would naturally lash out at her and Frank for being the ones to open this Pandora's box of horrors. "I do volunteer at the Prodigal Son Mission, but the real reason I went to your church is that one of the girls at your church was raped, and her attacker is probably one of your members."

For a moment, Mrs. Evans's stoicism broke. "Do you mean Grace Linton? Someone attacked that poor girl?"

"I didn't say—"

"Don't bother denying it," Mrs. Evans snapped. "You didn't know anyone in our church except the Lintons. It must be Grace."

"Her family doesn't want anyone to know," Sarah cautioned.

"Of course they don't. That poor girl. But didn't Grace tell her parents who is responsible?"

"She either can't or won't name the man."

"How awful for them. But how did you get involved, Mrs. Brandt?"

"I . . ." she glanced at Malloy who was trying very hard not to remind her that he'd warned her against this very thing. "I thought an outsider might have a better chance of finding the guilty man. I thought it was possible someone had somehow convinced Grace not to tell. It would have to be someone she trusts completely. And then I visited Mrs. Upchurch and—"

"That woman is evil! She'll say anything to cause trouble for her husband," Mrs. Evans said, her composure slipping badly. "Is she the one who told you these lies about him?"

"No, Mrs. Evans," Malloy said, startling Sarah. She'd almost forgotten he was there. "I already suspected something wasn't right between him and those boys. Mrs. Upchurch told Mrs. Brandt some things that made her think he had seduced Grace Linton, and I questioned him about it. I was pretty sure he wasn't guilty of that, but I still thought he was hiding something."

"He must have told his wife about Mr. Malloy's visit," Sarah added, "because in church on Sunday, Mrs. Upchurch told me I'd misunderstood her."

"I knew it!" Mrs. Evans cried. "She made up these terrible lies."

"She didn't make up the things Percy told me," Malloy reminded her. "She knew what was happening, and she wanted someone to stop it."

"If she knew, she should have done something sooner! How could she live with a secret like that?" she asked in outrage.

"The same way the boys could," Sarah said. "She didn't think anyone would believe her, and I think she was right about that. Most people wouldn't even believe a man *could* do those things to boys. They'd probably accuse the boys of lying, and Upchurch might even accuse his wife of being insane. She could end up in an asylum."

Mrs. Evans pressed her fingertips to her temples and squeezed her eyes shut. "I just can't . . . I don't know what to do. What do you *expect* me to do?"

"Help Percy stay away from him," Sarah said. "He's also worried about his mother finding out. He knows she's very ill, and he's afraid the shock will be too much for her."

Mrs. Evans looked up in surprise. "He said that? Oh, dear. We didn't think he knew. Well, it doesn't matter. She'll have to be told. She'd never forgive me for keeping a secret like that. And, of course, we'll keep him away. There's no question of that. But I think Mr. Malloy wants more of us than that. He wouldn't be here if he didn't."

Sarah watched Malloy carefully consider his words. "Most people would want to keep this kind of thing quiet. The boys won't want anyone to know what Upchurch did to them."

"Of course they won't!" she agreed. "Neither do I!"

"Thing is, that's how he's been able to get away with it all this time. We don't know when he started, but we know he's been doing it at least as long as he's been here. Isaiah was probably one of his first victims, and now he's too old, and Upchurch has moved on to younger boys. If the older boys had told someone in the beginning, we could have stopped him before he got to Percy. If we don't stop him now, he'll go on to other boys in the future."

Her eyes seemed to burn as she glared at Malloy. "You want us to announce that my grandson has been . . . *violated*? You can't expect me to publicly humiliate the boy I love more than my own life!"

"Someone has to stop him, Mrs. Evans," he said, making it sound perfectly reasonable.

"Not your way, Mr. Malloy. I won't destroy Percy."

"Then you're going to let Upchurch keep abusing other boys?" he asked angrily.

"No, I'm not. I'll stop him."

"*How?*" he challenged.

This time her eyes did burn, with a hatred so intense, Sarah had to look away.

"You'll see," was all she said. "But he'll stop, I guarantee it."

II

"WHAT IS YOUR MRS. EVANS GOING TO DO?" MALLOY asked Sarah when they'd found a coffee shop where they could sit, out of the cold, in relative privacy.

"She's not *my* Mrs. Evans, and I have no idea what she's going to do," Sarah replied tartly.

They waited while the waitress served them cups of steaming coffee. Malloy ordered them each a slice of pie. Sarah wrapped her hands around the cup, warming her bloodless fingers. She wasn't certain if she was so cold from the temperature outside or because of the horrors they had just been discussing.

"You said you knew a way to punish Upchurch without sending him to jail," Malloy reminded her. "What were you going to do?"

"I told you before, gossip. It's possible to ruin him without ever making a public accusation. In fact, it's more powerful because you have no idea what people are saying about you, so how can you defend yourself?"

"Mrs. Evans isn't going to start gossip about what he did to Percy," Malloy said.

Sarah took a fortifying sip of her coffee. "I know. That's why I have no idea what she's planning. Maybe she's hoping to remove him from his ministry somehow, although that isn't likely to stop him from lusting after little boys."

The waitress had just returned with their pie, and she almost dropped Malloy's into his lap in shock over what Sarah had just said. Malloy caught the plate just in time. He glared at Sarah, who smiled innocently at the waitress.

"Thank you very much," she said. "This looks delicious."

Her face still frozen in revulsion, the girl fled, probably to inform the rest of the staff what that respectable-looking lady at the corner table had been saying. Sarah sighed.

"At least keep your voice down," Malloy advised, taking an enormous bite of the pie. Apple, his favorite.

"You did say Upchurch might commit suicide if he was exposed," she remembered. "Do you think? . . ."

"That a sweet little old lady like Mrs. Evans intends to drive a man to suicide? No, I don't think that. She wouldn't have the slightest idea how to do it anyway, even if she could come up with an idea like that in the first place. Besides, Upchurch doesn't strike me as the kind to kill himself. He likes himself too much, and he could just move someplace where they don't know him and start over again."

"So, I guess my theory that I could stop him with gossip isn't very good."

Malloy gave her a look but graciously refrained from confirming her analysis.

"What *would* stop a man like that?" she asked.

"Death," he said baldly. "Sometimes they get too old and feeble or too sick to go to the trouble of finding and tricking the boys, but then he'd probably just hire boys off the streets."

Sarah shuddered. "I'd never thought of that. The street boys, I mean. I knew that girls sold themselves, but I never realized . . ."

"You don't need to know every ugly thing that goes on in the world, Sarah," he said softly.

She looked up in surprise to see a tenderness in his dark eyes that she'd never seen before, but when she blinked, it had vanished. Had she only imagined it? "If I don't know about it, how can I do anything to change it?" she challenged.

"Changing it isn't your job," he said, the usual gruffness back in his voice.

"Whose job is it, then? The police?" she scoffed. "They haven't had much success so far."

"Do you think your missions and settlement houses are going to do any better?" he scoffed right back.

"At least we're trying," she said belligerently, somehow angry that he'd shown her just a glimpse of his true feelings and now seemed determined to pick a fight with her. "We can't save them all, but at least we're saving a few."

He opened his mouth to reply, and Sarah braced herself, but all he said was, "Eat your pie."

Unable to think of a reason to argue with that command, she cut off the point with her fork and took a bite. It wasn't nearly as good as Mrs. Ellsworth's or even Mrs. Malloy's, but it would do.

When she'd swallowed it, she asked, "What are you going to do now?"

The look he gave her made her regret the question. "Nothing," he said, although she could see he hated it as much as she did. "If the families don't file charges against him, there's nothing more I can do. And don't try to convince them they should, either. They won't thank you for it, and Upchurch might bring charges against *you*."

"For what?" she asked in outrage.

"For not minding your own business," he replied. "It's called slander. People get sued for it all the time."

"Upchurch wouldn't dare do a thing like that!"

"Why not? He wouldn't have anything to fear. If the boys' families won't let them testify against him for abusing them, they aren't going to let them stand up in court and admit what happened just to protect you."

Sarah gaped at him, so furious she wanted to hit someone, and even more furious because she knew he was right. "But . . ." she tried, "I can't just forget about it!"

"Think about it all you want. Just don't do anything."

Sarah hated it when he was right. That's why she had to figure out some way she could still help.

SARAH HAD NEVER FELT GUILTY ABOUT ATTENDING church before. Usually, she felt guilty when she *didn't* go. Today, however, she had come only to see what might happen at the Church of the Good Shepherd, so she had left Aggie safely at home with Mrs. Ellsworth. Mrs. Evans wouldn't be at the worship service, of course, but could she have set her plan—whatever her plan was—in motion? Was she already working behind the scenes to punish Upchurch?

When Sarah arrived, the organ was playing as usual. Everything looked exactly as it had before—the winter sun streaming in through the stained glass windows, people sitting quietly in the pews, all wearing their Sunday best—but she sensed immediately that something was different.

The very air seemed charged, and no one engaged in friendly conversation. Instead, they looked around uneasily, as if watching and waiting for something to happen. The man who escorted her to her seat didn't smile as he had the week before. Instead he looked worried and preoccupied.

Sarah noticed the crowd was much smaller than it had been the previous Sunday. Mr. Linton sat in the same pew she'd shared with his family before, but he was alone. Mrs. Upchurch sat in what was apparently her regular seat near the front, as usual. Then Sarah saw Mrs. Evans just a few rows in front of her. At first she thought she must be mistaken, but then she realized that the woman next to her was her daughter, Percy's mother. Why would both of them be here after what they'd learned about Upchurch?

She remembered Malloy's warnings, about how families sometimes tried to pretend nothing was wrong or didn't believe their children at all. Could Mrs. Evans have decided she and Malloy were lying to her? Could Percy have changed his mind and denied everything when his grandmother confronted him? She could hardly imagine such a thing, but if the women believed that Upchurch had abused Percy, how could they sit here in his church?

Before she could make sense of it, an acolyte came down the aisle. Only one this time, and it wasn't Percy or even his young friend. Sarah recognized Isaiah. The expression on his face could only be described as grim as he marched down to the front of the church. A wave of whispers followed him as people remarked on something. Sarah knew that most churches used two acolytes, and they were usually younger boys. Were they commenting on the reduction in numbers? Or the fact that Isaiah was too tall for the robe he was wearing? Or perhaps on the fact that he was doing the job at all?

He began lighting the altar candles, and the whispers

died. When he was finished, the organ music swelled, and the choir filed in, their numbers also greatly reduced. Then the congregation rose for the opening hymn. As she always did, Sarah started singing out the words printed in the hymnal, but she quickly realized that no one around her was singing. In fact, when she glanced across the aisle, she saw that no one there was singing, either. The choir appeared to be the only ones giving voice to the words, but their few voices were subdued, a hollow echo of the magnificence she'd heard from them before.

The service proceeded, but it seemed almost a parody of last week's. The choir performed halfheartedly. The offering plates passed down row after row and emerged empty. Something was terribly wrong. Did Upchurch realize it? How could he get up and give a sermon in the face of such hostility? And what would happen if he tried? But first, Upchurch rose to serve communion.

He seemed unaware that anything was amiss. The elements were spread on a table in front of him, and he spoke in his eloquent tones of Christ's sacrifice, holding up the bread and a silver chalice of wine. Did his voice sound less confident than usual? Had he sensed the antagonism that hung like a miasma in the room? Did he understand that somehow they had all turned against him? He certainly didn't appear to.

Then he called for those in the congregation who wished to partake to come forward. Isaiah moved from his place to stand beside him, apparently to assist, but his expression was less than reverent. Sarah had seen that very expression on boys in the Lower East Side, desperate boys who had lost their faith in everything and everyone and whose souls had shriveled into black lumps of hatred.

A rustle of movement disturbed the stillness of the sanctuary, but it was only people shifting uncomfortably in their seats. No one rose. No one began to move toward the aisle and down to the altar to receive communion. Everyone simply sat, staring at Upchurch.

Long moments passed. Upchurch issued the invitation again, the edge of alarm in his voice this time. Still no one moved.

His face white, Upchurch turned to Isaiah, silently pleading for assistance. The boy simply glared back. What was going through the minister's mind? Did he understand what was happening? Sarah had no idea, but Upchurch wasn't going to surrender just yet.

He broke off two pieces of the bread and said, "Take, eat, this is my body which was broken for you." He offered one to Isaiah, who made no move to take it.

His eyes wild with desperation now, he stuffed the bread into his own mouth and swallowed it. The silence was almost deafening, as people seemed to hold their very breaths.

With unsteady hands, he lifted the silver chalice and spoke the scripture about the wine being Christ's blood, shed for the remission of sins. He turned slightly, ready to offer it to Isaiah, but the boy actually took a step backward, his chin raised defiantly in refusal.

Upchurch glanced around, as if looking for someone, anyone, to whom he could turn, but he was alone. Terribly alone. Holding the chalice in both hands he stared at it for a long moment, as if it held the answer to this mystery. Then slowly, deliberately, he lifted it to his lips and drank deeply, like a man dying of thirst. Some of the liquid ran down the corners of his mouth, and purple droplets stained the stole he wore over his robe. When he lowered the cup, he glared out at the congregation for a moment, then set it back down on the table with a thunk.

Sarah realized she'd been holding her breath, and the noise startled her into a gasp. What would he do now? Would he continue with this travesty? Would he insist on going to the pulpit and preaching whatever message he'd prepared? Would the congregation literally sit still for it or would they at last rise in protest? The tension made the air seem to hum as everyone waited.

Upchurch stood as if rooted to the spot, his eyes wide with disbelief. He put out a hand to brace himself on the table before him and drew an audible breath. His pale face flushed with color, and his breath seemed to strangle in his throat. For a moment, Sarah thought he was just having an emotional reaction to his congregation's silent rejection, but then his eyes rolled back in his head, and he keeled over backward.

Someone screamed, and a few people instinctively rose to their feet, Sarah among them. The sound of thrashing limbs told Sarah that the minister hadn't merely fainted.

"He's having a fit!" Isaiah cried, backing away in horror.

Responding only to her training, Sarah hurried up the aisle. Several men were there ahead of her, but they stopped short when they reached Upchurch's body. Sarah pushed past them. "I'm a nurse," she said to their startled looks.

Upchurch was indeed having a fit, his body convulsing violently. Her mind raced, trying to diagnose the problem. Could he have epilepsy? Could the strain of this morning have caused a seizure? Vomit dribbled from his mouth.

"Help me turn him onto his side," she said, kneeling down and grabbing one of his twitching arms. But no one moved to assist her. With all her strength, she heaved and succeeded in rolling him halfway over so he wouldn't choke to death. Aside from that, she could only try putting something into his mouth so he didn't swallow his tongue.

While she was glancing frantically around for an implement to use, the thrashing suddenly ceased. She looked down and saw Upchurch's face was oddly contorted, as if he were in pain. His body had relaxed, and his weight rolled him onto his back again, in an awkward position, as the seizure ceased as suddenly as it had begun.

She waited, expecting to hear him draw breath and begin to regain consciousness. Instead he simply lay perfectly still. Too still. He couldn't be dead, she reasoned. His skin was still a healthy pink. She found his hand and placed her fingers on his wrist but found no pulse.

An elderly gentleman had tottered to the front of the church, and the others made way for him. "What are you doing there, miss?" he challenged.

"I'm a nurse," she explained again, a little impatiently.

"I'm a doctor," the old man said, and when he tried to kneel down beside her, one of the other men hurried to assist him.

"Oh, thank heavens! I can't find his pulse," she explained, moving her hand to Upchurch's throat and finding no sign of life there either. "He doesn't seem to be breathing," she said, still puzzled. "But he can't be dead. Look at his color!"

The doctor frowned, rechecking the wrist and throat, then holding his hand on Upchurch's chest. "No heartbeat and no respiration," he concluded. "He's definitely dead."

"He's dead," one of the men standing over them reported to the congregation. Gasps and cries of surprise greeted his announcement.

"We killed him," one woman cried.

"No," the man at the front said. "God killed him. He smote him like the sinner that he is."

Vaguely, Sarah realized that they knew. They all knew. But she didn't have time to even wonder how.

The doctor was examining Upchurch more closely. He leaned over to sniff at his mouth, where the vomit was drying. He turned back to Sarah. "Can you reach that communion cup, miss? Be careful not to spill it. Hand it to me. There, that's good," he said as Sarah cautiously passed the cup to him. It was nearly empty. He sniffed it as well, and then frowned.

"What is it?" she asked.

He leaned the cup toward her face, tilting it so she could sniff it, too. "Do you smell it?"

She detected no odor except the communion wine. "What should I smell?"

"Bitter almonds," he said. "Not everyone can detect it. It's the telltale odor of cyanide. Victims' skin is frequently a pinkish color, which is what made me suspect. Leland," he said, looking up at the man who had announced Upchurch's death. "You were a bit hasty in your judgment. God didn't smite Oliver Upchurch. Someone else took matters into his own hands. He was murdered."

SARAH FOUND IT SURPRISINGLY EASY TO GET FRANK Malloy summoned to the church. The patrolman who arrived first was a Goo-Goo, what the men on the force called the new recruits. Sarah knew she could easily intimidate him by informing him that she was a personal friend of Police Commissioner Teddy Roosevelt. Then she suggested that he ask his captain to request that Detective Sergeant Frank Malloy handle the case since he'd already been investigating the victim's illegal activities.

By that time, several of the women in the congregation were weeping hysterically, and the few children present were also wailing. The poor fellow was only too happy for some guidance on how to handle this terrifying situation.

The man named Leland had taken charge. "We can't keep all these people here," he said to the doctor when the patrolman had gone for help.

Sarah knew her opinions would be ignored, so she whispered to the doctor. "Someone should get their names before they leave, in case the police want to question them later."

Dr. Thomas—he and Sarah had introduced themselves while waiting for the police to arrive—suggested that Leland and his friends organize an orderly retreat of those who wished to leave and make a list of their names as they went out.

Grateful for something constructive to do, the men standing around the body quickly mobilized and went to work. The congregation quieted after the announcement that they'd be allowed to go. Dr. Thomas had taken a seat in one of the chairs by the altar, and Sarah stood nearby, still not quite believing that Upchurch was really dead.

She looked around. Isaiah still stood almost exactly where he'd been when Upchurch first fell. His face was white, but his expression was still full of rage. Someone had pulled the cloth off the communion table and covered Upchurch, and Isaiah couldn't seem to tear his gaze from the shrouded body. Then Sarah was distracted by a figure moving over to where Upchurch lay. It was his wife.

Rachel Upchurch stared down at her husband's body for a long moment. Then, as if not quite satisfied, she reached down and lifted the corner of the altar cloth. She studied his face, turning her head this way and that, and before anyone could imagine what she had in mind, she kicked him sharply in the shoulder.

Sarah cried out in surprise, and Dr. Thomas jumped to his feet.

"What in heaven's name did you do that for?" he demanded, his wrinkled cheeks flushing scarlet.

Mrs. Upchurch gave him a mysterious smile. "I just wanted to be sure he's really dead. We wouldn't want to make a terrible mistake, now would we?"

At last Isaiah roused himself from his stupor and hurried to her side. "She . . . she's upset," he excused her, taking her arm. "Come on, ma'am, let's go sit down."

With one last wistful look at her husband, she dropped the cloth back over his face and allowed Isaiah to escort her to the front pew where they sat down, side by side.

Fortunately, no one else had witnessed this shocking display. Everyone else was either actually leaving the church or helping those who were.

"We'll have to tell the detective about that when he comes," Dr. Thomas said.

"He . . . Upchurch treated her very badly," Sarah said, offering another excuse.

"It's my understanding that he treated many people badly," Dr. Thomas said knowingly.

"Yes, he did," Sarah agreed. "That's why Mr. Malloy was investigating. Does everyone in the church know? Is that why no one would sing or take communion this morning?"

"Yes," a female voice said. Sarah looked up to see Mrs. Evans laboriously climbing onto the platform, taking the steps one at a time. Her daughter hovered close behind her, ready to assist if needed. "I told them."

"You couldn't have told all of them in just a few days," Sarah protested, stunned that she'd been willing to speak of her grandson's humiliation at all.

"I told the other families of the boys involved," she said, looking down at Upchurch's body. Mrs. York looked at it, too, staring as if transfixed. "I sent for them to come to my house and bring the boys," Mrs. Evans continued, "and I had the church elders there, too."

"At first the other mothers wouldn't believe it," Mrs. York said, her voice oddly flat as she continued to stare at Upchurch's shrouded figure. "I couldn't blame them, I didn't want to believe it, either, and the other boys tried to deny it, too, but then poor little Mark started crying."

"He's the youngest, a year younger than Percy," Mrs. Evans explained. "He said it was true, and the other boys finally confirmed it. They were reluctant, of course, but in the end, I think they were relieved that it was finally over."

"That was very brave of you," Sarah said, wondering if she would have had such courage.

"Why?" she asked gravely. "Because they might not have believed me? I'm an old woman, Mrs. Brandt. I don't have to worry what people think about me anymore. If I do something foolish, they'll just assume I'm getting senile. But they also take me seriously if I make sense. It's one of the few advantages of old age."

"Whose idea was it to poison him?" Dr. Thomas asked mildly.

Mrs. Evans looked at him blankly, but Mrs. York turned to him, her eyes blazing with hatred. "He died too easily," she declared vehemently. "He should've suffered more."

Mrs. Evans gave a little cry of distress, and for a few seconds, everyone simply gaped at her. Then the man named Leland came over quickly to intervene. "No one was going to poison him," he assured Dr. Thomas. "We were going to confront him this morning and tell him we knew what he was. We were going to dismiss him from his position and send him on his way."

Sarah felt an ache in her heart. They'd planned the best way they knew to protect their own children, but throwing

Upchurch out of their church wouldn't protect anyone else's. He'd probably have found another church in another city and done the same thing all over again. What had Malloy said? Death was the only way to truly stop him. Obviously, someone had figured that out.

FRANK HAD RARELY BEEN CALLED OUT TO INVESTIGATE A murder on a Sunday, but he'd known the instant he'd seen the patrolman sent to find him that it was Sarah Brandt's doing. All that poor fellow had known was that a minister had been killed right in his church on the Upper East Side, and the cops up there wanted him on the case. That was enough, though. How many ministers in the city were in danger of being murdered at any given time? At first he figured the Lintons or one of the other families he'd visited must have had them send for him, since he'd known the situation. He hadn't actually expected Sarah to be there herself, so when he saw her, he wanted to spit nails.

Luckily, she was all the way at the other end of the sanctuary, and there were a lot of people in between, so he had time to compose himself. First he had to deal with the group of churchmen who met him in the foyer. They wanted him to know they expected him to treat this matter with the utmost delicacy and discretion, and that he was forbidden from upsetting any members of the congregation. When he'd managed to extricate himself from them, the precinct captain and his detective met him halfway down the aisle and told him what they knew, which was less than Frank already knew.

"Seems he was doing something perverted, and they were going to fire him," the captain said. "Nobody'll say what it was, though."

"Young boys," Frank said. "One of the girls in the church

was raped, and I was looking into it. Found out about the minister's problem by accident."

"He rape the girl, too?" the detective asked. He was a round-faced Irishman who'd seen too much and didn't let it bother him anymore.

"I don't think so. He didn't seem to like females at all, according to his wife."

The two other men winced at such an abomination.

"That must be why the lady up there asked for you," the captain said, nodding toward where Sarah waited. "You're welcome to the case, too." He wouldn't be excited about a scandal like this. Irish cops investigating a Protestant minister wouldn't be popular.

"I can use some help," he said meaningfully to the other detective. "There'll be a lot of people to question."

The captain nodded. "Kelly will do whatever you need, and I'll leave a couple patrolmen, too. There was a bunch of people here when it happened. It was right in the middle of the Mass," he said, using the term with which he was most familiar. "They sent everybody home, but at least they got all the names, in case you want to question anybody."

Frank wondered if Sarah had thought of getting the names. It seemed like something she'd do. He wasn't going to ask her, though. He was too angry at her right now to be grateful for favors.

"Did you send for the coroner yet?" Frank asked.

"No, I figured you'd want to see the body first. I'll do it right now."

"Good. Let's find out what these people can tell us," he said to Detective Sergeant Kelly, who looked less than pleased at being selected to assist Frank.

They started toward the front platform, and Sarah walked down the aisle to meet them.

"Good morning, Mrs. Brandt," he said. "How nice to see you." His tone told her it wasn't nice at all, but as usual, she didn't flinch.

"I'm glad you were able to come," she said as brazen as you please, as if he'd done her a personal favor instead of responding to an order. "This is very shocking to everyone."

He introduced Kelly to her. "Mrs. Brandt was involved in a case I worked on last year," he said by way of explanation. "She was . . . helpful," he added, letting Kelly know Sarah wasn't just a brainless female. "I suppose you just happened by this morning," Frank said before she could speak, "while Mr. Upchurch was dying in front of his congregation." Beside him, he heard Kelly catch his breath at Frank's sarcastic tone.

"Oh, no, I came here to worship," she assured him innocently, lying through her teeth. He'd never understand how an upper-class lady could lie so well. Quickly and without wasting any words, she told him exactly what she'd seen when Upchurch died.

"I guess it *was* pretty shocking," he allowed, a bit mollified. He hated that she'd been there to see a thing like that.

"A lot of people stayed home today, because of the scandal, so fortunately there weren't many children here, or ladies, either."

"What scandal?" Kelly asked.

Sarah looked at Frank. "Does he know about Upchurch?"

Frank nodded, frowning.

"We were wrong about Mrs. Evans wanting to keep it a secret. She told all the other mothers and the church elders, too. Now everyone in the church knows. They were furious. No one went forward for communion, no one put money in the offering plates . . . no one even sang the hymns."

"You said he drank all the wine himself, after nobody else came forward, and that's when he died?" Frank asked.

"Yes, almost immediately, but everyone thought he was just having some kind of seizure or something. Dr. Thomas—he's that elderly gentleman sitting by the body—was in the congregation. He's the one who realized Upchurch had been poisoned. He said it was cyanide because he could smell bitter almonds in the communion wine."

"Somebody poisoned the communion wine?" Kelly asked in astonishment. "Wouldn't everybody die then?"

"Seems likely," Frank said. "How do Protestants do communion?" he asked Sarah.

"Different ways, but it seemed the people here go to the altar to receive it."

"And they'd all drink from the same cup?"

"I'm not sure. Sometimes people get a piece of bread and just dip it in the wine. You'll have to ask someone here how he usually served it. Like I said, no one went forward this morning, so I don't know."

Frank glanced around the room, taking a mental inventory of everyone still here. The cluster of churchmen who'd met him earlier still stood nearby, watching to make sure he behaved himself. He saw Isaiah sitting on the front pew with a woman he knew wasn't the boy's mother. Sarah had identified the elderly man sitting on the platform as Dr. Thomas. Lastly, he recognized Mr. Linton and Mrs. Evans sitting together off to one side.

"What's Mrs. Evans doing here?" he asked Sarah.

"She wanted to be here to see Upchurch's downfall, I guess," she replied.

"No, I mean why is she *still* here? Why didn't she go home when everyone else did?"

"I don't know," she said, "but I'm sure she'll tell you if you ask."

Frank remembered Kelly was listening to every word, so

he didn't say what he wanted. Instead he said, "I suppose it would be a waste of breath to tell you to go home yourself."

"It certainly would," she replied.

Kelly coughed behind his hand, and Frank refused to look at him. "Let's take a look at the body," he said and walked off without waiting for consent.

Up on the platform, Frank introduced himself and Kelly to Dr. Thomas. The old man looked remarkably calm for what he'd been through this morning, but then maybe doctors got to be like cops—things like this didn't bother them much after a while.

"Mrs. Brandt said you think Upchurch was poisoned," Frank said.

"Yes, I'm sure if you check what's left of the communion wine, you'll find cyanide. It has a distinct odor of bitter almonds. Not everyone can smell it, but I knew I could, because I had a patient once who took her own life with it. It's in some types of rat poison, and that's what she'd used. She'd put some in a drink—lemonade, I believe it was. She didn't die right away, so her family called me. She confessed what she had done before she died."

"So you recognized the smell of the cyanide in the communion wine?" Frank confirmed.

"Yes, and on Upchurch's breath. The poison causes convulsions, which is what happened to him, and it affects the blood, too, turning it bright red and making the victim's skin pink. See for yourself," he said, pushing himself out of his chair and leading the detectives over to the body.

Frank pulled back the cloth and saw what the old man meant. Not only wasn't Upchurch deathly white, he might have been blushing.

"You'll have an autopsy, of course," Dr. Thomas was saying, "but I'm sure that's what they'll find."

"Who sets things up for communion?" Frank asked, raising his voice so everyone in the room could hear the question.

Everyone looked at everyone else for a moment. One of the churchmen finally said, "I think the boys would help Upchurch get things ready."

"Which of the boys were here this morning?" Frank asked, looking down at where Isaiah sat wearing a ridiculous-looking robe.

He glared back defiantly. "Just me," he said.

"Did you help?"

He lifted his chin a notch. "I did it all. I poured the wine and put everything out on the table."

Frank saw the anger that simmered inside the boy, the rage over what Upchurch had done to him. Was he looking into the face of a killer? "Show me where you keep the supplies," he said.

The boy glanced at the woman beside him, as if for guidance. She nodded encouragement, and he rose to his feet and started toward the platform.

"Who is that woman?" Frank whispered to Dr. Thomas.

"Mrs. Upchurch," he replied.

Something stirred in Frank's memory, something he couldn't quite recall, but he'd think about that later. The communion cup still sat on the table, where someone had replaced it after removing the cloth to cover Upchurch's body. Frank sniffed it and realized he could smell the bitter-almond odor the doctor had mentioned.

"It's back here," Isaiah said, his attitude grudging as he led the men through a nearly hidden door behind the pulpit into a small room obviously used for preparations for the services. Robes of various colors hung along one wall, and cabinets held various supplies. The communion wine was stored under lock and key, probably to discourage the altar boys from sampling it. Isaiah produced the key and opened the appropriate cabinet.

"Who has a key to that cabinet?" Frank asked.

"Upchurch does . . . did," Isaiah said with a slight catch in his voice. "And me. That's all."

"Is this the bottle you used this morning?" Frank asked, reaching for it.

"Yeah," the boy said.

Frank gave him a look.

"Yes, sir," he amended, although reluctantly.

The cabinet held several bottles of cheap wine, and all but one of them were unopened. Frank pulled the cork out of the opened one and sniffed. He didn't smell almonds, but he'd have the police laboratory check it just the same.

"Tell me exactly what you did this morning, Isaiah," he said, keeping his voice neutral. No sense scaring him yet.

The boy shrugged. "I got here early. The other boys, they didn't come because their families wouldn't let them. I wanted to be here, though. I wanted to see him when they told him to get out."

"Can't blame you for that," Frank said encouragingly. "Then what did you do? Did you see Upchurch?"

"No, he was in his office with the door closed. I could hear him talking to somebody—one of them was talking pretty loud—so I came in here, to set up the communion table. I didn't know when they were going to tell him he was finished here—if it was before or after communion—but I wanted to make sure it was all set up so he'd expect everything to go like usual and then be surprised when it didn't."

"Was the wine bottle already open?"

"No, I had to open it. I poured it out into the cup we always use. The ladies in the church make sure there's bread here. Somebody had brought a loaf. I don't know who. It was here when I got here."

"Did you notice anything in the cup before you poured in the wine?"

"I didn't look," he said with a frown.

"Then what did you do?"

"I set up the table out there, like always, and put the bread and the cup on it."

"Was anybody else around?"

"No, like I said, it was early. Then I went to get a robe on. Since none of the other boys were here, I served as acolyte, too."

"What's that?"

"Lighting the candles at the beginning of the service. You walk down the aisle with a candlelighter first, then light them."

"So you left the communion table all set up in front of the empty church. How long was it before people started to arrive?"

"I don't know. A while. Nobody got here early this morning. They didn't want to see Upchurch and have to talk to him, I guess."

"Except someone was here early," Frank reminded him. "You said somebody was in his office with him. Did you ever see who it was?"

"No, I didn't. And I didn't kill him, either. I wish I'd thought of it, though. It was what he deserved."

Frank glanced at Kelly, whose eyebrows had risen in surprise.

"One more question, Isaiah," Frank said. "How do you usually serve communion to the people?"

"They come up front and get it," he said, puzzled by the question.

"No, I mean do people usually drink out of the cup you filled, or do they dip the bread in it?"

"They drink out of the cup. They come up and get a piece of the bread. One of the boys hands that out when they walk by. Then Upchurch gives them the cup to take a drink out of. Not much, just a sip."

"That's the way you always do it?"

"Yes, sir," he remembered to say this time.

"And when does Upchurch drink out of the cup himself?"

Clearly, he wasn't sure what these questions meant. "At the end. He'd serve the boy who was helping him, and then he'd serve himself last."

"Thank you, Isaiah," Frank said. "You can go now. If I think of anything else, I know where to find you."

Now the boy looked even more confused, but he recognized his good fortune and hurried out of the room and back to the sanctuary.

"He one of the boys this guy diddled?" Kelly asked.

"Yeah," Frank said with a sigh.

"Then he's the one did it, no question."

"Maybe," was all Frank said. "Let's talk to the others. We can use Upchurch's office."

They moved toward the doorway, but when they reached it, Mrs. Evans was blocking their way. "Don't bother that poor boy anymore, Mr. Malloy," she said. "I killed Reverend Upchurch."

12

"**D**AMN, YOU'RE GOOD AT THIS," KELLY WHISPERED. FRANK
ignored him.

"Mrs. Evans, that's a dangerous thing to say, especially if
it's not true," he said.

She didn't even blink. "I assure you, I am well aware of
the consequences, Mr. Malloy."

"Let's go into Upchurch's office where we can discuss this
privately," he said, taking her arm. As they passed through
the sanctuary, Malloy summoned one of the patrolmen to
take possession of the wine bottle and communion cup as
evidence. Then he called out to the group of churchmen
who had by now taken seats in the pews. "I'm going to
question everyone here one by one in the minister's office.
Stay where you are, and I'll call you in when I'm ready for
you."

"There's really no need to keep them here," Mrs. Evans scolded him. "I already told you—"

"I just want to make sure their stories agree with yours," he told her.

"Do you think I would lie about something like this?" she asked, affronted.

Frank had completely misjudged her once. He wasn't going to make the same mistake again, especially if it meant sending her to prison for the rest of her life. "I have to make reports, Mrs. Evans. It has to look like I investigated everything."

"Very well then," she said, letting him conduct her into Upchurch's office. Kelly closed the door behind them. He seemed to be thoroughly enjoying himself.

Frank put her in one of the chairs by the window, where he and Upchurch had sat the first time they'd met. He took the other chair and let Kelly pull one over from the chess table. "Now tell me what happened, Mrs. Evans."

She folded her hands in her lap, as calm as if she confessed to murder every day. "Where should I begin?"

"Let's see, Mrs. Brandt said you'd gotten all the boys and their mothers together and told them what Upchurch was doing," he said.

"That's right. I also invited the church elders. No one knew why I'd called them together, except perhaps the boys themselves. I doubt they believed I would speak about such things, but I did. It was very painful for everyone. At first they didn't want to believe me. A few even called me names and accused me of being . . . well, not in my right mind. I expected that. I just waited, letting them abuse me until one of the boys broke down and admitted the truth. That opened the floodgates."

"I can imagine," Frank said, not wanting to picture that scene at all. "And what did you decide to do?"

"It wasn't my place to decide. That's why I had called the

elders. They understood it was their responsibility to deal with it. There was some arguing at first. No one wanted the boys to be hurt anymore, so we couldn't take it to court and make it public, but we had to punish that man. In the end, they decided that the best they could do was to drive him from the church."

"How did you intend to do that?"

"The elders were going to confront him in front of the entire congregation. They were going to tell him they knew what he was and what he had done, and he was to pack up his things and be gone by Monday evening."

"And you managed to inform everybody in the church of this in less than two days?"

"We each took several families and called on them. I assure you, it wasn't difficult. The word spread even more quickly than we could spread it. Not everyone believed us, of course. Some of the doubters even came to church this morning to stand up for him, but in the end, they were too intimidated by the will of the majority to do anything."

Frank remembered Sarah's claims about gossip and imagined she was right. "Did you plan how people were supposed to act this morning? Mrs. Brandt said nobody sang or gave an offering or went forward for communion."

She thought about this for a moment. "We didn't really plan that part of it. I know I didn't feel like singing hymns of praise this morning, so I sat silent, as did most everyone else. I don't know why no one put money in the offering plate, but probably for the same reason. As for communion, I couldn't bear the thought of taking it from that beast, so I didn't go forward. Everyone else must have felt the same."

"What made you decide to kill Upchurch, Mrs. Evans?" he asked gently.

Her age-softened face colored delicately. "I . . . well, I understood that he could never be brought to justice unless the boys revealed what he had done to them. I couldn't allow that to happen, so . . . so I decided he had to die."

"Seems like that would be a hard decision for a good Christian woman like you, Mrs. Evans," Frank observed.

"I think God will forgive me, Mr. Malloy. He knows it was necessary."

She seemed very certain. Too certain. "How did you do it then?"

"How did I do what?" she asked.

"How did you kill him?"

"You know perfectly well. I put poison in the communion wine," she said indignantly.

"Tell me exactly how you did it—where you got the poison and how you got it in the wine and when you did it," he prodded, still gentle.

"Well, I got the poison from my home. I'm sure most every home in the city has rat poison. We certainly do." Frank supposed everyone had heard Dr. Thomas say that cyanide was found in rat poison. "I brought it to church and—"

"What did you carry it in?" Frank asked.

"What? . . . Oh, my . . . my purse," she said.

Frank looked meaningfully down at the small drawstring bag she carried. "How'd you get a box of rat poison in there?"

"Oh, no, I mean . . . I carried it in a paper sack."

"I see. Now tell me how you got it in the wine."

"I got here early this morning—"

"I suppose your family will vouch for what time you left the house this morning," Frank said.

"Well, yes, of course they will," she said but without much certainty.

"That's good. So you got here early this morning. Did you see anyone in the church?"

"No, no one was around. I went back into the room where they store the communion supplies, and I put the poison into the wine bottle."

"What did you do with the rat poison then?"

"What did I? . . . I . . . I threw it away. That's right. I went out into the alley behind the church and threw it away."

Frank nodded sagely. "I'm surprised at you, Mrs. Evans. You don't seem like the kind of person to take the law into your own hands."

This stung her. "I am the kind of person who does what's necessary, Mr. Malloy. I understood the consequences before I did it, and I am prepared to face them now. You may arrest me."

Frank rubbed his chin thoughtfully. "I'm not in a hurry to lock you up, Mrs. Evans. You don't seem like the kind of person to try to run away. Why don't you go home and pack some clothes and personal items. You'll want to explain things to your daughter and grandson, too. I'll come and get you later."

She blinked in surprise. "That's very kind of you, Mr. Malloy."

"Not at all. You've saved me a lot of work by confessing. I could've spent weeks trying to figure out who killed Upchurch."

She nodded. "That's true. I'm glad to have spared you that trouble. Well, then, I'll be going. When should I expect you?"

"Not until early evening. Have yourself a nice supper at home. Food at The Tombs isn't very good, so it might be your last decent meal. Pack warm clothes, too. The Tombs aren't very warm."

This sobered her, and when she rose from her seat, her

cheeks were pale. "Thank you for being so kind, Mr. Malloy," she said as he showed her out.

"Don't say anything to anyone about this, except your family," he warned her. "This is police business, and we don't want the newspapers involved, do we?"

"Oh, no, of course we don't," she said.

"Would someone see Mrs. Evans home?" he called to the men still loitering. "Whoever takes her home should come right back to answer questions, like everybody else."

Several men hurried forward to assume those duties, and Frank returned to the office to consult with Kelly, closing the door behind him.

"Why did she do that?" Kelly asked. "She didn't kill him anymore than I did."

"Damn, you're good at this, too," Malloy said, echoing Kelly's earlier remark.

"Maybe she carried rat poison to the church, although I don't see how, but she never put it in the wine bottle," Kelly said. "The cabinet was locked."

"And Isaiah said the bottle wasn't even opened when he took it out of the cabinet," Frank remembered.

"Who's she protecting?" Kelly wanted to know.

"Let's see if we can find out. Just in case, go out into the alley and see if you can find a bag of rat poison. I doubt you will, but just in case the real killer might've tossed it there. Then start questioning those men out there to see if anybody saw anything before the service started, like maybe somebody up on the stage near the communion cup. And try to find out if anybody knows who was in Upchurch's office with him."

"What're you going to do?"

"Talk to those other people out there, the minister's wife and Linton. His daughter is the one who was raped, but I don't know what he has to do with this mess. Then I'll help you finish up with the men you haven't gotten to yet. You know what we're looking for."

"Yeah, somebody who wanted him dead and could've put the poison in the cup this morning."

"And find out if anybody passed the word about not taking communion, too."

Frank opened the office door for Kelly, and they almost collided with the woman Dr. Thomas had identified as Mrs. Upchurch.

"I'm Reverend Upchurch's wife, and I need to speak with you immediately," she informed them.

Kelly gave Frank a questioning look. "Go ahead," Frank told him, and ushered Mrs. Upchurch into the chair where Mrs. Evans had sat.

"Did you have something you wanted to tell me, Mrs. Upchurch?" Frank asked as he took the other seat.

"I most certainly do. Don't waste your time questioning anyone else. I'm the one who killed my husband."

SARAH DEARLY WISHED SHE COULD BE WITH MALLOY as he questioned everyone, but she wasn't foolish enough to ask. He'd never allow it, even if he hadn't had that other detective with him. When she saw Mrs. Upchurch volunteering to be questioned, she could stand her inactivity no longer. She left her seat and moved up to where Mr. Linton was sitting all alone.

"May I join you?" she asked, surprising him. He'd been lost in thought.

"Certainly," he said without much enthusiasm.

"How is Grace doing?" she asked to make conversation as she sat down in the pew beside him.

A spasm of pain flickered over his face. "She's fine, I suppose. She doesn't understand what . . . what's going to happen to her, so she's not concerned."

"I guess you and your wife are worrying, though," Sarah said.

"Oh, yes. My wife, well, she's beside herself. We were already concerned about what will become of Grace when we're gone, but now we have the baby to worry about, too."

"Perhaps the child will grow up and take care of Grace when you no longer can," Sarah said.

He smiled sadly. "That's kind of you, Mrs. Brandt, but we know that's not likely. If we just knew . . ." His voice trailed off in embarrassment.

"Who the father is?" she guessed.

"We would never allow him to have anything to do with Grace or the child, of course, but we might make some arrangement for him to provide financially for the child in case it's . . . well, in case it's like Grace," he said, his voice breaking.

"She hasn't given you any more information about it?" Sarah asked as tactfully as she could.

"No. She acts like she doesn't know what we're talking about when we ask her, too. It's like it never happened. I can't believe she could have forgotten such a thing," he added bitterly.

"Shock can do strange things," Sarah said. "She may remember it later, but if she doesn't, you'll just have to consider it a blessing that she doesn't have that horrible memory."

They sat in silence for a while. Sarah tried to think of something less painful to discuss. "I'm surprised you didn't leave when everyone else did," she said finally. "Won't your wife be wondering where you are?"

"I suppose she will, but when I saw Mrs. Evans was staying, I couldn't leave. I had to make sure I set everything straight."

"Do you know something about the murder?" she asked in surprise.

"I do. I know far too much about it, and now I must confess."

FRANK WAS GLAD HE'D SENT KELLY OFF. HE WAS PRETTY sure the man would've laughed out loud. For himself, he managed not to sigh. "What did you say, Mrs. Upchurch?" he asked, just to be sure he hadn't misunderstood.

"I said, I killed my husband. I poisoned him. With rat poison. You can stop this travesty and let everyone else go home. Will you take me straight to jail, or do I have time to get my toothbrush and a change of clothes?"

"There'll be plenty of time for that later," Frank assured her. "First I need to ask you some questions."

"Why? I told you I killed him. What more could you want to know?"

"How you did it, for one thing, and why, for another."

"I did it because I could no longer bear knowing what he was doing to those poor boys," she said impatiently, as if surprised he hadn't already figured that out.

"Did someone from the church tell you what he was doing?"

"Oh, no," she said, surprised. "I've known for a long time, since shortly after I married him almost ten years ago. I was the one who told Mrs. Brandt, and I assume she told you, which is why you questioned Oliver about it."

"If you knew about it for ten years, why didn't you ever go to the police about it yourself?" he asked in amazement.

"I did," she informed him, anger roughening her voice. "Not long after I found out and came to understand exactly what was happening, I tried to report him, but no one believed me. A detective came to question Oliver, but my husband told the man I was crazy, an hysterical female who had been unhinged by the duties of the marriage bed and now I imagined all sorts of perversions in others. After that, Oliver told everyone I wasn't right in the head. How do you get people to believe you when they think you're crazy, Mr. Malloy?"

"Mrs. Brandt believed you," he reminded her.

"She was the first one. I knew she was different the moment I saw her. That's why I told her. I took a chance, but she proved me right."

"Yes, she did. And I believed you, and so did the families of the boys and even the church elders. So why did you have to kill your husband?"

"I didn't know for certain that anyone believed me, not until this morning, when I found out everyone had turned against him."

"How did you find that out?" Frank asked, being as gentle with her as he had been with Mrs. Evans.

"Well, I began to suspect during the service, when everyone was acting so strangely, but I wasn't certain until afterwards, when I heard people talking after Oliver was dead. That's when I realized everyone knew what he'd done."

"I want to make sure I understand, Mrs. Upchurch. You say you were afraid no one believed you and that your husband would just keep molesting those boys, so you killed him."

"Well, yes," she said thoughtfully. "Do you think that's a good enough reason? I have others, if it isn't."

"What others?" Frank asked in amazement.

She smiled mysteriously. "I needed to be a widow, Mr. Malloy, to protect my child."

"Your *child*?" he echoed stupidly. "I thought you didn't have any children."

"I don't, not yet," she said, still smiling. "But I will, in about six months. You see, I couldn't risk having Oliver denounce me. He'd know he wasn't the father, but no one else would. He might have tolerated it, just so he wouldn't have to explain how he knew the child wasn't his, but I couldn't be certain of that. He might have thrown me out or even locked me away in an asylum, and who knows what he would have done with the child? I couldn't take that chance, you see, so I had to kill him."

Frank had to agree, she had a much better motive than Mrs. Evans. "How did you do it, then?" he asked. "Tell me step by step."

"Isn't it obvious? I put the rat poison into the communion cup this morning, before anyone arrived," she said.

"Where did you get it?"

"Everyone has rat poison, Mr. Malloy," she chided him. "If we didn't, the rats would've taken over the city a century ago. I'm sure they even have some here at the church, but I brought mine from home."

"What did you carry it in?"

She hesitated a moment. "I put some into a medicine vial. I got to the church early and waited until Isaiah had set out the communion. Then I poured the poison into the cup."

"What did you do with the vial?"

She needed a moment for this one. "I threw it into the street."

If she had, it would be crushed to dust by now, so his chances of finding it were small. She would know that, too.

"Did you see anyone around the church? Did anyone see you?"

"No, no one," she said.

"Where was your husband?"

"I don't know. As I said, I didn't see anyone."

"Was he in his office?"

"I . . . I didn't notice."

"But you knew he'd already left home to go to the church," he tried.

"Oh, yes. He liked to go over his sermon one last time, so he always left the house very early."

"Mrs. Upchurch, weren't you worried about poisoning the entire congregation?"

"What?" she asked, confused.

"You know that everybody who takes communion drinks out of the same cup, and your husband is always the last to drink. Weren't you worried about poisoning a lot of innocent people?"

"I . . . I told you, *I killed my husband*," she said, angry now. "That's all you need to know. I don't have to explain every little detail to you. Now take me to jail!"

"Aren't you worried about going to jail in your delicate condition?" he asked.

She gave him a pitying look. "They won't keep an expectant mother in jail."

He didn't bother to hide his amazement. "Where did you get an idea like that?"

She stared at him in surprise. "Well, it's just . . . it's common sense! No one would be so inhumane!"

"You'd be amazed how inhumanely they treat murderesses, Mrs. Upchurch, especially women who murder their husbands to keep from being caught in adultery. A jury of twelve men wouldn't have a bit of pity for you. If they started letting women off for killing their husbands, there'd be a whole lot of new widows in the city, and nobody wants that. Now granted, they might not send you to the electric chair, but they'd surely lock you away for the rest of your life and take away your baby. After all, if you're crazy enough to kill your husband, you might kill it, too. Now, do you still want me to arrest you?"

The color had drained from her face, and Frank realized with horror that she looked as though she might well faint. He jumped up and hurried to the door, throwing it open. "Mrs. Brandt!" he shouted. "Will you come in here, please?"

SARAH STARTED AT THE SOUND OF MALLOY CALLING HER name. She looked at Mr. Linton, who had just told her he intended to confess to killing Upchurch, then at Malloy, who sounded desperate. Linton, she supposed, didn't intend to go anywhere, and even if he did, she'd just tell Malloy to go after him.

"Excuse me, please," she said to Linton, and jumped up. She hurried up the aisle and over to the doorway where Malloy stood. "What's wrong?"

"Mrs. Upchurch is . . ." He gestured vaguely, then grabbed her arm and pulled her into the office.

Rachel Upchurch did look ill. "What's wrong?" she asked, hurrying to the woman's side. Sarah took one of her hands. It was cold as ice. "What did you do to her?" she demanded of Malloy.

"Nothing," he claimed. "She's in a family way."

Sarah gaped at him for a few seconds before remembering she had more important things to do. She turned back to her patient. "I don't suppose you have any smelling salts with you?"

Mrs. Upchurch shook her head slightly, but Sarah was glad to see the color slowly returning to her cheeks. She took both of the woman's hands in hers and began to chafe them.

"Take some deep breaths," Sarah advised her. "Malloy, bring that chair over so we can put her feet up."

He did as she instructed, and in another few minutes, Mrs. Upchurch was looking almost normal again.

"What did you say to her?" Sarah demanded of Malloy again when she thought it was safe to take her attention away from her patient.

"Nothing," he said defensively. "She was trying to convince me she killed her husband. She thought she wouldn't go to jail because she's . . . expecting, so I had to tell her different."

Mrs. Upchurch moaned softly.

"Are you all right?" Sarah asked. "Should I call Dr. Thomas in?"

She shook her head.

"Would you like something to drink?" she tried.

"Not communion wine, I hope," Malloy said. Sarah glared at him, but he didn't look the least bit repentant.

"No, I just . . . I'd like to go home, please," Mrs. Upchurch said.

"I thought you wanted me to take you to jail," Malloy said innocently.

Sarah wanted to smack him. "Stop torturing her!"

"She's the one who confessed to murder," he reminded her. "I've got to be sure. Did you really kill your husband, Mrs. Upchurch?"

She raised terrified eyes to him. "No, I didn't. You must believe me. I didn't have anything to do with it!"

"Then why did you say you did?" he asked.

"I . . . I was afraid you'd arrest . . . someone else. I thought . . . I thought they wouldn't punish me because of the baby, so I lied."

"Who did you think I was going to arrest?" he asked. "Who were you protecting?"

The terror drained out of her eyes, and they turned as blank as glass. "If I'm trying to protect him, I'm not likely to tell you who he is, now am I?"

"So it's a man, is it?" he said, pouncing on her slip. "Is it your lover? The father of your child?"

She lifted a hand to her head and moaned again, this time with a theatrical flourish. "I'm really ill, Mrs. Brandt. Would you help me get home?"

Now Sarah had lost sympathy with her, too, but she wasn't going to let on. The woman might confide in her if she thought they were still friends. "Don't worry, I'll take care of her," she told Malloy, hoping he could hear her unspoken message.

He didn't look happy, so she wasn't sure if he did or not.

"I'll take you right home," Sarah said to Rachel.

"Get a couple of the men to go with you in case she faints," Malloy warned.

Sarah helped her to her feet and escorted her to the door. Malloy followed closely behind. When they opened the door, they found Isaiah standing right outside, looking distraught.

"Are you all right, Mrs. Upchurch?" he asked.

She gave him a sweet smile. "I'm fine, Isaiah. Mrs. Brandt is going to walk home with me."

"I'll go, too, in case you need help. You don't look so good."

"Ever the charmer," she teased, although he didn't seem to understand.

Sarah turned back to Malloy. "I'll take care of her," she

repeated more meaningfully this time, and this time he nodded as if he really understood.

FRANK WATCHED THEM MAKING THEIR WAY TO THE SIDE entrance of the church, which must be closer to the manse, then he looked out to see who remained to be questioned. Mr. Linton had already risen and was making his way to the front of the church, but Frank wasn't quite ready for him yet.

"I need to ask Dr. Thomas a few more questions first, if you don't mind, Mr. Linton," he told him.

The old doctor rose stiffly from his seat near the body. The coroner was just finishing up, and his assistants were loading Upchurch onto a stretcher. Dr. Thomas made his way around them and over to the office. Frank made him as comfortable as he could.

"What is it you need to know, because I don't know much more about cyanide than what I already told you?" he asked.

"I'm going to have the wine in the bottle Isaiah used to fill the cup tested, but near as I can tell, there isn't any poison in it. Isaiah said it wasn't opened when he took it out of the cabinet this morning. He filled the cup from the bottle after he opened it, and it appears that's about how much is missing from the bottle, so he seems to be telling the truth about that."

"So the poison was put in the cup, after the wine was poured into it."

"Or just before, but we do know it was only put in the cup. That means just about anyone could've done it once it was set out on the table in front of the church."

"Does that mean you don't think young Isaiah did it?" the doctor asked.

"I'm still not sure, but there's one more thing I need to know before I go any further. Suppose people had come up this morning to take communion and had drunk from that cup. Would they all have died?"

The doctor rubbed his cheek as he considered his answer. "I'm not an expert, so I don't know how much cyanide it takes to kill someone. You'd have to check with a chemist to be sure, but I think it probably depends on the person and his size and physical condition."

"You mean a large man would need more than a child, for instance."

"That's right, and someone in poor health might need less than someone in good health, although I'm just guessing."

"What if everybody took a sip from the cup, though. What would happen, generally speaking?"

"Again, I'm guessing, but I suspect that taking just a sip might not be fatal to many people. It would probably make a good many of them sick, but only some of them would die, perhaps only a few, and maybe not any at all."

"The weaker ones would be the ones who'd probably die," Frank said.

"That's right. But not even all of them, by any means."

Frank nodded and mulled over what he'd learned.

"What are you thinking, Detective?" the doctor asked.

"Right now, I'm thinking that none of this makes any sense at all."

"I doubt that murder often does," he said sympathetically. "Is Mrs. Upchurch ill? Should I go to see her?"

"Mrs. Brandt is a midwife," Frank said. "That's why I called for her, and if she needs help, I'm sure she'll send for it."

The doctor's bushy white eyebrows rose. "A midwife? Does Mrs. Upchurch need a midwife?"

Frank saw no reason to keep it a secret. "She will next summer."

"Ahh, I see," he said. "That's too bad, after all these years, that it had to come now. . . . Oh, well, I don't suppose you'd want a man like Upchurch raising a child, now would you?"

"No, you wouldn't," Frank agreed.

"Did you have any more questions?" the doctor asked.

"No, and I'm sorry to keep you here so long. You can go home now. If I need to know anything else, I'll find you."

The doctor rose from his chair. "Good luck to you, young man, although I can't say I'm too anxious for this killer in particular to be caught. If you ask me, he did the world a favor."

Frank had to agree. He hadn't been too eager to catch the killer either until innocent people started confessing to protect him . . . or her. If he didn't find the real killer soon, one of those people might end up in jail.

Wearily, he followed Dr. Thomas out and saw Mr. Linton, who was now sitting on one of the front pews, all alone. He jumped up as Frank and the doctor came out.

"Are you ready for me now, Mr. Malloy?" he asked.

"Yes, come on in," Frank said, wondering what Linton could have to offer. Maybe he'd seen someone at the communion table, acting suspicious, but that was probably too much to hope for.

"Have a seat," Frank said as he closed the office door, but Linton simply stood, staring at Frank with his hands clenched at his sides and desperation in his eyes.

"Mr. Malloy, I have a confession to make," he said.

Frank's heart sank. The last thing he wanted was to lock up Grace's father for murder. And what possible motive could he have had for killing the minister?

Before he could even think of a response, the door behind

them burst open and a frail-looking woman flung herself into the room. Her bonnet was crooked and her face flushed, as if she'd been running. "Are you the policeman?" she asked Frank breathlessly.

"Yes, I—"

"I'm Hazel York, Mrs. Evans's daughter. I know she told you she poisoned Reverend Upchurch, but she's just trying to protect me. I'm the killer, sir. You need look no further."

13

ISAIAH WAS KIND ENOUGH TO FETCH RACHEL AND Sarah's coats, and he let Rachel lean on him while they walked the short distance to the manse. At first Sarah had been merely grateful for his help in getting Rachel home, but after a while she began to realize he was much more concerned for Rachel's well-being than he should have been.

"Are you sure you don't need the doctor, because I can get him for you?" he asked for the third time.

"You're wearing me out, Isaiah," Rachel scolded. "I told you, I'm fine. I think it finally hit me that Oliver is really dead when I was in with that detective. I realized I'm quite alone in the world. For a moment, I was quite overcome, but I'm recovered now."

"You aren't alone," Isaiah insisted. Then he glanced at

Sarah, as if suddenly remembering her presence. "I mean, you've got lots of friends."

"Don't be silly, dear boy. I have no friends at all, but I shall be all right. Mrs. Brandt is a widow, and she has managed to make her way in the world, haven't you, Mrs. Brandt?"

"I . . . yes, I have," Sarah said in surprise.

"Then I shall, too."

Sarah watched the careful way Isaiah helped Rachel up her front porch steps. She tried to imagine any other schoolboy of her acquaintance being half so solicitous to a woman old enough to be his mother, and she couldn't, not at all. His care for Rachel was unnatural, just as her husband's abuse of him had been. Could that experience have changed him so drastically, or had something else changed him?

Sarah remembered the first time she'd seen the two of them. She'd gotten the impression Rachel was *flirting* with Isaiah. That's the very word she had used to describe the incident to Malloy, too. At the time she hadn't imagined it could have gone beyond that but now . . . now Rachel Upchurch was pregnant with a baby that wasn't her husband's, and she'd just tried to confess to a murder to protect someone else, someone who was probably her lover, and who must have had a good reason to want Upchurch dead.

Sarah noticed Isaiah put his hand on the middle of Rachel's back as he helped her up the stairs, a gesture that was inappropriately intimate. His head nearly touched hers as he leaned over to catch her every word. Had they been an old married couple, Sarah would have smiled at his obvious devotion. Instead, it made her heart turn cold in her chest.

"Mrs. Upchurch," she said before she could think better of it, "that was foolish of you to confess to killing your husband."

"*What?*" Isaiah cried in surprise. His head came up, and he turned to Sarah in amazement. "What did you say?"

"Nothing, Isaiah," Rachel said sharply, anger bringing the color to her face.

"I said, she shouldn't have confessed to killing her husband," Sarah said determinedly. "She could go to prison for the rest of her life."

He turned on Rachel. "Why did you do a thing like that?"

Rachel gave Sarah a look that should have raised blisters, but when she turned back to Isaiah, her voice was gentle and pleading. "We can discuss this later. Don't worry, everything is fine."

"No, it's not fine," he insisted. "I can't let you go to prison!"

His eyes wild, he bolted back down the steps, nearly knocking Sarah over in his haste, and sprinted toward the church.

"Isaiah, don't!" Rachel screamed after him, but he didn't stop. She was clutching the railing for support. "I have to go after him," she said desperately. "I have to stop him!"

"Did he kill your husband?" Sarah asked baldly.

Rachel turned to her, her face twisted with rage. "You! I thought I could trust you, and now look what you've done! That poor boy's life will be ruined!"

"Isn't it a bit late for you to worry about him?" Sarah asked. "Some would say you were the one who ruined him."

A gust of wind whipped around their skirts and nearly knocked Rachel over. She was weeping now, the tears leaking out of her eyes unnoticed as she stared after the boy. "I've got to stop him," she said weakly.

"No, you don't," Sarah said, taking pity on her, in spite of herself. "Come inside."

"But that policeman, he'll arrest him," she protested. "I can't let him go to jail!"

"If he's innocent, Mr. Malloy won't arrest him."

"How on earth will he know? And what if he's *not* innocent?" she asked in despair.

"Then God help him," Sarah replied, taking her arm and directing her toward the door.

"HAZEL, WHAT ARE YOU SAYING?" LINTON DEMANDED.

"This doesn't concern you, Wil," Hazel York said, laying a hand over her heart as she fought to catch her breath.

Both men instinctively went to her. Between the two of them, they escorted her to the nearest chair and sat her down. Her color had faded, and she looked as if she could barely breathe.

"Should we get Dr. Thomas back here?" Frank asked Linton.

"I don't need a doctor," Mrs. York insisted. "I just need a minute to recover."

"Hazel, you know you're supposed to avoid exerting yourself," Linton said.

"I had to exert myself," she informed him. "I can't let my mother go to prison for killing Reverend Upchurch." She looked up at Frank, her eyes swimming with tears. "You can't put my mother in prison. She didn't kill Reverend Upchurch. I did! She was only trying to protect me when she confessed."

Frank squeezed the bridge of his nose to ward off a threatening headache. "Mr. Linton, could I ask you to go back out and wait for me a little longer?"

"I won't leave Hazel alone," he said. "She obviously doesn't know what she's saying."

"I know exactly what I'm saying," she informed him. "Please leave us so I can get this over with."

"She can't know what she's saying," he argued to Malloy. "She thinks her mother confessed to killing Upchurch!"

"She did," Frank told him.

Linton's mouth dropped open.

"Tell me, Mr. Linton," Frank said. "Were you going to confess to killing him, too?"

"Me?" he said incredulously. "No, no, of course not!"

"Then what *were* you going to confess?"

"I . . . I'm afraid I played a role in what happened here this morning, and I wanted to explain—"

"Good," Frank said, cutting him off and slapping Linton on the back in a friendly gesture. "Then you won't mind stepping out for a few minutes while I talk with Mrs. York, will you?" Giving him no choice, he fairly shoved Linton out the door and slammed it shut behind him.

When he turned back to Mrs. York, she seemed to have recovered a bit. At least she didn't look like she was going drop over anymore. "Can I get you something, Mrs. York? I don't want you to make yourself sick."

"The only thing that will make me feel better is if you allow me to clear my conscience," she said.

Obligingly, Frank pulled a chair over to her and sat down. "All right, Mrs. York, tell me your story."

She stared at him uncertainly for a long moment. "What do you want me to say?"

Once again, Frank managed not to sigh. "Tell me the truth. Tell me what happened."

"Well, I . . . I couldn't let him get away with what he'd done to my son."

"You're Percy's mother, aren't you?"

The tears welled in her eyes again. "Yes," she whispered.

"He's a fine boy," Frank said. "You should be very proud."

"I gave him to that monster," she said as the tears spilled down her cheeks. "It's all my fault."

"He tricked you. He tricked all of you, not just the boys. He was a liar and a good one. You don't have anything to be ashamed of. You couldn't have known."

She covered her mouth and squeezed her eyes shut to stop the tears.

Frank waited, hating the feeling of helplessness he always got when he saw a woman cry. She fought hard for control and eventually won. She dug in her purse and pulled out a handkerchief. Dabbing at her eyes, she apologized for her emotional outburst.

Frank ignored the apology. "Why did you kill Upchurch, Mrs. York?"

"Because of what he did to my boy," she said indignantly. "Why else?"

"You weren't happy that they were going to run him out of the church?"

"No, that wasn't enough of a punishment for what he'd done. He'd still be out there, and other boys would be in danger. Someone had to stop him."

"Where did you get the poison?"

"I got it from home. I put some in a paper bag and carried it to church. I saw the communion cup at the front of the church, and I put the poison in it. Then I threw the bag out in the alley."

She looked very satisfied with her story. It was, of course, the same one he'd elicited from her mother, and it was just as false.

"Did you know that nobody was going to take communion this morning?"

"What do you mean?"

"I mean, did everybody decide ahead of time not to go up this morning?"

"No," she said, then caught herself, suspicious that she'd been tricked. "At least, no one said anything to me about it."

"So you expected the people in the congregation to go up and drink out of the cup you'd put poison in."

"Yes . . . I mean, no," she said, laying her hand on her heart again. "I . . . I didn't think of that."

"We didn't find a bag of rat poison in the alley, Mrs. York." He wasn't sure of that, but Kelly would certainly have returned to tell him if he had.

"What? I . . . Maybe it blew away," she tried.

"Was there any poison left in it when you threw it away?"

"Yes . . . No . . . I . . . I don't remember." She was starting to cry again.

"It doesn't seem very responsible of you to throw a bag with poison in it out into the alley. Some poor dog might've found it. Or a child."

"I . . . I didn't think of that."

"You didn't do it, either, did you?"

She stared at him, fear darkening her eyes. "I did! I killed him. I swear I did."

"Why are you wasting my time, Mrs. York? Have you considered what would happen to you if I believe you and put you in jail?"

She swallowed loudly. "I know what would happen. I would go to prison. I have a weak heart, Detective. I wouldn't live very long in prison. That's why my mother is taking the blame for this. She thinks she's protecting me, but I won't live much longer in any case. If I'm dead and she's in prison, what will happen to Percy? That's why I can't let her take the blame."

"Does she know you're here?"

"I . . . I don't think so. I didn't tell her I was coming."

"Mrs. York, your mother didn't kill Upchurch, and neither did you. Your mother was trying to protect someone, maybe the real killer or maybe somebody she thought was the real killer. Do you have any idea who that could be?"

"I . . . No, I don't think so," she replied uncertainly.

"Could Percy have done it?" he asked baldly.

"Oh, no!" she cried in alarm. "He was at home this morning. He didn't want to come to church, and we wouldn't have let him, even if he had. Our maid can vouch for him."

Frank believed her. She wasn't a good enough liar to fool him. "Could she have been protecting you? Could she have thought you did it?"

Mrs. York stared at him for a long moment. "Oh, dear, she might have. I said something unkind about Upchurch—I don't even remember what it was—right after he died. We were standing right over his body, and Mother looked at me so oddly, almost as if she was afraid of something," she added in dismay.

That was it then, Frank decided. They'd been trying to protect each other. "Whatever her reason was, she didn't convince me she's guilty, so you don't have to try to convince me you're guilty to protect her. Go home, Mrs. York, and take care of your son."

"Oh, Mr. Malloy!" she cried and began to sob.

Frank wondered how she would've reacted if he'd arrested her. He didn't have much time to think about it, though, because the door burst open again, and this time it was Isaiah Wilkins.

He'd been going to say something he probably considered very important, but when he saw Mrs. York sobbing her heart out, he stopped dead.

"What did you do to her?" he demanded.

"Nothing," Frank snapped, getting tired of being falsely accused of abusing women. "Didn't anybody ever teach you to knock?"

"I . . . I had to tell you something," he stammered, still looking at Mrs. York, who was making an effort to stop crying.

"Let me guess. You killed Upchurch," Frank said.

"Well, yeah . . . I mean, yes, sir, I did," he said with some amazement.

This sobered Mrs. York instantly. "Isaiah!" She looked at Malloy in confusion. "Could she have been protecting *him*?"

Frank doubted it, but Isaiah said, "That's right, she was, but nobody needs to protect me. I can take my own punishment. That's why I'm here."

"Oh, Mr. Malloy, what will happen to him?" she asked in despair.

"That's up to a jury to decide, Mrs. York. Do you feel able to get yourself home? There's probably some men from the church still here, if you need help."

"Perhaps I'll wait for Mr. Linton to be finished. He passes my house on his way home, so I could go with him."

"That's a fine idea," Frank said, escorting her to the door. "Please tell him I'll be with him as soon as I can. And tell your mother I'm sorry, but I won't be calling on her this evening after all."

Mrs. York smiled wanly. "I'm sure she won't be too disappointed. Thank you very much, Detective." She turned to Isaiah. "You have many friends here. We won't desert you."

Isaiah blinked a few times, as if to clear tears from his eyes, and he nodded solemnly in reply.

When she was gone, Frank closed the door behind her and turned back to Isaiah. "Have a seat, young man."

The boy frowned, as if he thought the offer was some sort of trick, but when Frank took a seat, he followed suit.

"Now tell me what you forgot to tell me when I questioned you before," Frank said, the edge of annoyance sharp in his voice.

"I didn't forget," he said belligerently. "I just . . . I didn't want you to know, is all. I didn't want to go to prison."

"Or the electric chair," Frank said blandly. "Don't forget, murderers usually get to sit in Old Sparky."

Isaiah blanched, but to his credit, he didn't falter. "I don't want no woman taking the blame for something I did."

"That's noble of you, son. You do owe Mrs. Evans a debt, though."

"Mrs. Evans? Why?" He seemed genuinely puzzled.

"For confessing to the murder to protect you," Frank said impatiently.

"She did?" Now he was flabbergasted.

Now Frank was confused. "Who did you think had confessed for you?"

"Mrs. Upchurch," he replied. "Mrs. Brandt said so."

"Mrs. Brandt said Mrs. Upchurch confessed to protect you?" Frank asked, still confused.

Isaiah frowned. "No, she just said Mrs. Upchurch confessed. I knew she didn't really do it because . . . because *I* did it," he realized, quite satisfied with his logic. "So I had to come and tell you, so you wouldn't arrest her."

Frank didn't like the way this conversation was going. He and Sarah had been certain Rachel Upchurch was trying to protect her lover. Isaiah Wilkins couldn't possibly be her lover.

Or could he?

"That's very gentlemanly of you, Isaiah," Frank said, using the word he knew Upchurch had always used.

Isaiah winced a bit, but he didn't drop his gaze. "It would be worse than ungentlemanly to let a lady go to prison for something she didn't do, wouldn't it?"

"Oh, yes," Frank said. "That's why I'm careful to find out who's really guilty before I arrest anybody. Now tell me, how did you kill Upchurch?"

"With rat poison," he said confidently.

Frank silently damned Dr. Thomas for voicing his theory so publicly. "Where did you get the rat poison?"

This stumped him, but only for a few seconds. "From here. We keep some downstairs in the church kitchen. The rats come around even though there's not much food here."

"Where do you keep it?"

"It's in the kitchen pantry, on the top shelf. I can show you," he offered, starting to rise.

"Maybe later," Frank said. "How do you happen to know so much about the rat poison here at the church?"

"Because I put it out a few times, whenever Reverend Upchurch . . ." He hesitated, his lip curling in distaste for a moment. "Whenever he saw rats, he'd tell me to put it out."

"All right," Frank said, satisfied with that explanation. "When did you put the poison in the cup?"

He had to think about this one, too. "I got the idea when I was getting the wine out this morning. I figured it would be a good way to kill him, and nobody would ever know it was me that did it."

Frank nearly winced at his naïveté, but he soldiered on. "How did you get the poison in the cup?"

"I . . . I took the cup downstairs and put some of the poison in it," he said. "Then I took the cup back upstairs and put the wine in it and set up communion like I usually did."

"Weren't you worried about the people who were going to come up for communion that morning?" Frank asked.

"What do you mean?"

"I mean, what made you think Upchurch was the only one who'd drink out of that cup?"

"I . . . I wouldn't've let them," he said, his eyes wide as he realized what could have happened. "They were all so mad at him, why would they want to take communion from him? I was pretty sure they wouldn't come up, and I didn't drink any, either. He was the only one who did."

Frank nearly sighed. That was the trouble with honest people. None of them could lie worth a damn. "If I look downstairs, will I find the rat poison where you left it?"

"Yes. That's where it always is."

"Let's go downstairs now, and you can show me."

Mr. Linton rose to his feet as they walked through the sanctuary, but Frank had to ask him to be patient just a bit longer. Downstairs, they passed one of the churchmen waiting in the hallway to be interviewed by Kelly. He ignored the man's curious stare as he and Isaiah found the kitchen.

The room was spotlessly clean. If rats indeed visited here, they were surely disappointed. Isaiah went straight for the two-door wooden cabinet at the far end of the room and pulled the doors open. Inside were tins of various sizes, obviously holding whatever supplies a church kitchen needed. Everything was arranged in neat rows across the front of each shelf. The boy looked up at the top shelf where one slot stood empty. It looked like a missing tooth in an otherwise perfect smile.

"That's funny," he murmured. He stood on tiptoe and reached up to feel around in the empty spot, to see if the box could have gotten pushed back. "It's not there," he said in surprise.

"When was the last time you saw it there?" Frank asked.

"I don't know. A couple weeks ago, I guess," he said, then caught himself. "Until this morning, I mean."

"So you saw it there this morning, but now it's gone."

"Yeah, I mean, yes, sir, that's right. I saw it this morning. . . . I mean I *used* it this morning and put it right back there, but now it's gone."

"Maybe the killer took it," Frank suggested.

Isaiah stared at him blankly for a moment, and then he got mad. "Stop trying to trick me."

"Why would I try to trick you into saying you didn't kill Upchurch?" Frank asked quite reasonably.

"Because you don't like Mrs. Upchurch, and you want to get her in trouble. Nobody likes her, and people are always saying mean things about her, but they're wrong. She's not like they say. She's not crazy."

"What is she?"

"What do you mean?" he asked suspiciously.

"I mean is she the kind of woman who seduces young boys? That would make her no better than her husband."

His face flushed scarlet, and his eyes blazed with fury. "You don't know anything about it. She loves me!"

"And you love her, too, I guess."

"Yes, I do," he admitted proudly.

"So does that make what you did with her all right?" Frank challenged.

"More right than what Upchurch did to me!" he cried. "He was the one who told me what to do with the girl I loved. He said you should only do it with somebody you loved. That was important."

"So you got your revenge by doing it with his wife."

"No, it wasn't like that! It wasn't revenge!"

"What was it then?"

"I told you, I love her!"

Frank waited a few moments for Isaiah's anger to burn down to a simmer. "Did Upchurch tell you that what you were doing with the girl you love could make a baby?"

He was puzzled again. "No."

"Well, it can."

He didn't seem too concerned. "Only if you're married. Only married people can have babies."

Frank nearly groaned aloud at this further example of the innocence of privileged youth. "Did Upchurch tell you that?"

"He didn't have to. Everybody knows it!"

Frank rubbed his forehead. Plainly, the boy didn't know why Mrs. Upchurch had been so eager for his affections or that she was now carrying his child. With any luck, he'd never find out, either.

"Do you believe me now that Mrs. Upchurch didn't kill her husband?" the boy asked when Frank didn't reply.

"Yes," Frank said wearily.

"Are you going to arrest me now?"

Frank looked into his eyes, still so innocent even after two people he'd trusted had betrayed him so mercilessly. "Not just yet. Because you're still a child, I can't arrest you without notifying your mother," he lied.

The boy's face crumbled. "Oh, I didn't think about her."

"You should have. She loves you more than anyone in this world, and this is going to break her heart."

"Oh, God," he breathed, covering his face with both hands.

"Maybe you'd like to spend a little time with her before I come to arrest you," Frank suggested. "Don't tell her what you've done, though. Just be nice to her and tell her you love her and spend the rest of the day with her."

He lowered his hands to reveal red-rimmed eyes. "I will.

I'll do that! Thank you, Mr. Malloy. I'll never forget you for this."

Without a backward glance, he ran out. Frank heard his feet pounding on the stairs as he raced up and out to the street. Wearily and much more slowly, Frank followed. In the sanctuary, he found Mrs. York still keeping Mr. Linton company.

"Sorry you had to wait so long," Frank told him. "Come on into the office."

Maybe, just maybe, Frank thought, Linton has the missing piece that would solve this puzzle.

Or maybe he didn't.

Sarah made Rachel Upchurch lie down on her chaise while she fixed some tea, then took it to her.

"He didn't kill Oliver," Rachel argued between sips. "He couldn't have."

"Why not?" Sarah challenged. "He's obviously in love with you, and he has good reason to believe you love him, too."

"What do you mean by that?" Rachel said, trying to sound affronted.

"I mean he's the father of your baby, which means you seduced him. To him, that would be proof that you love him."

"I didn't seduce him," she insisted. "I didn't have to. Oliver took care of that."

"Are you saying your husband brought the two of you together? That he knew about it?" Sarah scoffed.

"No, of course not, but he's the one who filled their heads with all that nonsense. He told them he was just teaching them how to make love to a woman. I never realized that until Isaiah told me. He'd always liked me, you see, right from the first, and I encouraged him. It annoyed Oliver when any of his boys paid me attention, so naturally, it gave me pleasure."

"So when you found out Isaiah was interested in you, you used him to get the child your husband wouldn't give you." Sarah didn't bother to disguise the contempt she felt.

"It wasn't like that . . . not entirely," she amended when she saw Sarah's skepticism. "Isaiah had finally realized that Oliver had lied to him, and I think he needed to prove to himself that he was a man. The only way he could do that was by being with a woman, and being with Oliver's wife would be the ultimate . . ."

"Revenge?" Sarah offered when Rachel hesitated. "That's a romantic reason to start an affair."

"You must understand," she pleaded. "He loves me. No one had ever really loved me like that before. It was intoxicating."

"I'm sure it was, but that still doesn't excuse what you did to him. What's going to happen when he realizes you lied to him just like your husband did?"

She covered her eyes for a moment, as if she really did feel the guilt for what she had done. When she looked up again, her voice was flat with despair. "He may never know it if he ends up in prison. Dear heaven, why would he have killed Oliver?"

"Maybe he was thinking about marrying his widow," Sarah suggested.

To her credit, Rachel began to cry. "What have I done?"

Sarah had no answer for her.

"Now, what is it you've been waiting so long to tell me, Mr. Linton?" Frank asked.

Linton looked uneasily around the minister's office. "I

came by this morning early, before anyone else was at the church, to see Upchurch."

Ah, Upchurch's mystery visitor. "What did you want to see him about?"

Linton had folded his hands in his lap, and now he began to twist them. "I didn't sleep at all last night, after I heard what Upchurch had done to those boys. I didn't even know a man could . . . could use boys like that."

"Not many people do," Frank said, wishing he was one of them.

"I kept thinking about Grace and what happened to her. I've been trying to figure out who could have done it ever since we found out. I keep coming back to the fact that if a man had attacked her, she would've told us. I know if he'd frightened her or hurt her, she would've told us. Then I remembered what you'd said, that maybe the man who did it was someone she knew and liked and maybe she hadn't been frightened at all."

"The way the boys weren't frightened of Upchurch," Frank offered.

"That's right. Until I heard about that, I could never have imagined such a thing could have happened to Grace, too."

"Why did that make you go see Upchurch?"

Linton nervously smoothed his lapels. "I wanted . . . I had to find out if he'd done the same thing to Grace that he did to those boys. She would've trusted him like they did, and she would've believed any lie he told her."

"Did you ask him outright?"

Linton nodded stiffly.

"What did he say?"

"At first I didn't let him know I'd heard about the boys, so he denied it. He was horrified that I could think him guilty of such a thing. He even hinted that he was going to mention my accusation to the church elders. He wanted to be sure someone knew that he'd been falsely accused in case I decided to start rumors about him."

"That took a lot of gall," Frank said in disgust.

"I thought so, too, and that's why I told him it wouldn't do him any good to complain to the elders because they knew—and everybody else did, too—what he'd been doing with those boys he pays so much attention to. I told him the boys had exposed him for what he was."

"What did he say then?"

"He was angry at first. He called me a liar, but I didn't back down, and pretty soon, he realized I was telling the truth. Then he started to look . . . afraid."

"Afraid?" Frank wished he'd seen it. He wanted Upchurch to suffer for what he'd done, even if it had only been for a little while. "What do you think he was afraid of?"

Linton had to think about this. "I'm not sure. He must have known that no one would tolerate him as our minister another day, but he'd also know the scandal would ruin him. He'd lose his livelihood and even his house—the church owns the manse, you see. He might never get another position, either."

"Did he say anything about his fears to you?"

Linton shook his head. "I was too angry to sit and listen, even if he'd tried. I just told him we'd all make sure he paid for what he'd done to those boys, and then I left."

"When was this?"

"I'm not sure exactly. I didn't check my watch, and I don't remember hearing any clocks striking, but it was at least a half-hour before the service started, maybe longer."

"Did you notice if the communion things had been set out yet when you left?"

"I'm afraid I didn't. I was in a hurry and didn't pay any attention. Does it matter?"

"Probably not, unless you poisoned Upchurch."

Linton smiled sadly. "I can't help you there, and I'm afraid I'm not very eager to see the real killer caught, either."

"We're pretty sure Upchurch isn't the one who . . . who hurt Grace," Frank assured him. "He doesn't seem to like females at all."

"Even if he isn't, he deserves to burn in hell for what he did to those boys."

"There's not many would disagree with you, but I've got to find the killer to keep some innocent person from going to prison for it."

"What do you mean?"

"I mean just about everybody I've questioned so far has confessed to the murder except you."

Linton's eyes widened in amazement. "I knew Hazel—Mrs. York—had confessed, of course, and she told me she did it to protect her mother, who had also confessed. May I ask who else?"

"Mrs. Upchurch and Isaiah Wilkins."

"Oh, my!"

"I don't think any of them did it, either, which is why I've got to find the real killer. Please try to remember, Mr. Linton. Did Upchurch say anything else? Did you see anybody else in the church when you were leaving?"

His brow wrinkled as he concentrated. "I know I didn't see anyone. I was glad of it, because I was very upset, and I didn't want to have to explain why to anyone. We'd wanted to surprise him, you see. He wasn't supposed to know anything was wrong until they confronted him during the service."

Frank felt the first hope he'd had all day. "So he knew even before the service started that he'd been exposed."

"Yes, he did, thanks to my impulsiveness. Is that important?" he asked when he saw Frank's expression.

"It could be. Let me ask you something else. Did anyone instruct you not to go forward for communion this morning?"

"No," he said, frowning. "I hadn't even thought of it until I saw the table set when I came back for the service. I remember thinking I couldn't take communion from that man, but I didn't say it to anyone else, and no one mentioned it to me, either. I'm sure everyone felt the same way, though, which is why no one did."

"Thank you, Mr. Linton. You've been a big help."

"I have? In what way?"

"I'll explain it all to you when I'm finished investigating. In the meantime, would you see Mrs. York home and then you can enjoy the rest of your day."

He rose, still looking uncertain. "Are you sure that's all I can do?"

"Very sure."

"Good luck to you, then, Mr. Malloy."

"Thanks. I'm going to need it."

14

WHEN SHE GOT BACK TO THE CHURCH AFTER LEAVING Rachel Upchurch wallowing in her guilt, Sarah found Malloy in Upchurch's office alone. He didn't look happy, but then he apparently hadn't taken anyone off to The Tombs, either.

"Did Isaiah do it?" she asked.

"No," he said wearily. "And neither did Mrs. Upchurch, Mrs. Evans, or Mrs. York."

"Mrs. Evans and Mrs. York?" Sarah echoed in surprise. "Did they confess, too?"

"Yeah, Mrs. York was trying to protect her mother, who was trying to protect her, near as I can figure."

"Rachel Upchurch was trying to protect Isaiah. She thought he must've done it because he was the one who set up the communion table, I guess, and because he's in love with her and might've wanted her to be a widow, although I don't think he knows about the baby. Rachel admitted that he's the father."

"I figured, and I'm *sure* he doesn't know. He doesn't even know that what they did makes babies," he said in exasperation. "Even still, he confessed to protect her, but he didn't do it, either."

"How can you be sure?" she asked, taking the chair the suspects had used.

"The same reason I knew all of them were lying. See, all they knew was what happened. They knew nobody from the congregation went forward to take communion, and Upchurch was the only one who drank from the cup. They also knew the wine was poisoned with rat poison, thanks to Dr. Thomas, who told them. It's easy to figure out that the cup was sitting there for a while with nobody around, and somebody put the poison in it during that time."

"So?"

"So they all said they put rat poison in the cup to kill him."

"Then how do you know they're lying?"

"Because," he said, rubbing both hands over his face. "First of all, none of them knew that nobody was going to take communion this morning."

"I thought they must have decided it ahead of time."

"So did I, but they didn't, or at least nobody I talked to had heard anything about it. So as far as they knew, a lot of people would've drunk from the cup before Upchurch, and according to Doc Thomas, none of them would've gotten enough to be a fatal dose unless they happened to be elderly or sick already. That goes for Upchurch, too, who usually would only have taken a sip like everybody else."

"That doesn't make poisoning the communion cup a very reliable way of killing Upchurch then," she realized.

"Right, and then you've got the problem with the rat poison."

"What problem is that?"

"If they wanted to kill Upchurch, why would somebody bring rat poison from home to put in the communion cup that everybody in the church might drink out of? The killer might not even have known that a little sip wouldn't necessarily be fatal. He'd be putting the whole congregation at risk."

"You're right," Sarah agreed, trying to put herself in the killer's place. "Bringing poison from home would require planning ahead, and if you thought about it at all, you'd know it was a stupid idea. Did everybody claim they'd brought the poison from home?"

"Everybody except Isaiah. He said he used the poison they keep downstairs in the church kitchen, but when he took me down to show me where it was kept, it wasn't there."

"Maybe he got rid of it somehow."

"No, he was surprised it wasn't there. He claimed he'd used it this morning and put it back on the shelf. Since I don't believe he used it, that means the killer might have and then not put it away again."

"Then it's probably still here in the church somewhere."

"Maybe. Or maybe it disappeared along with the real killer."

He sounded discouraged. Sarah had seldom seen him discouraged. "You could give up," she suggested. "A lot of murderers are never caught, and in this case—"

"I can't take that chance. Too many people already know what went on here today. What if the newspapers find out four people confessed and the police didn't arrest anybody?" Sarah knew the newspapers would love a story like that. It would sell thousands of copies. "I'd be out of a job, and they'd arrest the wrong person just to close the case."

He was right, and they both knew it. Sarah sighed, and they sat in silence for a few minutes while she tried to think of something to help or at least something to say to make him feel better. Before she could, he turned to her and said, "I've been trying to remember the last time I had a case where somebody was poisoned by cyanide, but I can't."

"Do you see a lot of poisonings?"

"I get my share, between murders and suicides, but they're usually arsenic. In fact, I thought that's what rat poison was."

"It's odd you should say that. I was thinking the same thing when Dr. Thomas told you cyanide was in rat poison. I'm certain every rat poison I've ever used has been arsenic."

"Wait a minute, what he really said was that it's in *some* rat poisons."

"That's right, he did!" she remembered. "If it's only in some of them, then all we have to do is find out who has the right kind, the kind with cyanide, and we'll probably find the real killer!"

He gave her one of his looks that told her this wasn't a good idea. "Do you suggest we go door to door in the city until we find somebody with the right kind?"

"Don't be ridiculous, but we could check the families in the church, or at least the ones who were here today. You have a list of the names. You could start with the people who confessed, to make sure they're eliminated, then go from there."

She could see that he thought this was a good idea but didn't want to admit it. "Do you know how long that would take?"

"Most of the people live right here in this neighborhood. You could do it in a few hours."

"Do what?" Kelly asked from the doorway. Sarah was happy to see he didn't look as irreverent as he had this morning. She hadn't thought he was taking the case seriously enough earlier.

"Did you find out anything useful?" Malloy asked him.

"No, just that everybody agrees they didn't decide ahead of time not to take communion. What about the lady that confessed?"

"Which one?" Malloy asked sarcastically.

Kelly frowned. "The old one who confessed to us out there," he said, pointing in the direction of the sanctuary.

"She didn't do it, and neither did anybody else who confessed."

"How many did you get?" he asked in wonder.

"Four, I think that's a record for me. Did you find any trace of the bag of poison Mrs. Evans said she threw outside?"

"No, and not inside, either. Somebody said you took that boy down to the kitchen."

"He claimed they keep rat poison down there, but it wasn't in its usual place, even though he claimed he'd put it back there when he was finished with it."

"You ever know a boy to put something back where it was supposed to go?" Kelly asked.

Malloy smiled a bit. "How do you think I knew he was lying in the first place?"

Sarah cleared her throat. "You still have plenty of time to check people's homes this afternoon," she reminded him.

"Check people's homes for what?" Kelly asked, turning back to Malloy.

"Mrs. Brandt reminded me that most rat poison is arsenic, not cyanide."

"I thought the doc said it was rat poison that killed him."

"He said that cyanide killed him, and that it's in *some* kinds of rat poison. If we check each family in the church to see what kind they have, then we can narrow down the list of suspects to those who have the right kind."

Kelly made a face. Plainly, this was not how he wanted to spend a Sunday afternoon.

"They all live nearby," Sarah said by way of encouragement. "I'll be glad to help."

Kelly's eyes nearly bugged out of his head at such a suggestion. Malloy just grunted. "You're staying here."

"What am I supposed to do here?" she asked, annoyed.

"You can go comfort the widow if you want, or you can look for the rat poison that Isaiah said was in the kitchen. If it's the right kind, we'll have it checked to see if it matches what was in the wine, which reminds me . . ."

He pushed himself out of his chair and went out into the sanctuary. Sarah and Kelly followed, having nothing left to do in the office. Malloy called for the two patrolmen who had been left on duty to provide assistance. He found them sleeping on a back pew. After making sure they were properly chastised, he sent one of them off with the wine bottle and communion cup to have the contents tested. That wouldn't happen until the police laboratory opened tomorrow, but at least the evidence would be where it needed to be.

Then he, Kelly, and the remaining patrolman got the list of attendees from this morning's service and began dividing it up after consulting a city directory they found in Upchurch's office for addresses.

"I'll check with Mrs. Upchurch," Sarah offered, and Malloy grudgingly accepted her offer.

Before they left, Malloy warned Sarah not to get in trouble, and she returned the warning, to Kelly's amusement.

When they were gone, she set to work in search of a box of rat poison that might or might not exist.

Frank had taken the other three confessed suspects for himself, and he'd left them for last. So far, he'd found only one box of rat poison containing cyanide in his visits, and the elderly couple who owned it hadn't even known it was in the house, much less where to find it if they'd decided to poison a minister. Their cook had finally produced it, grumbling about being pestered and confirming no one had moved it from the cupboard where she kept it in weeks.

He smiled a little as he knocked on Isaiah Wilkins's door. The boy was going to be mad when Frank didn't arrest him. The maid escorted him into the parlor where Isaiah and his mother sat. He was on his feet instantly, his young face pale but determined. His mother looked a bit alarmed, but not unduly so. She obviously had no idea her son expected to be carted off to jail.

"I'm sorry to bother you, Mrs. Wilkins, but we're checking with everyone who was at church this morning to see what kind of rat poison they keep in their house," Frank explained, not looking at Isaiah.

"Whatever for?" she asked.

He used his diplomatic smile. "We're trying to find out where the poison that killed Reverend Upchurch came from," he said. "It's an unusual kind, and we think that when we find it, we'll have found the killer."

She glanced at her son, then back at Frank. "Surely, you don't suspect any of us here?" she asked anxiously.

"No, ma'am, but I have to check everybody."

"You don't have to do this," Isaiah cried.

His mother thought he was talking to her. "Of course I do, dear," she said. "I want Mr. Malloy to know that we had nothing to do with that man's death."

The boy gave Frank a desperate look, but he ignored it and allowed Mrs. Wilkins to take him to the kitchen where he found, much to his relief, an arsenic poison.

Isaiah was lurking in the kitchen doorway. "What about the poison at the church?" he tried.

"We're still looking for it," Frank said mildly. "We think the killer might've taken it with him, though." He thanked Mrs. Wilkins for her help and apologized again for bothering her. Then he let her show him to the door, with Isaiah following doggedly in their wake.

"Is that all?" the boy asked when Frank started out the door. He still looked terrified, but now he was desperate, too.

"No, it's not all," Frank said, turning to Mrs. Wilkins. "You should be very proud of your son. He's a little headstrong, but he's got a good heart." He looked at Isaiah. "You're old enough to make your own decisions now, Isaiah. Be sure that from now on, you make good ones."

"But . . . but don't you need to . . . to ask me some questions?" he asked, his eyes wide.

"No, I'm satisfied that you didn't have anything to do with Upchurch's death."

"But—"

"Stop bothering Mr. Malloy," Mrs. Wilkins chided him. "He has work to do, and I'm sure he'd like to be on his way."

"Yes, I would," Frank said and left, aware of Isaiah's frustration and taking a perverse satisfaction in it.

Rachel Upchurch answered her own door, and she seemed relieved to see Sarah again. "What happened to

Isaiah?" she demanded as she stood aside for Sarah to enter. "Do you know? Has he been arrested?" To her credit, she looked as tortured as a woman who might have driven a boy to murder should have.

"Mr. Malloy doesn't believe Isaiah killed your husband," Sarah informed her.

"Oh, thank God," Rachel breathed, laying a hand on her heart. "Thank you for coming to tell me."

"That's not why I came," Sarah said, feeling no sympathy for her. "I came to see what kind of rat poison you keep in your house."

"I thought Mr. Malloy didn't believe I'd killed Oliver," she said in surprise.

"I still need to check. He's checking everyone who attended church this morning. Will I find it in the kitchen?" Sarah asked, heading in that direction without waiting for a reply.

"I'm sure you will," Rachel said, following. "Our maid quit the other day—I told you I have trouble keeping servants—so I'm not sure, but it shouldn't be hard to find it."

Apparently, she wasn't lying about not being sure. She helped Sarah look, throwing open cupboards and searching through the pantry until they located a half-empty box.

"Arsenic," Sarah read from the box.

"What does that mean?" Rachel asked with a worried frown.

"It means this isn't what killed your husband."

"Did you think it was?"

"No, but as I said, we have to be sure. Isaiah said they keep rat poison at the church. Do you know where it would be?"

"Heavens, no," Rachel said. "Did you look in the kitchen? That seems the most logical place."

"That's where we looked first, but it isn't there. Where else might it be?"

"How should I know a thing like that?"

"You're the minister's wife," Sarah reminded her.

Rachel gave her a pained look. "And that must mean I know everything that goes on at the church, I suppose. It might if I were the typical minister's wife, but as you well know, I'm not. The only time I ever went over there was for Sunday services."

"And to seduce young boys," Sarah reminded her.

She flinched, but she didn't back down. "I don't know anything about rat poison at the church," she insisted, her eyes filled with a pain Sarah felt she deserved to feel.

As angry as she was with Rachel Upchurch, she couldn't help feeling sorry for her, too. Her entire life had been lonely and loveless, and now she was more alone than she had ever been.

"What will you do now?" she asked.

"If you're worried that I'm going to get Isaiah to marry me, don't be concerned," she replied defensively. "He doesn't know about the baby, and I have no intention of telling him."

"I'm glad to hear it," Sarah replied tartly. "He wouldn't be much of a provider in any case. You'll have to go someplace, though. They won't let you stay here."

"I know. Actually, I've been trying to figure that out while you were gone. If Mr. Malloy doesn't change his mind and put me in jail, I suppose I'll contact my aunt and uncle. He's my mother's brother. When they hear I've been widowed and am expecting a child, they'll most likely feel obligated to take me in. They live near Albany, so it's unlikely the scandal of Oliver's murder will follow me there."

"Do you think Isaiah will let you go?"

"He's just a child," she said dismissively. "What could he

do to stop me? I'll simply tell him I no longer care for him. He'll recover soon enough."

Sarah wondered if he'd ever recover from what both of the Upchurchs had put him through, but she wasn't going to argue. She knew Rachel's leaving him was the best thing for him. "I have to get back to the church," she said.

"What are you going to do there?"

Sarah sighed. "Try to find the poison that killed your husband."

JUST A BLOCK AWAY FROM THE WILKINS'S HOUSE, FRANK came to the Evans-York household, his last stop. Mrs. Evans greeted him when the maid showed him into the parlor. She looked tired and much older than she had the first time he'd met her.

"Have you changed your mind about arresting me, Mr. Malloy?" she asked with a touch of irony.

"No, I know you didn't do it," he replied kindly.

"I'm afraid I owe you an apology," she said. "And a debt of gratitude."

"Yes, you do, but don't give it another thought. How's Mrs. York?"

"She's resting. I'm sure she'll be fine now that she knows I'm not going to prison. You were right, Mr. Malloy. I did think she'd killed that awful man. I couldn't bear the thought of her going to prison, so I lied. I was very angry when I found out she'd confessed to protect me, of all things, but I also have to be grateful for the love that moti-vated her."

"Yes, you do," he said. "Not many people would sacrifice themselves like that for somebody else."

"And not many people would refuse to accept a confession of murder, Mr. Malloy," she said gravely.

He chose not to respond to that. "The reason I'm here is that I have to make sure there's no real evidence against you and your daughter, in case somebody else gets assigned to this case later. Can you show me where you keep your rat poison?"

"How will knowing where I keep my rat poison prove I'm innocent?" she asked in confusion.

"Because not many kinds of rat poison are cyanide. Most of them are arsenic. Do you know which kind you have?"

"I never paid any attention," she realized.

"Then show it to me, and we'll find out."

She readily complied, and as Frank had hoped, it was arsenic.

"I wonder if another detective would have taken the time to check my story," she mused as she walked him back to the parlor.

"I don't think anybody would believe you're a killer in the first place, Mrs. Evans," he told her. "I just need to ask you one more thing. Do you know if there was rat poison in the church kitchen?"

She looked up at him in surprise. "Why, yes, now that you mention it. I think we kept a box there. The rats get in everywhere," she added almost apologetically. "We tried to keep the church clean and not tempt them, but even a crumb is enough to draw them."

"Do you know where the poison was kept?"

"There's a cabinet in the kitchen. The last time I saw it was on the top shelf, so the children couldn't reach it, you understand. I can show you, if you like."

"That's not necessary. Isaiah took me down there, but it wasn't there."

"Oh, dear," she said, instantly seeing the significance of this. "Do you think? . . ."

"Who else knew it was there?"

She considered. "Any of the women who worked in the kitchen could have seen it, and that's all of us at one time or another."

"Mrs. Upchurch?" he suggested.

This made her frown. "I couldn't really say. I can't actually recall her ever helping us down there, so she might not have known it was there, but then, she's the minister's wife, and she's got access to the church all the time. I have no idea what she knows and doesn't know."

"What about the men?"

"You said Isaiah knew about it," she said. "Some of the other boys might have, too, I suppose. I don't know who else might have. The men seldom go into the kitchen, but that doesn't mean they wouldn't know about it."

"Would you by any chance know if the poison at the church was arsenic or cyanide?"

She shook her head sadly. "I wish I did. I didn't even know there were different types."

It was the echo of the story he'd heard over and over this afternoon. He thanked Mrs. Evans and took his leave. As he walked back to the church, he hoped Kelly or the patrolman or even Sarah had been more successful.

Sarah was sitting in Upchurch's office, taking advantage of the comfortable chairs in there, when she heard the sanctuary door open and close. She tensed for a moment, realizing she was alone in the building where a murder had taken place. If the killer had returned . . .

"Sarah? Where are you?" Malloy called.

She hurried out into the sanctuary to meet him. "Did you find anything?"

He looked even more discouraged than he had before, and Sarah's heart ached for him. "No, and I met Kelly and that idiot patrolman a couple blocks from here. Neither of them did, either, so I sent them home. You should go home, too."

Sarah sighed. "I will. I just wanted to let you know that I searched every nook and cranny in this building, and I didn't find any rat poison. Oh, except for Upchurch's desk, which is locked. I couldn't find any keys, either."

"Upchurch probably had them in his pocket, in which case they're at the morgue. I'll take a look, though. Maybe I won't need any keys."

Before Sarah could ask what he meant by that, he was on his way to Upchurch's office. Did police officers learn how to pick locks the same way burglars did? She wondered idly as she watched him examine the end of a letter opener that had been lying on the desk. He leaned down and inserted it into the slot above the center drawer. A little jiggle produced a click and the drawer slid open.

"How did you do that?" she asked in amazement.

He ignored her and began pulling open the other drawers.

"Hello, what's this?" Malloy said, staring down into the largest drawer.

The tone of his voice made the hairs on the back of Sarah's neck stand up. She hurried over as he pulled a box out of the drawer.

"Is that rat poison?" she asked incredulously. "Is it the right kind?"

"Yeah, it is," he confirmed, setting the box down in the middle of the cluttered desk top. "Says so right here: cyanide." He pointed to the boldly printed words.

"Why would it be in Upchurch's desk?" Sarah asked, hardly able to believe it had been right there under their noses all along.

"I don't know, unless . . ."

"Unless what?" she prodded.

"Unless Upchurch put it there himself," he mused.

"Why would he have done that? Why would he have had it in the first place?"

"Something's been bothering me about this case from the beginning, and I couldn't figure out what it was, but now . . . now I think I might have it."

"What?" she demanded. "Tell me what you think."

"Remember when I told you that the confessions didn't make sense with what really happened?" he asked.

"Yes, because putting the poison in the communion wine probably wouldn't have killed Upchurch, and it could've made everyone else who drank out of the cup sick."

"But we know that somebody *did* put the poison in the cup."

"And we know that Upchurch drank it and died," she added.

"But the killer couldn't have known that when he put the poison in the cup. Nobody knew the people weren't going to come up for communion, and nobody knew Upchurch would drink it all himself."

"Then we're back where we started, and it doesn't make sense," Sarah said.

"Unless . . ."

"Unless *what*?" she snapped impatiently.

"Unless the person who put the poison in the cup wanted to make the people in the congregation sick," he said.

"Who would want to do that?" she scoffed.

"Somebody who hated them or wanted to get even."

Sarah gaped at him. "You mean Upchurch? But he didn't know what they were planning," she argued.

"Yes, he did. Wilfred Linton told him this morning."

"Why did he do a thing like that?"

"He thought maybe Upchurch had tricked Grace the way he'd tricked the boys. He wanted to find out before the church members confronted him because he wouldn't be likely to cooperate after that."

"Did Linton find out? Did Upchurch rape Grace, too?"

"Not from what he said to Linton. Linton didn't intend to let him know what was going to happen, but Upchurch got a little self-righteous and threatened to report Linton to the church elders for making false accusations. Linton got mad and told him everybody knew the truth about him."

Sarah thought back to that morning and how Upchurch had looked when he came out to lead the service. He'd seemed composed at first, but he'd rapidly lost that composure as things began to go awry. "He was upset when no one sang and the offering plates came back empty, but I thought that was because he didn't know what was wrong."

"He knew, all right," Malloy confirmed, still trying to put all the pieces together. "He knew they'd turned against him. He knew they were going to run him out of the church and probably out of the city."

"And you think he put poison in the communion wine?" she asked uncertainly.

"It had to have been him. Who else would've locked it in his desk?"

"But why did he do it?"

"Who knows what his reason was, but he must've wanted to get back at them somehow," Malloy suggested. "Maybe he hoped they'd all die, but he knew they'd get sick at least.

He could even drink some to divert suspicion from himself. He wouldn't even have to swallow it, just pretend to, and then pretend to be sick like the others."

"But no one came forward." Sarah remembered the scene too well. "He called for them twice, but no one moved. I'll never forget the expression on his face. I thought he was just humiliated."

"What did he do then?" Malloy asked. "Tell me exactly what you remember."

She pictured it in her mind. "He looked desperate. That's the only word to describe it. He offered the cup to Isaiah. He'd offered him the bread first, and he didn't take it, so Upchurch ate it himself. Isaiah wouldn't take the cup, either. He even took a step backward. I remember thinking how embarrassing it was for Upchurch to have even his assistant refuse him. And then . . ."

"Then what?" Malloy prodded.

"Then he looked around the room. His eyes were terrible, almost crazed. I actually felt sorry for him. Then he lifted the cup to his lips and drank it down."

"He didn't just take a sip?"

"Oh, no. He tipped the cup up like he wanted to empty it. Some of the wine even ran down his face and stained his stole, that thing he wears around his neck. You probably noticed those stains."

Malloy rubbed a hand over his face. "Then it's what I thought. Upchurch poisoned the wine."

"If Upchurch had poisoned the wine, why would he drink it himself?" she protested.

"Because he saw his life crumbling around him," Malloy said with a sigh. "He knew they'd expose him and ruin him. He might never get another church, and he might even go to prison. He'd wanted to punish them for what they were going to do to him, but they even ruined that by refusing to cooperate. He must have been desperate, just like you thought. He didn't see any way out, and he knew the wine was poisoned, so he drank it. That's why they call suicide the coward's way out."

15

ON TUESDAY EVENING, SARAH SAT IN THE WARMTH OF her kitchen after supper, enjoying the newspaper reports of Upchurch's unusual death. Malloy had given his version of the story to an old friend of theirs, Webster Prescott, who worked for *The World*. The other papers had picked up the story and embellished it in various ways, but no one had discovered the truth behind the minister's suicide. Malloy's version had the church ready to dismiss him for stealing money from the offerings, and Upchurch choosing to end his life on the altar to avoid the accompanying scandal and what it would do to his career as a minister. It was close enough to the truth to be believable, and far enough to protect those most vulnerable.

Once again Malloy had shown himself to be discreet and trustworthy and even kind. Sarah remembered the first time they'd met, when she'd been certain he was none of those things. Now she knew him to be all of that and more. She had no more than formed that thought when she heard the doorbell ring.

Probably a baby to deliver, she thought, hearing Maeve and Aggie bolting down the stairs from the second-floor playroom to answer it. Then she heard a familiar voice and Maeve's delighted laughter, and she knew these were welcome visitors instead.

She found Malloy and Brian removing their coats while Aggie literally jumped up and down with excitement to see her playmate again. When Brian saw Sarah, he ran and threw his arms around her skirts, looking up adoringly. He was getting too big for her to lift anymore, so she could only reach down and give him a hug of greeting.

"I'm so glad you came," she told Malloy. "I know Aggie has missed Brian."

"I thought she might, and I didn't want you to have to put up with my mother again so soon," he said with a twinkle.

She decided not to reply to that provocation. "Aggie, why don't you take Brian upstairs and show him your new toys?"

Aggie grabbed his hand and fairly dragged him toward the steps before he got the idea and began to race her up. Maeve followed at a more dignified pace.

"New toys?" Malloy echoed, still teasing. "You aren't spoiling her, are you?"

"My mother sent over some of my old things. I think it's her way of telling me she approves of having Aggie as a member of our family."

"You're going to adopt her, then?" he asked in surprise.

Sarah felt the twinge of disappointment all over again. "I

looked into it, and I just found out yesterday that I can't legally adopt her because I'm not married," she said. "But I'm going to keep her. I can be her legal guardian, so that will have to do. She'll be my child in every other way."

She waited, half-afraid Malloy would tell her she had no business taking on a child. Other people had already warned her, and she knew they were probably right. Instead Malloy said, "Aggie's a lucky little girl."

Sarah felt her face melt into a joyful smile. "No, I'm the lucky one. Come on into the kitchen, and I'll get you some coffee."

He saw the newspapers still spread out on the kitchen table. "What did you think?" he asked, pointing at Prescott's article as he arranged them into a neater pile.

"I think you're an excellent liar, Mr. Malloy," she replied with a grin as she set a cup of coffee before him.

"It helped that Prescott owed us a favor, too. He didn't ask any questions when I told him he was getting first crack at the story."

"He did a very nice job. Did anybody at Police Head-quarters ask any questions you didn't want to answer?"

"No. They were too relieved to get the mess cleared up so neatly. I didn't exactly have proof Upchurch killed himself, but they were all willing to believe my theory, considering the evidence we did have."

"Thank heaven for that," Sarah said, "and thank heaven none of the boys were guilty. I don't know what would've happened if you'd had to arrest one of them. It would've been impossible to keep the secret then."

Malloy didn't respond to that, and when she looked up, he was frowning.

"What is it? Did someone find out after all?"

"No, it's not that."

"What then?" She knew him too well to be so easily dismissed.

"I've been thinking about Grace Linton."

Sarah felt a knot of dread forming in her stomach. "You don't think Upchurch was responsible after all, do you?"

"No," he assured her quickly. "At least not directly."

"How could he be *indirectly* responsible?" she asked. "He either was or he wasn't."

He sipped his coffee, and Sarah waited. Time was when she would've badgered him for an explanation. Now she knew he was looking for the proper words to use to tell her something he didn't want her to hear. She was too grateful that he'd come to trust her enough to confide in her to rush him.

"When I questioned Wilfred Linton on Sunday, he told me that he'd been thinking about what Upchurch had done to the boys, and how he'd convinced them it was a perfectly normal thing so they wouldn't be frightened. He said that got him to wondering if Grace's attacker might've done the same thing."

"You mean tricked her?"

"Well, yeah. He could've convinced her it was something that happened to every girl. Maybe he even said he loved her and told her it was something people in love did. She's so trusting, she'd believe it."

"Of course she would," Sarah said, considering all the new possibilities this raised. "Oh, dear!" she cried suddenly.

"What?" he asked with a worried frown.

"I just realized that all this time I've been asking Grace if someone hurt her or frightened her or did something she didn't like. If she was really seduced by a lover, those are the wrong questions! No wonder she kept insisting that nothing bad had happened to her!"

"You mean you didn't ask her if somebody had . . . ?" He hesitated, as always uncomfortable with delicate subjects. "You didn't describe it?"

"No," she said, feeling stupid. "I didn't want to . . . well, I guess I didn't want to make myself uncomfortable by talking about what I assumed had been a horrible and frightening experience for her. I thought she would've been terrified and that it would've been painful, but if it wasn't . . ."

"Then that explains why you didn't get the right answers from her," Malloy concluded.

Sarah considered all the possibilities. "That still leaves us with the fact that Grace is never alone with anyone male. And if it's true, who could that male have been? You've already eliminated Upchurch."

"I've been thinking about that a lot. One thing all the boys said is that Upchurch told them he was teaching them what to do when they loved a woman. We know one of the boys put his lessons to good use in fathering another child."

"Isaiah!" Sarah exclaimed.

"We've got pretty good evidence that he knew exactly what to do."

"But Rachel Upchurch pursued him," Sarah argued. "She knew he'd figured out that Upchurch had been lying to them, and she took advantage of his anger and bitterness against her husband."

"Maybe he wasn't satisfied with just one woman, though. Maybe he wanted to try it with someone else, too."

"Oh, my, Rachel did say that Isaiah wanted to prove he was a man," Sarah remembered. "But why Grace?"

"Maybe he couldn't find any girls who are . . . well, smart, that were willing. Maybe he was afraid to try. Grace is a pretty girl, and he'd know she'd be easy to fool."

It made sense, but something wasn't right. She just couldn't imagine Grace being charmed by Isaiah. "She told me she doesn't even like him," she remembered.

"Maybe she stopped liking him after he did it."

"She did say he'd called her stupid."

Malloy nodded his head in understanding. "Boys can be mean when they've had their way with a girl."

"I don't know," Sarah mused. "It seems logical, but . . ."

"There's one way to be sure," he said. "Ask Grace."

SARAH HAD SENT MRS. LINTON A MESSAGE REQUESTING A private meeting, and Mrs. Linton had agreed. Sarah imagined the poor woman was wondering what she could possibly want to discuss this time. She probably thought it had something to do with Upchurch's death. If only it were that simple.

Over tea that Sarah was too nervous to drink, she explained to Mrs. Linton what she and Malloy had concluded about Grace having been seduced instead of raped, based on her own husband's theory.

"Yes, Mr. Linton did mention that to me," Mrs. Linton said slowly. "And it does make a certain kind of sense. I've been thinking about it myself, wondering if it could have happened, but even still, I can't imagine who it could have been. You know how closely we watch her. It just doesn't seem possible that . . . that anyone would have had an opportunity to be alone with her, much less . . ."

"Mr. Malloy discovered that one of the boys Upchurch . . . harmed," she said, choosing her words carefully. "One of them has . . ." How could she put this delicately? "That one of the older boys has had relations with another . . . female and gotten her with child as well."

"Oh, no! How awful!" Mrs. Linton exclaimed. "Is it another girl in the church? Someone we know?"

"Oh, no," Sarah lied. "But since we know one of the boys has already, uh, persuaded another female, without resorting to force, it seems possible he could have persuaded Grace, as well."

"Oh, my, how awful! A boy we know. . . . This is almost worse than what we'd imagined!" she said, literally wringing her hands. "But where could it have happened?"

"Perhaps at the church," Sarah said apologetically. "It's just about the only place we could think of. I'm so sorry to bring you such distressing news, Mrs. Linton, but I thought it might help if you knew Grace hadn't been brutalized, at least. That is, if this is what really happened," she added lamely.

Mrs. Linton pulled a handkerchief out of her sleeve and dabbed at her eyes. "I suppose it would help a bit to know she wasn't terrorized," she allowed. "Do you . . . ? Who is the boy?"

"I'd rather not say, in case I'm wrong. If I'm right, though, Grace will tell you who it was."

Obviously, Mrs. Linton hadn't thought about asking Grace. Her eyes widened as other possibilities occurred to her. "Should we punish this boy, whoever he is? Or have him arrested for what he did to Grace and the other girl? He must be stopped!"

"I agree, but it's possible he didn't know what he was doing was wrong. Perhaps he was just . . . Well, Upchurch twisted the boys' minds as well as assaulting their bodies. I think they'll all need some help and guidance figuring out what's right and wrong for some time to come. Mr. Malloy is willing to deal with him outside of the law, if that's what you choose. I don't think he's a bad boy, Mrs. Linton. Don't forget, he was a victim, too."

"I suppose you're right, but I still can't stand the thought of him getting away with it."

"Remember, this is just a theory. Grace is the only one who can tell you what really happened. Now that you know what to ask her, it shouldn't be hard to find out, either."

"Oh, I couldn't ask her," Mrs. Linton protested, dabbing at her eyes again. "Every time I think about what happened to her, I start crying, and then she gets so upset . . . Mrs. Brandt, could *you* ask her about it?"

"It's not really my place," she hedged, not wanting to usurp a mother's role.

"Please. I'd be so grateful, and I know Grace trusts you. She'd tell you the truth, no matter what it is. And I imagine you could get through it without crying and upsetting Grace."

Touched by her confidence, Sarah was still reluctant to assume such a heavy responsibility alone. "If you really want me to, I'll do it, but I'd like for you to be in the room," Sarah said. "In case Grace needs your support."

She drew a fortifying breath. "All right. I think I can control my emotions if I don't have to talk. I'll call Grace down right now, before I lose my courage altogether."

The girl's stomach had swelled noticeably since Sarah had seen her last. She saw Sarah looking at it and grinned. "I'm getting fat," she said, patting her belly. "Mama said that's supposed to happen."

"She's right," Sarah confirmed with what she hoped was a natural-looking smile. "Would you sit here beside me, Grace?" she asked, patting the sofa seat. "I'd like to talk to you about something."

Grace sat down obediently and looked up at Sarah with such innocence that it made her heart hurt.

She took a breath and plunged in. "Do you remember when we asked you if anyone had ever hurt you, Grace?"

Grace nodded, her pretty little mouth screwing up in disgust. "I told you and told you, *no*."

"We believe you now, but I still need to ask you about something that happened last summer."

"All right," Grace agreed. "If I can remember. Last summer was a long time ago."

"I think you'll remember. It's about a boy," Sarah said. "This boy would've been very nice to you."

"Most boys are mean," Grace informed her solemnly.

"I know. That's why you'll remember. This boy told you he liked you. He wanted to be alone with you so he could kiss you and touch you. Do you remember that, Grace?"

Grace hunched her shoulders and covered her mouth with both hands to hide an impish grin. She nodded, her eyes dancing with a delicious secret, and her mother made a strangled sound.

"What's wrong, Mama?" Grace asked anxiously, turning to where her mother sat on the far side of the room.

"Nothing dear," she said, her voice strained. "I . . . something was in my throat. Go ahead and answer Mrs. Brandt's questions."

Grace turned expectantly back to Sarah.

"He wanted to do things with you," Sarah said, wishing she knew the right words to use, the ones that would describe without revealing her true feelings. If Grace got the idea that what she'd done was wrong, she might never tell them what really happened. "He probably took off some of his clothes, and you did, too."

"I wasn't wearing clothes," Grace informed her.

Sarah winced inwardly, expecting Mrs. Linton to cry out

again, but miraculously, she didn't. "You weren't wearing anything at all?" Sarah asked, her throat dry as she experienced the same dread Mrs. Linton must be feeling.

"Just my nightdress," Grace said. "But I didn't take it off. That wouldn't be nice."

Sarah glanced at Mrs. Linton who gazed back in baffled surprise. "Where did this happen, Grace?" Sarah asked.

"In my bedroom. That's why I was wearing my night-dress, silly."

"A . . . a man was in your bedroom?" Mrs. Linton said in a strangled voice.

"Not a *man*," Grace told her. "You're not supposed to let men in your bedroom. Everybody knows that."

"If he wasn't a man, what was he?" Sarah asked, mystified by how her mind worked.

"He's a boy," she said, as if that were the only possible answer. "I know it's all right for boys to be in my bedroom. Sometimes we play there, and Mama said it was all right."

"But . . . but that was just Percy," Mrs. Linton said, "when you were both children."

Grace seemed puzzled. "But we're still children," she said. "That's what you always call us. Mrs. Evans and Mrs. York do, too."

"Grace," Sarah said, drawing her attention back from the fruitless argument. "How did he get into your room?"

"I'm not supposed to tell anybody, because he's not allowed to be out after dark. His mother would've been mad at him."

"It's all right to tell us now, Grace," Sarah said. "It was a long time ago. How did he get into your room?"

"Just like he always does. He climbed up the fire escape," she reported with a hint of glee.

"Like he always does?" Sarah echoed. "Has he come more than once?"

"Sure, lots of times, and we'd play these funny games. I didn't like all of them, but mostly I did. They felt really good."

This time Mrs. Linton couldn't hold back the sob that wracked her.

"Mama, what's wrong?" Grace asked in alarm.

"Nothing, nothing," she hastily assured her, although her face betrayed her anguish.

"Are you sick? Maybe Mrs. Brandt could take care of you." She turned to Sarah. "I remembered you're a nurse."

"That was very smart of you, Grace," Sarah assured her, although the smile she managed felt almost painful. "I think your mother will be fine. I just want to ask you a few more questions."

"All right, but I think Mama really doesn't feel very well," she said, glancing at her mother again.

"I'll make sure she's all right before I leave," Sarah promised. "Now tell me, when Isaiah came to your room, did he—"

"*Who?*" Grace asked, interrupting.

"Isaiah," Sarah said. "Isaiah Wilkins, the boy who came to your room."

Grace wrinkled her nose in disgust. "He never came to my room. I'd never even *talk* to Isaiah Wilkins. He's mean!"

"Is Isaiah the one who . . . the one you told me about?" Mrs. Linton asked Sarah raggedly.

Sarah nodded, not taking her eyes from Grace's face. "If it wasn't Isaiah, then who came to your room?"

She glanced at her mother, then lowered her voice to a whisper. "I promised not to tell. He'll get in trouble."

"No, he won't. I promise, Grace, and it's important that you tell me who it was."

She considered, idly pleating the fabric of her skirt as she weighed the options. "I don't want to get him in trouble, because he's my beau. We might even get married someday," she added shyly. "That's what he said."

A memory stirred in Sarah's mind, slender and fragile and seemingly unimportant at the time. Grace telling Aggie how to behave in church, and then, seeing the acolytes coming down the aisle, she'd bragged . . .

"Grace, is *Percy* your beau?" Sarah asked, her heart nearly stopping in her chest.

Grace nodded proudly. "But I didn't tell you. You guessed, so I didn't break my promise. And you said he wouldn't get in trouble. You promised!"

"Yes, I did," she said faintly as the enormity of Upchurch's sins began to dawn on her. A scripture verse echoed in her head, something about the sins of the fathers being visited on the children. So many children, so many lives scarred by his evil. Some of them weren't even born yet.

Mrs. Linton was weeping softly into her handkerchief, and Grace went over to comfort her, still having no idea why she was upset. Sarah prayed she'd never be able to understand the evil that had touched her.

FRANK HAD HARDLY BEEN ABLE TO BELIEVE THE LETTER Sarah sent him. He supposed he should be grateful that the Lintons had no intention of pressing charges against young Percy. Enough harm had come to both those children, and Frank had no heart for causing any more. No one outside the families would ever learn the truth about who had fathered Grace's baby, and Mrs. Evans would make sure Percy understood that what he'd done with Grace had been wrong. Frank could imagine how heartbroken the boy would be to learn how horribly Upchurch had twisted his understanding of the world, and he was glad he wouldn't be present for that conversation.

The only good news her letter brought was that he no longer needed to concern himself with the Church of the Good Shepherd and its parishioners. He'd been spending every moment of his spare time on that, so now he could afford to return to investigating Tom Brandt's death.

Whenever he could during the next few days, he tried to track down the three other women who had suffered from the same strange obsession as Edna White. At the first woman's house, a maid told him the tradesmen's entrance was in the back, and she didn't seem impressed when he told her he was the police investigating a murder. After consulting with someone inside, she'd returned to tell him they knew nothing that could help him and slammed the door in his face. If he'd been officially assigned to this case, he would've brought a squad of patrolmen back to make a rather messy and destructive search of the premises, but since he wasn't officially assigned, he decided to try his luck elsewhere.

At the second woman's house, a servant let him in, but a forbidding woman with a face like a prune and a disposition to match informed him no one there cared a fig who'd killed that quack of a doctor who'd only succeeded in upsetting poor Amelia more than she had been already.

Frank asked if he might speak to Miss Amelia's father— he didn't mention the man might well be a suspect in Tom Brandt's murder—but the old woman told him he most certainly could not and told him to leave. Since she herself left the room, he didn't have much choice. She hadn't even confirmed whether this Amelia even had a father.

The fourth woman was the one who'd had the dementia, what Dr. Quinn had told him was far more serious than just imagining herself in love with a man she hardly knew. But when he finally found the right house, the family no longer lived there. The new family wasn't home, and the maid had no idea where the previous owners might've gone.

He knew from experience that every street in the city had a resident like Mrs. Ellsworth, so Frank started knocking on doors up and down the street until he found an elderly lady who had nothing better to do than mind her neighbors' business. He had to sit in her parlor and drink tea and eat Sally Lund cake, but he found out everything he needed to know.

"Oh, yes, that poor girl behaved terribly," Mrs. Peabody informed him. "They had to keep her locked in her room so she wouldn't run out into the street in her nightdress. I felt sorry for her family. She'd been a promising young thing, very smart and pretty. She sang, too, as I remember. Voice like an angel."

"So she wasn't always like that," Frank said between mouthfuls. The cake was very good.

"Heavens no. She was perfectly normal, at least as far as anyone knew, until . . . let me see, I suppose she must've been around twenty when her brother died."

"How did he die?"

"Oh, it was the most horrible thing. He was riding one of those bicycle contraptions, and a carriage ran him over. Broke his neck, they said. They should be outlawed, if you ask me. The bicycles, I mean. I can't imagine why any sane person would get on one in the first place."

Frank didn't point out that the police department had found them so useful that they'd started a bicycle squad. "Was it her brother's death that, uh . . ." He struggled to find the right words, but she was ahead of him.

"'That unhinged her?'" she supplied helpfully. "Oh, my, yes. They were twins, you see, so they'd always been close. She took to her bed for weeks afterwards, her mother told me. No one could console her, and then she started acting so strangely. She thought people were talking to her when no one was there, and she decided everyone was lying to her and her brother was still alive."

"I suppose they called in some doctors," Frank said.

"For what little good it did. They said to keep her locked in a dark, quiet room and make sure her life was as calm as possible. As if they had any choice. They certainly couldn't let her out of the house in her condition."

"You said 'they.' How much family did she have left? Were both her parents still alive?"

"They were the last time I heard anything about them."

"What sort of man was her father?" Frank asked, finishing off the last of his cake and hoping Mrs. Peabody would offer him some more.

She seemed puzzled by the question. "He was a businessman. I'm not quite sure what business he was in, but they were quite comfortable, if that's what you mean."

"Did he have a temper?"

"Not that I ever saw, but then, I wouldn't, would I? He was devoted to his children, though. I do know that. They both were. Losing the boy was terrible, but then they lost their daughter, too, in a way. I don't know how they bore it."

"When did they move away?"

"Oh, dear, let me think. Two years ago at least. Yes, it was before my last grandchild was born, and he'll be two in May. I remember because I'd just told Mrs. Alberton we were expecting him when she told me they were moving out of the city. They hoped Christina would improve if they lived in the country, you see."

"Do you know where they went?"

"Yonkers, I believe. Mr. Alberton still works in the city, so they couldn't go far. Would you like some more cake, Mr. Malloy? You seemed to enjoy it so much."

"Yes, I believe I will, Mrs. Peabody," he said, holding out his plate. "You wouldn't know their current address, would you?"

"I don't think so, I'm sorry to say, but they shouldn't be too difficult to find. Alberton isn't a common name."

Frank accepted the second helping of cake and tried to think of something else she might know that could help him. "I don't suppose you know if the move to the country helped the girl or not."

"Not for certain, of course, but I did hear through some mutual friends that they finally had to put her into a sanitarium. For her own safety, you understand."

Frank winced inwardly. Under those circumstances, the Albertons weren't going to be eager to speak to a policeman. If Mr. Alberton had killed Tom Brandt, he'd avoid the police like the plague, and even if he hadn't, he wasn't likely to want to talk about his poor daughter's tragedy.

He had to face it: he wasn't going to be able to get any further on this case. He was the wrong social class, the wrong nationality, and the wrong religion, and as if that weren't enough, he was a policeman. No respectable Protestant family in the city would allow an Irish Catholic cop into their home unless compelled by some horrible event that had made them the victim of a crime. Even then, their cooperation would likely be perfunctory and reluctant. He'd just been reminded of that when dealing with the members of the Church of the Good Shepherd.

As Mrs. Peabody chattered on about inconsequential things, Frank thought about going back to Felix Decker to tell him he'd failed. The prospect turned the cake he was eating into sawdust in his mouth. No, he'd rather be horse-whipped than do that, but what else could he do?

SARAH WAS HELPING AGGIE PUT TOGETHER A PUZZLE UP-stairs in the playroom the following Sunday afternoon when the doorbell rang. Aggie frowned, knowing it was probably someone summoning Sarah to a delivery. Sarah felt a stab of disappointment herself. She'd been looking forward to spending this gloomy winter afternoon with Aggie.

The girl followed her down the stairs, clinging to her skirt as if she could keep her from going, but Sarah's mood lifted instantly when she saw a familiar silhouette on the frosted glass of the front door.

She was already smiling when she opened it to admit Malloy and Brian, who was fairly bouncing with anticipation. When everyone had been properly greeted and coats removed and hung up, Aggie and Brian raced upstairs to the playroom.

"Where's Maeve?" Malloy asked, chafing his hands to warm them.

"She has the day off. Come into the kitchen."

He glanced up the stairs. "Do we dare leave them alone?"

"Not for long. We'll check on them in a few minutes."

When they were settled at the kitchen table with coffee and some of Mrs. Ellsworth's apple pie, Sarah told him what she'd heard from Mrs. Linton.

"Mrs. Linton is taking Grace to stay with some friends in New Jersey, and she'll have the baby there. They're going to bring it back and announce that they've adopted it. There may be some gossip, but they plan to ignore it and stick to their story."

"What about Percy? Does he know he's going to be a father?"

"They aren't going to tell him until he's older. I imagine he'll eventually figure it out for himself, even if they don't. Mrs. Evans and Mrs. York have promised that they will help support the child in case . . . well, in case it's like Grace and needs that support."

"Any word on the Widow Upchurch?" Malloy asked sarcastically.

"None at all! Apparently, she just packed up her things and disappeared. No one even knows where she went, although she told me she had an uncle in Albany who would take her in."

"Young Isaiah must be heartbroken," he observed.

"I suspect he is," Sarah said, "but he'll get over losing her soon enough, I imagine. Someday, he'll even count his blessings."

They sipped their coffee in companionable silence for a few minutes, and then he said, "Remember when I told you about those women your husband treated?"

"The ones who were . . . deluded?" she asked, not pleased with the word she'd chosen, but knowing it made sense to him.

"That's right. I found out at least one of them is in a sanitarium."

"How awful," she said. "Do you still think they have something to do with Tom's death?"

"It's possible, but I can't find out for sure."

"Why not?" she asked, feeling a stab of disappointment.

"Because none of their families will talk to a cop."

"But you're investigating a murder," she argued.

"Not officially," he said. "And if I offend these people, and they didn't have anything to do with your husband's murder . . ."

"They'll complain about you," she supplied. "Maybe even get you fired."

He hadn't wanted to tell her that, but she certainly didn't think any less of him for it. He had a son to support, and he needed his job.

"Is there something I can do?" she asked. "Could *I* talk to the families? Surely they'd speak to me," she argued.

He fairly cringed at the prospect. "No, you can't," he informed her. "If one of them killed your husband, he might decide to kill you, too, if you come snooping around."

Sarah hadn't considered that possibility, and it sobered her. "Then what *can* I do?"

She could see he'd thought this through carefully, but he still hated to ask her. "If I was officially assigned to the case, I wouldn't have to worry about offending anybody."

She understood instantly. "I could ask Teddy to reopen the investigation and assign you," she said, referring to her old friend Teddy Roosevelt. "He'd be happy to do it, I'm sure."

He didn't seem as pleased by her offer as she'd expected. "Think about this before you make any offers. Don't forget that solving a murder isn't always good. Sometimes people find out things they didn't want to know."

"You mean like with Upchurch."

"Exactly like that."

She stared at him, trying to see behind his neutral cop's expression. "Tom was a good man, Malloy. You won't find anything I don't want to know."

"But if I do . . ."

"You won't. I just want to find his killer. I need to know why he died."

"It won't change anything," he warned her. "He'll still be dead."

She hadn't thought of it that way. Was that what she wanted? Of course it was. She wanted Tom back, alive, and everything the way it had been. But that would never happen. He was gone forever. "The man who killed Tom robbed me of my husband and robbed the world of a great doctor and a wonderful person," she said. "He has no right to be walking around free. I want him punished."

He stared back at her for a long moment, as if judging her resolve. Then, as if satisfied, he nodded once. "Talk to Roosevelt, then."

Just then they heard a loud thump from upstairs, reminding them they'd left the children alone too long.

"I guess we'd better check on them," Sarah said, glad to change the subject.

Malloy followed her through the house to the stairway. From above, she could hear someone talking, and for an instant she simply wondered whose voice it was. In the next instant she realized whose it had to be.

It was Aggie's voice. She was talking to Brian. Sarah stopped dead, her heart pounding in her chest as she looked up the stairs toward the sound.

Behind her, Malloy started to speak, but she hushed him, putting a finger to her lips. From above, the tiny sounds floated down to them.

"I know you can't hear me, Brian, and that's why I'm telling you. Everybody thinks my name is Aggie, but it's not. My name is Catherine."

Sarah turned to Malloy as tears flooded her eyes. She saw her own wonder reflected on his face. "She can talk," she whispered.

She never knew which of them moved first, but in the next second she was in his arms, clinging to him as she sobbed against his chest. She wept out her joy for the child that was now her daughter, her grief for the husband she had lost, her sorrow for the pain she'd seen so many innocents suffer these past weeks, and her gratitude that she had Malloy to share it with.

As he crushed her to him, she knew that no matter what happened, they would be all right.

Author's Note

I HOPE YOU ENJOYED THIS BOOK. YOUR SUPPORT HAS made the Gaslight Mysteries a success and helped ensure there will be more books to come! I've heard from some fans who were interested to know why I chose to have Brian learn American Sign Language instead of attending a school where he would learn to speak. After researching the various schools of thought about teaching the deaf, I came to the same conclusion that Frank Malloy did. If Brian had lost his hearing after he had learned to speak, I would have sent him to a school where he would learn to speak. Since he has never heard the spoken word, and my research indicated that those who are born deaf have a difficult time learning to speak, I chose to have him learn to sign.

Please let me know how you enjoyed this latest install-ment of the Gaslight Series. You may contact me through my web page at victoriathompson.com.

Enjoy the rich historical mysteries from Berkley Prime Crime

Margaret Frazer:
Dame Frevisse Medieval Mysteries
Joliffe Mysteries

Bruce Alexander:
Sir John Fielding Mysteries

Kate Kingsbury:
The Manor House Mysteries

Robin Paige:
Victorian and Edwardian Mysteries

Lou Jane Temple:
The Spice Box Mysteries

Victoria Thompson:
The Gaslight Mysteries

Solving crimes through time.